WICKED RIDE

(The Wicked Horse Series)

By
Sawyer Bennett

ISBN: 978-1-940883-47-2

Find Sawyer on the web!
www.sawyerbennett.com
www.twitter.com/bennettbooks
www.facebook.com/bennettbooks

Table of Contents

Prologue
Logan

I THINK THIS woman may be the death of me.

A dire prediction, but probably true.

Probably true because she's not mine to have and I'd probably take her, even at the risk to my own safety.

I'm fixated on her... obsessed really. That black-as-midnight hair and huge, blue eyes the color of the Wyoming sky. Her skin pale... almost translucent. She looks otherworldly, in fact, and it's no secret that every man in The Silo is obsessed with her as much as I am.

I have to have her, and maybe tonight will be the night. My dick is already hard and aching with the thought, and if I'm given the pleasure of her company, my cock won't even get to touch her pussy, which I'm betting is sweeter than honey. I try to look nonchalant as her "owner" walks around The Silo, chatting up the various patrons and deciding who gets to play with her tonight. He's passed me by on three other occasions. I expect tonight won't be any different because he knows I don't have the type of bank he'll be asking for when he ultimately auctions her off. So many men slobbering to get a taste of her, but only one sweet, virginal girl to go around.

That's right.

She's a virgin.

Twenty years old and looks like a porcelain china doll that would break if not carefully handled. But I also know she's stronger than she looks as I've watched her take a mouth fucking like a champ.

She's a contradiction.

She's most likely my downfall.

Like I said, she'll probably be the death of me, but it's a risk I'm willing to take.

Chapter 1

Logan

I'M IN THE *viewing room again. Three rows of seats, stadium style. I'm in the front row, so I have a completely unobstructed view of what's going on fifteen feet down below us. I've been here before and it's all familiar to me, but not in a way that provides comfort.*

But it's familiar in a way that I know I have to see this nightmare through to the end, even if I'm not sure exactly where it's going.

While the lights in the viewing room are bright and astringent to my eyes, the room below is dark and shadowy with only the center being visible because of the round surgical lamps surrounding the operating table. And I know it's an operating table below because I can hear the soft whoosh of a respirator and the faint beeping of the EKG monitor, but mostly because several doctors and nurses clad in scrubs and face masks congregate around it. There are so many of them that they stand with their shoulders pressed against one another, forming a tight ring around the table as they do their work. The circle of medical professionals is so tightly formed that I can't even see who is on the table.

I lean forward in my chair, getting closer to the clear

glass. My eyes narrow and I lean left and right in my seat, trying to get a better look. Trying to see past the surgeons and nurses.

Trying to get just a tiny peek of who is lying on that table.

Maybe if one of them would just move a tiny bit, I could see.

It's so frustrating, and I'm wondering if I'm the only one in this room having a hard time trying to see what's going on down below. The seats are filled to capacity, this I know, but I'm not sure who all is here with me.

I turn my head to the right, see a row of people, but their faces are all blurred and indistinguishable.

To the left, it's the same, but no one is leaning forward the way I am. By their body language alone, none of them appears to be distressed that they can't see who's on the table.

I slide my gaze back down to the surgical room below, my nerves tingling with an awareness that I just can't quite put my finger on. The doctors and nurses work, murmuring words I can't understand.

Then it happens… the doctor at the very end of the table at the patient's feet shifts slightly, and then straightens until his spine is perpendicular to the floor. His head slowly turns, lifts, and his eyes come right to me. I can't see any of his face below said eyes as it's covered by his mask, but I don't need to see what's under that thin, protective covering to know that his lips are flattened in a disappointed grimace.

His eyebrows slant inward and his eyes narrow; I feel the icy disgust permeate every molecule of my being.

Then he moves again... this time turning his body to the right, which creates a slight opening at the end of the table. His gaze is so hostile now that it's not a chore for me to tear mine away, and I cut it to the operating table.

It's a small body on the table, covered in a white sheet, the feet not even reaching to the end. One by one, each of the doctors and nurses step away from the table, creating more space for me to observe what's really going on.

My gaze drifts up the small body that I inherently know is female, covered all the way up to the chest. I first notice the long, dark hair spilled out from under her head, but I can't see her face as it's covered with a large mask attached to the respirator.

I'm so frustrated, not being able to quite recognize who it is.

Then a nurse reaches a hand outward to the patient, puts it on the mask, and slowly pulls it away.

My heart rate speeds up with anticipation... dread... near hysteria. I want to look away, but I can't.

I won't let myself.

Then I see who it is just as the respirator goes quiet and a long, steady beep emits from the EKG machine.

And I scream, and scream, and scream.

I shoot straight up in the bed, my abs clenched tight from the move, but then my stomach turns to liquid as I come awake. My mouth is wide open, but no sound is coming out. I'm soaked with sweat, trickles running down my temples and down the middle of my bare chest.

My lungs are rapidly expanding and deflating, yet it doesn't feel like any oxygen is getting in. I swing my legs to the side of the small mattress, the box spring underneath squeaking, and I place my feet on the floor, slightly spreading my legs. Leaning forward, I dip my head down in between my knees as wave after wave of nausea rolls through me. I suck in deep breaths of air, mentally telling myself it's just a nightmare.

But I'm awake and cognizant enough to know it's not.

Images flash through my head of the little girl on the operating room table. The vague smell of antiseptic remains in my nostrils so vividly, my eyes water in response.

I swallow hard against the vomit threatening to rise up my throat and fling myself back on the bed. Shutting my eyes tight, I conjure up the most pornographic images I can think of to try to redirect my thoughts. I've tried deep breathing, meditation, prescription drugs, illegal drugs, and alcohol. I've tried it all before, but nothing wipes my mind clear of the nightmare quite like refocusing my attention to something that is almost antithetical to the pain that particular dream produces.

So I choose to focus my mind on the extreme pleasures of perversion to wipe out the raw desolation of my sorrow.

It always works.

At least, it has for the past year I've been a member at The Silo. As long as it continues to be my mental

Novocain, I'll continue to submerge myself into a cloud of sexual haze to keep the insanity at bay.

I think about last night and the amazing sex I had with Rand and Cat.

So fucking hot.

Tiny, frail body under a sheet.

Squeezing my eyes shut, I remember what it was like to kiss Rand… feel his roughened hands on my cock while Cat fingered herself. I call up the memory of Cat commanding me to fuck Rand and the shiver it sent up my spine, knowing that watching two guys get it on was making her hot.

Long, steady beep from the EKG machine. She's flat-lined.

I squeeze my eyes shut harder, forcing myself to recall the image of when I pressed my lube-slicked dick to Rand's pucker and the way it felt when the head popped through that tight ring. As I slide my hand down my stomach, in between my legs, I almost beg my cock to get hard from the memory, but it doesn't.

It refuses and that worries me, because I know from having this nightmare many times, I can usually chase away the dredges of horror by jacking myself off to any number of memories I have stored up from my sexual escapades over the past year. I'm usually able to crudely spit in my palm, wrap it around my shaft, and allow the first touch to completely free my mind. By the third stroke, I'm habitually lost to pleasure and I forget all about that little girl lying on the table. Sex is a drug and

I'm possibly a sex addict, but it does wonders at keeping my misery at bay.

But even as hot as last night was with Rand and Cat… regardless of the fact I came hard while lodged balls deep in the tightest of asses, my dick stays limp.

"Fuck," I mutter as I come up to my elbows and look down my body in the early morning light. The memory of last night should do the trick, but I feel nothing but overwhelming guilt and sadness holding my body hostage. For the first time in a long time, I have the urge to get utterly and fantastically shit faced. Drown myself in a bottle of vodka, perhaps preceded by a few Xanax. My palms actually itch, not with the urge to jack myself off, but with the need to shove some pills down my throat or crack open a bottle of liquor.

Not. Good.

I flop back on the small mattress, the sheets all bunched up under me, which is testament to the shitty sleep I had, and breathe out a frustrated sigh. Everything from my mind to my dick seems broken.

Closing my eyes, I wonder what gruesome image will flash before me since I'm utterly wallowing right now, but I'm surprised when a bright and vivid vision pulses before me.

Long hair falling to mid-back… dark as raven's wings. Large, blue eyes blinking with innocence. A luscious, curvy body with an ass made to be held on to tight while I fucked her.

I groan as I think about the virginally sweet Auralie

who has been gracing The Silo the last three days, and my cock starts to react.

And it reacts swiftly.

My balls tingle as I wrap my hand around my increasing length, and I immediately start stroking as I think about the woman who has greatly intrigued me these last few days. In fact, while I was fucking Rand last night, who was fucking Cat at the same time, I was actually imagining I was riding Auralie. It was her face I imagined when I came.

She's an enigma, and I'm not the only one whose dick stands at attention when she's around. Her "owner" is a douche-looking asshole who likes to parade her around, letting the men sniff but not touch until he says so. Sometimes, he has her walk around The Silo naked, her large breasts swaying with pert, stiff nipples that make me think she's turned on by the experience. But that only makes her more intriguing, because the rumor is that she's a virgin.

That's not to say she doesn't have sexual experience, but Magnus—her owner—has insinuated to several of the patrons that her pussy is untouched. Therefore, that makes it even more tantalizingly sweet to all the horny men looking to add a virginal notch in their belts.

Me?

I've never cared much for virgins. Too stiff and unyielding, and when I fuck, I don't want to have to worry if I'm hurting her. I want a woman who begs me to ram my cock into her, who won't mind the swift bite of pain it might cause. Doesn't mean I'll give into that desire, because I find just as much pleasure with a slow, sweet, and tender fuck. It's all good to me.

But there's something about Auralie that speaks to me. I don't care she's a virgin, and if I were ever lucky enough to get a crack at her, I'd take great care to ensure I didn't hurt her. I'd make it good her first time, and, when she was ready, I'd give it to her harder the second time if I felt she could take it.

No, that's not what intrigues me about her.

I can't put my finger on it, but there is something in her eyes that I recognize. Call it perhaps one soul possibly speaking to the other through our looks, and trust me… we've shared plenty of looks each night I've seen her in The Silo.

In fact, just last night, I swear we had an entire conversation with each other just through stolen but meaningful gazes. There was a moment last night, just before Magnus picked the lucky bastard who would get a little one-on-one time with her, that she looked at me, and I swear her gaze said, *I wish I didn't have to do this. I wish I could be free to pick who I want. I really wish I could pick you.*

And I couldn't help it. The look I gave back to her said, *I'll help you get out of this. Tell me what you need, and I'll do it.*

But then Magnus gave a big, booming laugh that broke our connection, and he was enthusiastically shaking one of the patron's hands. My stomach cramped for a moment, thinking that he had "sold" Auralie to this guy… someone I really didn't know who had started coming to The Silo in the last few months… but then I realized he had merely been chosen for a tiny interlude with her.

Magnus cut his eyes to Auralie and jerked his head toward the man. The chosen patron was older than me by about ten years, which put him about twenty years older than Auralie's rumored "twenty" years of age. But I suppose he was relatively attractive—not that I really looked at guys that way. I mean, sure… I've fucked Rand a few times and he's fucked me, but that's really just me looking for new and innovative ways to get my rocks off. It's all about consuming my mind with the most intense and surreal experiences I can muster, so I don't think about… other things.

Auralie's head dropped slightly, and she took a deep breath. She walked up to the man, who was clearly sporting a hard-on against his dress pants, and took him by the hand. And because The Silo is a private sex club that people join so they can express their sexual perversions in an enlightened and accepting atmosphere, showmanship is often the name of the game. It's why The Silo is nothing more than a round building with glass rooms on the interior, so that no fucking is done in private, but is there for all the other patrons to enjoy and be titillated by.

I watched last night, dreading and anticipating in equal measure, as Auralie led the man over to a set of low-slung, black leather chairs formed in a circle and pushed him down into an empty one. Even though I didn't want her to be messing with that guy, I was also turned on by the prospect, a feeling that completely baffled me.

Yes, I wanted those pale, delicate hands to be working at my belt the way they were working his. Wanted her to be pulling my cock out. I wanted her to lean over me and have those breasts sway like hypnotic pendulums, just the way they were for him. And Christ… when she opened her mouth and wrapped her lips around his cock—which was nowhere near the size of mine—I swear I almost felt the sensation on my own dick. Even though I'd just fucked Rand not an hour prior—having left him and Cat curled up sweetly together on their bed—I became insanely horny again watching the lovely Auralie give another man a blow job.

I was jealous, turned on, and angry all at the same time. I wanted to tear her away and push her to her knees before me. Wanted to punch the man sitting in the leather chair, his face slackened from lust, and then I wanted to kick the shit out of Magnus, who seemed to take pleasure and pride in pimping out Auralie's mouth since he wouldn't let anyone touch her pussy for free.

I watched for a few minutes as Auralie bobbed up and down on his dick, my own thumping in my pants for release. Locking my jaw, I watched, wishing it were me and knowing it would never happen. The "rumor" was that Magnus was going to auction her hymen off to the highest bidder—and I could never afford her on my salary—but for now, he was doing nothing more than guerilla marketing. He was whipping the male patrons into a frenzy by parading her around and letting her suck a few dicks so they could have a little test run first.

I knew I was a goner when, on an upstroke with her cheeks hollowed out, Auralie lifted her eyes and pinned them on me. I read her expression loud and clear, for it said, *I wish this were your cock.*

Fuck… I was a total goner.

I broke eye contact with her, spinning around and stomping off toward the short hall that led to the outer perimeter hall that circled The Silo. Following it about a quarter of the way around, I chose a glass door that housed "The Orgy" room. It was the best choice because it was always filled with people who were nothing more than a writhing mass of cock and pussy begging to be fucked. Grabbing a condom from a large bowl on a table by the door, I headed toward the center of the mass. I was going to get fucked or sucked, didn't really care, but I needed release.

And I'd be imagining it was Auralie the entire time.

Chapter 2
Auralie

I WALK DOWN the staircase, one hand trailing along the knotty pine banister, the other holding my long robe up so I don't trip. I suppress a yawn, I'm not sure why, then just let it loose. As it is, I don't bother to cover my mouth as manners would dictate. The only other one who could possibly be offended is Magnus, and I don't care if he's offended. I can hear his voice, low and controlled, as I head through the small living room and into the kitchen.

Magnus Albright sits at the round kitchen table that seats four. It's also done in a blond pine with dark knotholes patterned throughout. I'd never been to Wyoming before Magnus brought me here five days ago and moved me into this cute little western chalet just on the outskirts of Jackson. But I love everything about it so far, from the stunning peaks of the Teton Mountain range to the pine log homes that sparsely cover the vast landscape.

Yes, I love Wyoming from what little I've been able to see, but I hate why I am here.

Magnus is already showered and dressed, his thinning blond hair meticulously slicked and combed to the side to hide his impending baldness. His face is freshly shaven except for long sideburns that he doesn't realize went out of style back in the 1800s. Magnus is all about impressions, and he always dresses as if he's going to be handling "business" at any given moment. That means he's wearing a custom-tailored suit in dark navy with a pristinely starched white dress shirt underneath. His tie will be added later if he leaves the chalet, but I'm guessing he won't since he really has no place to go other than The Silo, and he doesn't even bother to drag me there until the late evening hours when the place will be hopping with horny customers.

His muddy-brown eyes shift up to me as he holds his cell phone to his ear, listening to whoever is on the other end. He rakes his gaze over me impersonally, as he is neither attracted to me, nor does he care for me. I am nothing but a business deal, which does make me important to him, but not in the way the heart works. I appeal to his mind and his ego, and he equates me to nothing but a good score.

I'm his long con that's going to be a decidedly easy trick to pull, even though it might take some time and effort to get all his ducks in a row.

I'm his pawn... his shill... and sadly, I have no choice in the matter.

"Well, I don't give a darn if he's demanding to cash out immediately," he says snippily.

I roll my eyes as I pour myself a cup of coffee because

Magnus refuses to curse. He thinks it's impolite, which is ridiculous given the fact he made me suck some stranger's dick last night without blinking an eye.

"Tell him that the terms of agreement clearly state we get five days. You have to be tough, Mickey. I don't have time to come back and handle this."

Magnus listens for a moment, and then nods in affirmation of whatever is said in return. "That's good. And go ahead and deposit the Anderson investment into the outsource account, let it clear, and then on the fifth day, cash him out with a four-percent rate of return."

A slight pause, and then Magnus says firmly, "You heard me right. Four percent. The man may be insufferable but he's well connected. He'll refer more people to us."

Another slight pause and a nod. "That's good, Mickey. Now… would you like to talk to your daughter?"

My spine stiffens slightly and I turn around to face Magnus, my eyes dropping to the phone in his outstretched hand. Magnus gives me a cool smile and nods in encouragement for me to take it. "He wants to check in on you."

I reach a shaky hand out and take the phone from Magnus. Just as I start to tug it from his grasp, he tightens his hold on it to stop my momentum and get my attention. My eyes slide up slowly to meet his, and his look is clear. *Don't upset your father.*

Giving a curt nod, I pull the phone from Magnus. I then give him my back as I put it to my ear and say,

"Hey, Dad."

"Hey pumpkin," he says in that faded Boston accent. He's been in New York for almost thirty years now, and it's hard to detect unless he says words like *park,* which comes out like *pah-k.* "How are things going?"

I swallow hard against my lie and hope my voice doesn't quaver. "Awesome. How are things with you?"

I purposely turn things back on him so he doesn't push me for more details. Not that he would. Deep down, my dad doesn't want to know the details and I'm happy for that.

"It's all good here," he says with a roughened breath. I can tell he's stressed. "But I'm holding it together."

"That's good, Dad," I say. My words come out shakily, and I know I'm about to lose it. So I lie again. "Listen, I'm on my way out the door... important business and all that. I'm going to hand you back to Magnus."

"Okay, baby," he says, but his voice is already fading as I turn on Magnus and shove the phone back at him. He takes it with a cool smirk to his lips and doesn't even bother to look at me.

I grab my cup of coffee and head back toward the staircase, to the safety and privacy of my room, just as I hear Magnus murmuring to my dad again. I'm sure my dad is pressing him for assurances that I'm truly doing okay, but Magnus will never give him more than the bare minimum to keep him pliant.

In my room, which is more knotty pine walls, furniture, and flooring, the monotony of which is broken up by a thick comforter with a Native American design done in taupe, coral, and muted greens, I take a sip of my coffee and look around. The walls are covered with western-themed prints of cowboys and Indians, the matting inside matching the colors of the comforter so it all ties in together. On the bedside table is a copper lamp with a bucking bronco etched into the shade. A large rack of elk antlers hangs over the bed, and while the decor sounds more masculine than not, it actually is very soothing.

I've pretty much been holed up in here when I'm not working it at The Silo, trying to drum up as much horny anticipation and fevered need to fuck me as possible.

After I take another sip from my cup, I set it down on the dresser that has a large mirror attached. I take a careful look at my reflection. My skin is clear and translucent, apparently one of the few things my mother ever gave me that was good. Magnus has forbidden me to wear makeup, something I very much enjoy doing, but he says it makes me look older and that would defeat his marketing prowess.

I do, in fact, love playing with makeup and putting it on because it does make me look older. This I like because I believe I look abnormally young for my age. Even though I have large breasts, and, if you saw me naked, there's no denying I'm a woman fully grown, my face could sometimes pass for a teenager. Magnus says dirty old men like that.

I shudder, hoping to God he doesn't auction me off to some old perv. Every night in The Silo has been an absolute torture as I wait to see what he'll make me do. For the past three nights, he's kept it fairly simple. The first night he did nothing but parade me around, fully clothed, which lulled me into a false sense of security.

The next night, he struck up a conversation with one of the other patrons and quickly found out he was a cattle baron, which are frankly a dime a dozen out here, but they are incredibly wealthy. Hell, all the patrons at The Silo are sinfully rich.

They'd have to be to afford the $50,000 membership fee.

So with the cattle baron looking at me with undisguised lust, and Magnus calculating mentally how much I could sell for, he decided it wouldn't hurt to give the man a "freebie".

Now, since my "virginal" status is what's being peddled, the freebie did not mean sex. Magnus made it very clear when he told the man—whose name I do not even know because we were never introduced—that there could be no penetration of my vagina.

I mean, that's literally how he said it in that formal, polite way. "You may not put anything in her vagina."

I winced because it sounded so clinical. I also winced because that left a lot of other things the man could do to me, and while blow jobs were not unknown to me, I did not want anything near my ass.

Turns out my worries were for nothing, because the

man was more than happy to accept a blow job.

And it was awful.

I mean… blow jobs aren't awful, if you're with someone you are genuinely attracted to and maybe even have a measure of care for. But sucking a stranger's dick who you are in no way attracted to is just nasty, and I suppose the only good thing is that the man put a condom on and I was spared from having to swallow.

He was also a fast shooter so I didn't need to suck more than a minute or so before he was blowing, so that was good too.

Last night though, Magnus upped his game. He told me as we pulled into the parking lot he wanted me naked for the night. I immediately balked and told him to go to hell.

He just clucked his tongue and chastened me, "Now, Lee-Lee… you know you have to do this. You know you have to do it right. You know I won't accept anything but full effort from you on this deal, and I don't have to remind you of the consequences if you don't."

So I got naked.

Because I didn't need the reminder.

And Magnus led me around, introducing me to patrons, letting them ogle my breasts. After the first fifteen minutes or so, I lost the red tinge of embarrassment from my cheeks and I let my alter ego take over. I had developed it over the last few days, and it wasn't a chore.

Acting came naturally to me, and if I needed to act like the innocent seductress, I could do it. So I lowered my eyes a lot, knowing my fabulous black lashes stood out starkly against my pale skin, and I fidgeted shyly when one of the patrons would roam his eyes all over my body.

Magnus even let one of the members pinch my nipple. "Just to get a feel of how firm they are," he'd said.

My nipple didn't even react, just stayed soft and yielding. This didn't even seem to register with Magnus—who never really looked at my naked body—or the other man, who didn't care if I was turned on or not. He was just trying to get in good with my "owner" so that he'd be in the running for that evening's "experience" with me.

Yeah, it shouldn't be a surprise that nothing about this experience would turn me on, given that this was something I was not fully on board with, and that I was sort of being coerced. Being paraded around and forced to bestow sexual favors, knowing that made me a filthy whore because money would eventually change hands, really wasn't conducive to stiff nipples or wetness down below.

That is… until *he* walked in.

No clue his name, but I saw him on the first night Magnus brought me in. Saw him on the second night too. Last night, he was still just as beautiful and just as perplexing.

Oh yes… he's beautiful. Dark hair, slightly longish and messy like he just doesn't care one bit about how it looks. A goatee surrounding beautiful lips. His skin olive toned, his jaw solid, and his cheeks angled.

Those eyes though.

From the color…

Hazel with subtle shades of green, brown, and gold.

To the level of pain I saw within them…

Deep and consuming.

To the way in which he communicated his emotion…

Confidently and without ambiguity.

Those eyes captivated me from the start. The rest of his packaging was beautiful as well, as he was tall and built. There wasn't a woman in that circular house of perversion who didn't have their tongues hanging out when he walked by.

But it was his eyes.

They simply spoke to me.

For the past three nights, this stranger, with a heavy burden on his shoulders I'm not sure anyone else truly recognized, played a subtle game of secret communication using stolen glances and subtle body language.

It's not that we spoke on any deep level using the power of our gazes, but there was clear meaning.

Lust, intrigue, frustration.

I took one look at the beautiful man with the soulful eyes and my nipples got hard. They did that each night I saw him.

Even as I was sucking another man's dick, they were hard. I looked at him once in mid-bob, and I hoped he understood my message.

I wish this were you.

I understood his response. It was short, and then he stalked off.

I wish it were me too.

But it never would be. I didn't know the man at all... not even his name... but I could tell he didn't have the money to be a real patron at The Silo. His jeans were always worn and some of his shirts a little frayed. I heard Magnus talking with the owner, Bridger, one night, and he said that some of the men and women in The Silo are Fantasy Makers. Extra people who are on hand to add to the numbers of people wanting to fuck and be fucked. They are paid employees, I guess, which probably made the beautiful, sad man as much a prostitute as I am.

That is something we have in common.

Perhaps why we understand each other with just the merest of glances.

A knock on my bedroom door startles me out of my thoughts, and I look down to see if my nipples are poking out against my robe. They are... straight out and completely reflective of my wayward thoughts toward a man I'll never be able to touch.

I open the door just a crack and peer outside, keeping my traitorous body from his view.

Not that he'd look.

I don't think Magnus is into women.

Or men for that matter.

I think he's just into money.

"Yes?" I ask crisply as I open the door. He knows I

don't like being around him when it's not needed.

"We're going to leave a little early tonight for The Silo," he says coolly. "I want you to wear that pink dress tonight."

I grit my teeth and nod, thankful on one hand I'll be clothed since he's choosing my wardrobe, but also on edge, because I know he has something different planned for tonight.

The dress is pretty and demure with a flowing skirt that comes to just above my ankles. He had bought a pair of pale, pink ballet flats to go with it.

It is demure and virginal, and he wants to remind everyone at The Silo that he's got a product to sell.

Fresh, tight pussy.

"And leave your hair long," Magnus adds on.

I nod again and stare at him with hard eyes.

"We're upping the "wow" factor tonight," he says thoughtfully, almost as if he's trying to get a rise out of me. Which is ludicrous. Magnus does not like to fight and does not like confrontation. He merely expects obedience. "I want you to really put on a show for the crowd."

"Understood," I grit out, and then I shut the door in his slimy face.

Oh, I'll give a show all right if that's what he wants. If I can do anything to facilitate this matter so we can just get it over and done with, I'm all for that.

I'm going to see this through to the end, because I have no choice in the matter.

And when I'm done, I'm done.

Finished.

Never coming back to this life again.

And in my new life, I'm going to make it my mission to find a way to make Magnus suffer for what he's doing to my family and me.

Chapter 3

Logan

I WALK INTO The Silo tonight tense and on edge. I spent all day out on the Snake River with a father and son visiting from Maryland. The boy was eleven years old and the first cutthroat trout he pulled out of the water had him screaming with excitement. I maintained a lucid smile on my face while I removed the hook from the corner of the fish's mouth, trying not to show how much it hurt when the father reached an affectionate hand out and ruffled his kid's hair with pride.

Those twinges of pain are to be expected, but are usually alleviated by the mere fact that my job during the summer and fall months consists of taking tourists out on float trips down the Snake River for a taste of some Wyoming fly fishing. While I certainly can't speak for all careers and professions out there, I can say, without a doubt, this is probably the best job I've ever had. Even more so than fucking myself into a stupor at The Silo.

There is nothing more peaceful or restorative to my soul than three or four hours spent floating lazily down a meandering river with blue sky and gentle breezes washing your worries away. Now granted… that restorative fix is usually destroyed by my nightmares, but I can say that there are great chunks of my day that are pleasant and even happy at times.

Today was no exception, except that as the evening got nearer and I knew I'd be heading to The Silo, I started to get knotted up with unease. This was very strange because I go to The Silo almost every night, and I fuck almost every night. I love sex. It's amazing and addictive and freeing and numbing.

So I try to do it as much as possible.

It is something that causes my steps to become lighter once I walk toward a guaranteed orgasm within that building.

But not tonight.

I walk in that door, and I immediately tense up with wondering what Auralie will be wearing. How will she smell? Will her hair be up or down? Nipples hard or soft? Will her eyes look at me with the same meaning as last night, and will I absolutely hate watching her touch and taste another man if Magnus so deems that to be the night's main attraction?

I'm late getting here, perhaps even subconsciously hoping that Magnus will have already paraded her around before I arrive, but the minute I step into the circular opening of The Silo, my eyes are immediately drawn to the pale pink of Auralie's dress.

I know what Magnus is doing. He's playing up every bit of youthful innocence she possesses, and I have to say, it's a brilliant move for most of the perverts in here that want to pop her cherry.

Who wouldn't want to be the big, studly man who gives the virgin her first sweet orgasm?

I hate to break it to these fools in here, but I know something about Auralie that they don't. I've never talked to that beautiful woman once, but I know that she knows exactly what an orgasm feels like. It may not be by a man's cock if Magnus is to be believed, but she's had a finger, tongue, or vibrator up against her tight bud before.

I can tell.

It's in her eyes.

She may not like sucking the dick she's had to suck, and she might not like having her flesh peddled—all things that are patently clear—but when she looks at me and she conveys that message of want and desire for yours truly, I know it's because she knows how fucking good an orgasm feels and she's imagining one with me.

God knows… I've sure as shit been fantasizing about it from my end.

Her slender back is to me with her long hair that is so black it shines blue hanging down her back almost to that rounded ass, but she stiffens slightly when I walk in. Almost as if sensing me, she turns her head slightly and lets her gaze roam the room until it comes to a complete stop right on me.

She gives me a soft smile, but the real meaning simmers in those cobalt eyes. *You're here. I'm so glad.*

I'm not trying to be a dick, but I'm angry and frustrated by these circumstances, and I can't help my return look. *I'm not so glad. I can't have you, and it's going to kill me to watch you be given to someone else.*

Sadness fills her eyes, making them shimmer briefly before they shutter closed. Her lips draw down, and, with a regretful sigh, she turns from me to listen in on the conversation Magnus is having with the Cleimdens, a married couple who are into some seriously kinky shit that includes the wife pegging her husband in the ass while he brays like a donkey. I hope to fuck Magnus is not going to let Auralie play with them tonight.

Turning away, I make my way through the crowd up to the center bar that's circular like the room. A black lacquer top and contemporary chrome stools upholstered in buttery black leather are heavily occupied except for an empty seat right beside Bridger.

He's sipping on water, ass sitting on the edge of a stool while his foot is propped up on the chrome railing at the bottom of the bar. He rests an elbow casually on top of the bar, but his gaze is pinned on Magnus and Auralie. He's clearly unsettled by the couple as his gaze is wary, but I can tell by the loose set to his shoulders that he's also accepting of their presence. Bridger does not try to curtail the kinky shit that goes on in this establishment as long as all participants are willing and consenting.

Knowing Bridger as I do, which isn't all that great really because the guy is a complete mystery to most, I'm sure he's thoroughly checked out this Magnus dude as well as ensured Auralie was a willing participant in his shenanigans, contrary to what her eyes have told me in the past.

"What's up?" I announce my presence behind him with a slight clap of my hand on his back.

He's not startled because he's Bridger and nothing rattles him, so he merely swivels his body my way and nods. "Not much. What's up with you?"

I shrug. Not much is up other than my blood pressure and feelings of guilt and anger over the thought of Auralie touching someone else tonight, but I'm not going to tell him that.

This Bridger notices all in one skilled glance because my emotions are painted clearly on my face, but he tries not to make a big deal out of it. "You seem tense."

I don't respond but call out to Heather, one of the bartenders, who looks my way. "Maker's Mark… neat."

"Must be tense," Bridger comments. "You don't ever drink on work nights."

"I might take the night off," I muse, trying not to get insulted by Bridger's snort of disbelief. Me coming to The Silo and not getting my rocks off is just… unheard of.

"Seriously," he prods at me. "What's up?"

Taking the drink, I slug back a hefty swallow and set it back down, enjoying the burn. I shouldn't even bother to engage, and I'm better served by walking out of here and staying away until sweet Auralie is sold off, but I can't fucking help myself.

"What's the deal with the virgin auction?" I say, carefully veiling my feelings by not even daring to mention I know Auralie's name. I mean, it's hard not to given that everyone is talking about her and her "owner" Magnus—which is a seriously stupid fucking name—but I don't want him to see how affected I am.

Bridger's head swivels back to Auralie and Magnus, and my gaze follows. I receive a jolt that makes my legs shake as I realize she's staring straight at me. Time seems to stand still as she gives me that wistful look before turning away. Bridger looks at her for just a moment more, and then turns back to me.

For a moment, I can't even move, but then I tear my gaze away from that pretty pink dress and look back to Bridger, trying to seem unaffected. I'm met with a highly arched eyebrow of curiosity.

"What?" I say with a belligerent tone. "I'm curious about them, that's all."

"Have you been fucking her?" he asks in a low voice, leaning in toward me. "Because if he's advertising her as a virgin, someone's going to be disappointed."

"No, I'm not fucking her," I mutter, but damn… I so wish I were fucking her.

"That look she just gave you," Bridger says knowingly. "It's carnal."

"I haven't touched—"

"Maybe not carnal as in physicality, but you two know each other in some way," he presses.

Yeah, if you give any credence to silent, wordless com-

munication, then sure... I know her. I know she doesn't belong here selling that sweet pussy to someone, and that I should be the one to have her.

I think this all in a sullen tone inside my head.

"You don't have enough money," Bridger says flatly, but not unkindly. He's just trying to make me see reality.

Oddly, I do have some money if I was so inclined to bid on a virgin, but no one here knows that and besides... it's probably not enough for the amount Auralie will eventually command. So it will continue to sit in my savings untouched... just as it's been for the past two years. As far as anyone here knows, I'm practically a vagrant who wanders the country in search of the next big rush. I've landed in Wyoming and stayed longer here than I have anywhere in the last two years, mainly because I love my job as a fishing guide and I love the unlimited sex that lets me have some measure of solitude. The fact that I live on a permanent campsite in a small tin trailer with wheels that I pull behind my beat-up old Ford truck lends to the air that I'm pretty much penniless. And that's really how I exist. My income is nominal from my job, but it's enough to pay for my campsite, put good food in my belly, and clothing on my back when I need it.

I don't respond to Bridger's comment about money, but instead I ask, "You sure she's doing this of her own free will?"

"So she says," he responds. "I talked to her at length, and she was adamant that she was."

"So she's selling her virginity?" I ask incredulously. I mean, who does that? Fuck… who still has their virginity at her age?

Which is?

"How old is she?" I ask hesitantly.

"Says she's twenty," Bridger says, and I wince. Christ… I'm thirteen years older than she is. Not a huge difference, but enough to know we're probably worlds apart in our emotional mentality.

And she certainly could pass for twenty.

But damn… she looks like she sucks cock like a pro, and I remember what it was like when a twenty-year-old would blow me. Most don't know what the fuck they're doing at that age. Women are infinitely better in the sex department as they get older and their confidence grows.

"If I can have everyone's attention please," I hear called from across the room. The chatter slowly dies down. I'm stunned the announcement comes from Magnus, and he beams out to the patrons with a smarmy smile.

"What a tool," Bridger mutters, and this confirms what I had suspected.

He doesn't like the dude any more than I do.

"As you all know," Magnus says as he picks up a lock of Auralie's hair and brings it to his nose to sniff in dramatic fashion, "my pet here… Auralie… is a young and fresh innocent. Smells so sweet."

My gaze slides to Auralie. Her face is tilted to the ground, her eyes shyly hiding from the spectacle Magnus is creating. The crowd presses in a little closer to listen to what he has to say.

"A select few of you have felt the pleasure she can give the past few days, but I want to offer up something different tonight. I'm going to choose one of you lucky men tonight who want to get a crack at something so sweet and pure that you won't be able to think of anything else after. A chance to feast between the lovely Auralie's legs and see that, although she may be virginal, she is more than ready to be pleasured by someone."

Auralie keeps her face down, but I can see the pink tinge to her cheeks and the tightening of her jaw as he's just offered her pussy up to someone's greedy mouth. I involuntarily stand from my stool, but Bridger claps a hand on my shoulder and growls, "Stay out of it."

But how can I?

When my mouth is fucking watering at the chance to eat her out.

My dick starts to swell at the thought. I give it a frustrated shove over in my jeans to get it out from behind my zipper, but I refuse to sit back down on my stool. Bridger's hand falls away from me, but he stands up on high alert. I think he's afraid I might run over to her, pick her up, and throw her over my shoulder like a caveman to jet out of here with my virginal prize.

Instead, I pick up my drink and slug the rest of it back, slamming the highball glass down on the bar top. Heather walks over and looks at me with eyebrows raised.

"Another," is all I say.

In the meantime, Magnus, with his captive crowd and blossoming beauty ready to be devoured, looks around contemplatively at the potential customers he wants to milk for semen and money. Finally, his eyes come to rest on Jacob Johnson, a local lawyer who made a fortune suing pharmaceutical companies for several years while he practiced in L.A. The rumor is his last settlement yielded a twenty-million-dollar fee, so he retired and owns several homes around the United States. He spends the summer months here in Wyoming, fucking most nights at The Silo.

While he's generally a nice guy and we once got our dicks sucked together by the same girl who alternated between the two of us while we shot the shit, I hate him right at this moment as he steps up to Magnus and shakes his hand with a grateful smile.

"How about you take her into The Orgy room?" Magnus suggests with a sweep of his hand that way.

There are only five people in there right now. Two guys lying on a silk mattress kissing and caressing each other, not in a hurry to get it on just yet. And a three-some going at it… guy fucking a girl from behind while she sucks another guy's dick.

Been there done that.

Several times.

I watch as Jacob takes his hand and wraps it behind Auralie's neck, giving her a subtle push toward the hallway that leads to the back doorways to the rooms. He pushes her along, not roughly but with command, as if he's confident in his abilities. But I've watched him eat pussy before. He's sloppy at best and won't give her what she deserves.

My fingers itch to do something, but I'm not sure what.

Heather returns with my drink and I take it from her, knocking it back in one long swallow that burns my guts up but gives me a slight head rush. I don't do liquor very well anymore.

She starts to turn away, but I say, "Hold up."

Heather stops and looks expectantly at me. I turn to Bridger, who is facing me again now that Auralie has been led away. I tell him, "I need to borrow Heather for a bit."

Bridger just shakes his head with a flat line to his lips, not denying my request but rather empathizing with my poor, fucked-up head.

"Go ahead," he says, and Heather's eyes light up.

She and I are very well acquainted with each other, and she's a favorite fuck of mine. I jerk my head toward The Orgy Room and say, "Let's go."

"Absolutely," she says with a grin as she walks toward the other side of the bar that houses the swinging pass through so she can exit.

Chapter 4

Auralie

O H, SHIT.

Shit, shit, shit.

I cannot do this.

I. Cannot. Fucking. Do. This.

The man who Magnus called Jacob keeps his hand firmly on my neck as he guides me to the back hallway that leads to the entrances to the glassed rooms.

The Orgy Room?

My skin crawls thinking about having a complete stranger do something so intimate to me. For reasons that I'm sure are completely fucked up, I found I could turn off my emotional switch when Magnus made me blow those other two guys. That was a job and nothing else.

It was acting at its finest.

No different than pulling a change-raising short con.

But now he's talking about letting a man—a stranger—attempt to pleasure me in a way that I've never had done before. I'm very aware as to how my clit functions, as well as its response to stimulation. I've never had a man's lips and tongue there before, but I have a trusty vibrator that makes short work of me and I'm terrified as to how I'll respond.

I'll either be so wigged out that I'll stay dry as the desert and embarrass myself, probably ruining my sale value, or I'll react like a shrieking banshee because my clit is so sensitive, and I'll embarrass myself. It's a no-win situation.

On top of that, the beautiful man is here and I don't want him watching me. I can't bear to have him watch me react, or possibly not, and the humiliation will be awful.

Or, the worst of all things that could possibly happen is that the beautiful man watching me could cause me to have a reaction that would be unforgiveable. He'd know I was more turned on by him watching me than what was actually being done to me.

I just can't.

"Wait," I say suddenly as he starts me down the perimeter hallway, which is dimly lit with wall sconces about every ten feet.

"What?" he says, using his grip on my neck to turn me to him.

We're completely hidden from the patrons on the interior of The Silo, as well as the members of each room since the back wall of said rooms is made out of concrete staves that match the exterior. I take a deep breath, knowing Magnus is not going to be happy with me, and say, "I'm on my period… you can't."

Total ballsy lie, but it's all I got. I hope to God he

doesn't ask for proof.

"You're fucking kidding me, right?" he mutters, his hand falling away from my neck.

I shake my head a little too enthusiastically, my voice raising an octave. "No… it started this afternoon. I had no clue Magnus was going to offer this to the men here, or I would have told him."

I sort of expect him to be a little more put out over the wasted opportunity, but instead, he grabs me by the back of the neck again, not roughly but more in a controlling way, and says, "No worries. I'll take a blow job. I was going to get one anyway when I was done, right?"

Before I can respond, he starts to push me down the hall again. The heels of my feet instinctively dig into the concrete flooring, bringing me to a stop. "Wait—"

"For fuck's sake, what now?" he growls, his hand gripping me a little harder, which causes my heart to start pounding.

"Is there a problem here?" I hear from behind us, and I don't even need to turn around to know who it is. While I've never heard his voice before, I know without a doubt it's the beautiful man standing behind us.

Jacob whips around, spinning me with him since he doesn't let me go. My first close-up look at the man who is softly washed in the glow of the sconces is almost too much to take in. He's just perfection, and his eyes are pinned right on me. I vaguely notice he has a woman with him… one of the bartenders, it seems… and he's holding her hand. But what I notice most is the hard glint in his eyes and the way his jaw is locked so tight that a tiny muscle jumps in the lower portion of his cheek. While his gaze seems full of anger, I inherently know it's not directed at me.

This is confirmed when he slices his eyes to Jacob and says, "I repeat… what's going on?"

"None of your fucking business, McKay," Jacob bites out, his fingers gripping me even harder as if I'm his favorite toy and he's afraid the neighbor kid is going to take it.

And McKay? That's his name?

The beautiful man—McKay—drops the woman's hand he's with and takes two steps to bring himself almost toe to toe with Jacob. His voice is low and commanding when he says, "She looked like she didn't want to go with you, and you know Bridger's rules… she has to consent."

Oh, fuck.

I have no say in this really. Sure, I had a very awkward conversation with the owner, Bridger, a few days ago when he grilled me for affirmation I was here of my own free will. Another fine acting job was completed when he seemed to accept my lies.

"She's on the rag," Jacob mutters. "So I'm getting a dick suck instead."

"Nice," McKay mutters sarcastically, and his eyes slide down to mine. "You want to go with him?"

His first words spoken to me. Even if he hadn't

voiced a single syllable, he could have looked at me with that same question in his eyes and I would have known just what he was asking.

My expression back to him is pointed. Eyebrows knitted with tension, biting hard on my lower lip with unease and eyes filled with a desperate plea for help, I still manage to say, "Yes."

Because that's what Magnus would expect of me.

McKay stares at me for a long moment, seemingly undecided as to which answer he should deem as the truth. Even though there's nothing he can do to stop my fate, I hope he accepts my silent answer as the one I mean, so he knows I want nothing to do with this creep. I wonder if he can also glean just by my look that I would have gladly gone into that room with him.

"Auralie." I hear Magnus' cultured voice behind McKay, who is so tall and broad shouldered I hadn't seen Magnus walk up. "What's going on?"

Before I can answer, McKay turns to Magnus and says, "She's not feeling well. You can take one look at her and tell."

Thank God he didn't give my "period" lie to Magnus. Magnus would demand an inspection for proof because he'd be pissed I was messing up his grand display of showmanship and superiority.

Magnus' gaze cuts to me, and in a tight voice that he tries to pass off as concerning but doesn't quite make it, he asks, "Auralie, love… is that true?"

I give a slight nod, trying to look pathetically sick,

but I know I come off as terrified of how this situation has gotten out of control. When I risk a look up to McKay, I see that muscle in his cheek jumping harder as he takes in the fear in my eyes.

With a surprising amount of humility that I wouldn't have guessed this big, powerful man would possess, but with complete manipulation that I admire, he turns to Magnus and says, "With all due respect, sir… perhaps you should let her rest tonight. She's put on quite a show the last few nights, and you've admirably whipped up everyone in here. It's been a real treat to watch for sure. And if she doesn't make an appearance tonight, it's only going to increase every man's appetite for her."

Magnus looks at McKay. For someone who regularly takes advantage of and manipulates people, he still immediately buys into the flattery that McKay gives to him. His chest puffs out a bit, and he says, "You have an excellent point."

Jacob's hand falls away as he growls in frustration. McKay looks right at me, but he says, "Jacob… why don't you and Heather head into the Orgy Room? I'm sure she'll make things better for you."

"Yeah, fine," he mutters, but as he reaches past me to grab Heather's hand, who looks just as happy to be going with Jacob as she was with McKay—weird girl—he looks to Magnus and says, "I want another crack at her though before you make the sale. I'm going to make a serious bid you don't want to miss."

Magnus smiles magnanimously and says, "Of course, Jacob."

Without another word, Jacob and Heather head off down the hall. I'm left alone with a man I despise and a man who I feel an intense connection with even though we've hardly spoken at all.

Magnus reaches a hand out and asks, "And you are, sir?"

"Logan McKay," McKay—well, not McKay—says as he shakes Magnus' hand. While his tone is warm and inviting to further conversation, I can tell by the look in his eyes that he despises Magnus as much as I do.

Logan.

I like that a lot.

"And what exactly do you do for a living?" Magnus inquires politely, although I think it's overly rude. He's asking because he wants to know if Logan will be a serious suitor for me. If he's got the bank to make a good bid on my poor, underused vagina.

But I already know the answer to this because while I know Logan is intense, sexy, deep, concerned, protective, and commanding, I also know he's a simple man who lives a very simple existence outside of The Silo. I can read it all over him loud and clear.

"I'm a fishing guide," he says, confirming my instinct as he releases Magnus' hand. "I guide fly-fishing trips, mostly on the Snake River, but sometimes I'll go over to the Yellowstone or Gros Ventre."

"Really?" Magnus says with interest. "I've always

wanted to try fly fishing. I think I'd be very good at it."

I roll my eyes, seeing that Logan notices as those gorgeous lips tip upward slightly as he looks back to Magnus. "I'd be happy to take you out any time you'd like."

"Let's go tomorrow," he immediately demands.

Weird how I can read so much from Logan's posture and eyes. He clearly doesn't want anything to do with Magnus. The offer was just politeness with a suspicion Magnus was not the type of guy who would really go fishing, but he still says, "We would have to leave early. Six AM? You'd have to meet me at the South Fork boat ramp."

"Then I should get my little dove home so I can get to bed," he says with the exuberance of a little child trying to play grown up. "I'll Google directions to the boat ramp and see you there."

God, he's so freakin' weird.

Logan's eyes slide back to mine. This is not noticed by Magnus because he's reaching for my hand as he says, "Come, Auralie. If you're not feeling well, you probably need some rest too."

I tip my head to the right a little and give Logan a smile that is nothing but gratitude for saving me from the terrible situation I was walking into.

Granted… it only makes me safe for tonight as no telling what Magnus will make me do tomorrow, but I've gotten a reprieve and I'm grateful for it.

I let Magnus pull me back toward the exit door, risking a glance over my shoulder back at Logan. He watches me carefully until I round a bend in the hall. When I can't see him anymore, I look at Magnus' stiffened back. He's definitely pissed at me.

I have to trot to keep up with his long, skinny legs. As soon as we step out into the crisp evening air, he releases my hand and rounds on me. "You better not be messing things up, Auralie."

I'd like to say Magnus scares me, but he doesn't. He knows I'll do my part when required because he knows I have no choice.

"I'm really not feeling well, Magnus," I say apologetically. To smooth his ruffled feathers, I point out, "You wouldn't want me puking on a potential sale, would you?"

His pinched expression goes lax, and he gives me a curt nod in acceptance. "Well, it's not like this really hurts anything. I'm not going to be making a quick decision on this. I want the absolute top dollar for you, so not only do we have to rile up their horny little senses, but I also need to make sure I'm waving you under the proper noses. Everyone who is a paid member in there can afford what I'm going to ask, but not everyone will want you. I need to focus on those who do."

Logan does, I think bitterly. I not only see it in his face, but I also feel it in my bone marrow when he looks at me.

Which makes me wonder…

"Why in the world are you going fishing?" I ask curiously, because Magnus in his fine custom suits and gel-slicked hair has never struck me as a person who would want to go fishing. He's too… prissy.

"To schoomze, of course," he says simply as I follow him to his rental car. A Porsche something or other, because he has to maintain an image.

"Schmooze?" I ask astounded. Surely, he has to know just by looking at Logan that he doesn't have that type of money.

"Oh, I don't expect that yokel to bid on you," he says primly. "But I've been watching him, and he's well connected in that establishment. He's been a member since its inception according to someone I talked to last night, and thus he's going to be my in as to who I should be focusing my attentions on."

Figures.

He's going to use the "man of my very own dreams" to sell me to someone else.

Chapter 5
Logan

B Y SIX AM, I have everything set up to take Magnus fishing, and I'm waiting patiently at the back of my boat trailer for him to arrive. I'm almost betting he doesn't show, and it's going to piss me off because I actually had shit I had to do today that was far more important than guiding his ass down the Snake River.

Nothing I hate worse than taking a prissy douche fishing. I bet he won't even touch a fish if he's lucky enough to catch one.

My sixteen-foot drift boat sits in the shallow water off the bank of the South Fork ramp, held in place against the current by a pyramid shaped anchor I dropped to the rocky bottom. I then pulled my truck and trailer up to a parking spot, where two local kids will pick it up and move it to another ramp a few miles downriver where we'll end up porting at the end of the trip. I pay them ten bucks each to do this, which doesn't sound like a lot, but there is so much fishing in this area and so many one-man crews like me who operate that they can work at this solidly for eight hours a day moving vehicles and make pretty good money for a high school kid.

I hear the crunch of gravel under tires and look up from my brooding toward the river to see a black Porsche pulling in. Nice car, but he's still a douche.

Magnus gives me a little wave as he pulls in beside my truck. I push away from the boat trailer and start walking down toward my boat, not even waiting for him. I hear his car door open, then close, and the sound of his feet crunching over the gravel to catch up to me.

"Good morning," he says pleasantly from behind me.

"Mornin'," I say, forcing a jovial tone to my voice that I'm just not feeling. I peer over my shoulder at him and see he's weirdly dressed in a fancy-type tracksuit in black with silver racing stripes down the legs. It's apparent he sees my look of amusement at his outfit as he gives me a smarmy grin and says, "I didn't have much in the way of clothing options. Afraid all I brought with me to Wyoming was fancy suits and a few of my workout outfits. Left all my jeans and cargo pants at home back in New York."

I call bullshit because I can tell that prissy motherfucker abhors the idea of sweat. I'd cut off my left nut and hand it to him if he's ever worked out a day in his life… skinny, pasty, weak motherfucker.

"You're good," I force myself to say lightly. "Doesn't matter what you wear, really. Except… you're going to need a hat. Once that sun gets up, it will burn your head if you're not careful."

"I didn't bring one," he says worriedly as we reach

the boat.

"No worries," I say as I stop at the bow, which rests only about two feet off the bank in water that's only a few inches deep. "Let me just help you in, and I'll get one for you."

With my right hand on the bow, I hold my hand out to Magnus in an offer to steady him as he climbs in the boat. But he doesn't make a move, looking worriedly back and forth between the water and what I'm guessing are very expensive and never before worn tennis shoes.

"I have to get in the water?" he hesitantly asks.

"Yup. Although you can take your shoes and socks off to get in so they don't get wet," I explain, not thinking he'll be that big of a sissy.

But to my surprise, he sits down on the gravel and pulls the fuckers right off. With his pale, bony bare feet, he gets back up, hobbles over the gravel, and lets me help hoist his body into the boat. I pick up his shoes and socks and hand them to him, trying hard to keep my facial expressions pleasant and not downright disgusted.

Because everything about this man disgusts me.

I had a crappy night of sleep. You'd think I'd have slept great since I'd succeeded in getting Auralie out of something she clearly didn't want to do. I just assumed she'd had some experience with oral since she sucked dick like a champ, but she was clearly wigged out about having Jacob put his mouth down on her unmentionables.

I was wigged out by it too, which is utterly ridiculous. It smacks of jealousy, which is an emotion I haven't felt in years. In my life, I've been envious of many things.

People's ability to handle stress.

Other people's skills.

Hell… other people's jobs.

Love.

Security.

Season tickets to the Bulls.

A speedy metabolism.

The ability to yodel.

Whatever.

But not once in the past two years has jealousy even flitted through my senses when it comes to sex and a woman. That's because in order to be jealous, you have to desire something as if it's precious to you, and while it's true I desire Auralie's body, I most certainly don't desire the purity of it in a way that makes me proprietary.

As I said… don't care if she's a virgin.

Don't care she's sucked other guys' dicks at The Silo.

Okay, well… that does bug me, but whatever.

The point is I shouldn't care one bit if another man touches her, but for some reason last night, the thought of Jacob having her pissed me off so badly, I was on the verge of taking Heather in that Orgy Room and fucking her pussy with my mouth right beside Auralie so she could see what she was missing.

It was utter madness, and it actually frightens me the lengths I was willing to go to try to foil Magnus' plan to display Auralie out like a piece of meat and let another man touch what isn't mine but I wished to hell was.

I shake my head and try to get my head in the game. Because while I have absolutely no desire to spend the next four hours with this jackass—which is how long the trip will take downriver—I most certainly am going to use this opportunity to try to find out exactly what his plans are. The "rumor" has been heavy that Magnus intends to sell her virginity, and I say rumor only because I haven't heard it straight from his mouth. He's told other people—namely Bridger—but he's not made a formal type of announcement.

I almost hope to God it's true. If so, it means these people will be gone from The Silo soon after the sale. If Auralie's out of sight, she'll most definitely be out of my mind.

Fucking liar.

No way will she be out of my mind when I've been using the fantasy images of her lying beneath me to get myself off at night, or to chase away bad dreams.

Fuck... even last night after she left with Magnus, I waited a sufficient time for them to be able to get out of the parking lot, and then went to my little camper in the woods. What does it say about me—what does it say about what she's done to me with her sweet eyes and curvy hips—that I gave up an opportunity last night for some amazing sex at The Silo?

I just wasn't fucking into it, and that scares me more than anything. I need the lure of sex. I need the numbing power of the almighty orgasm. If I don't have those available to me, I'm only stuck with my thoughts and my bad deeds. I cannot live life that way. I won't survive it.

Chasing away those particularly morose thoughts, I lift a leg over the edge of the boat, my Teva-clad feet splashing down briefly into the shallow water before I haul myself in.

My drift boat is a source of pride for me. It's necessary for me to make a living, and it wasn't cheap even though I bought it used. It's aluminum with a swivel, high-backed chair at the bow and at the stern, as well as a bench seat in the middle where I sit in between two nine-and-a-half foot oars on either side. I use those oars not to propel me downriver, because the current does that— hence the name drift boat—but to steer me past small rapids and to move me from one side of the large river to the other to hit certain fishing holes I know are guaranteed catch spots.

When I take a party out on my boat in the summer, I dress in cargo shorts and a tank top. While it never gets overbearingly hot in Wyoming, the sun in still strong and I'm always tanned to a golden brown. I remember a few weeks ago I was in The Silo eating some pussy, and I must have looked up at the girl—can't remember her name—and she gasped, "Oh my God... your eyes... they pop against your tan. So hot."

That caught me off guard. I missed a targeted lick to her clit, but then I got back on my game and got her off quickly thereafter. I put her words out of my mind then, and the only reason I'm thinking about them now is because five minutes ago, I was just thinking about Jacob eating Auralie out and how jealous I felt. I wonder if she would think my eyes were amazing as she stared down at me when I—

Fuck!

Get your head in the game, Logan.

"All right," I tell Magnus as I move past where he's seated in the bow seat. I sit down on the middle bench, use a winch crank to pull the short length of rope and anchor holding us on the bank, and I use the oars to push us off into deeper water. The aluminum bottom scrapes along the rocks, but my upper-body muscles easily get us dislodged. "Let me get us to the middle of the river, and then I'll take a few moments to show you some casting techniques."

"Okay," Magnus says as he looks around at the stunning scenery, although I have a vague notion he's not the type to appreciate the blue waters, summer green buttes, and rocky crags as we float downriver. I release an oar, which is held in place by an oarlock that prevents it from falling into the water, and reach down to my backpack at my feet. Fishing around inside, I pull out an old baseball cap that I keep in there.

Handing it to Magnus, I say, "Put that on your head. And grab that life vest at your feet and put it on."

"You're not wearing a hat," he says as he does my bidding.

"I'm used to the sun," I tell him as I direct the boat to mid river, lock the oars so they're out of the water and won't drag, and then pick up a fishing pole I'd readied by putting a dry stonefly nymph onto the hook. They're hatching now and the fish are tearing them up. And I can't help adding on, "Your skin looks a bit delicate to go without a hat."

He doesn't seem to take offense and just nods, watching me with interest. Over the next ten minutes, I teach him how to cast the rod from a seated position on the boat. I try to show him how to stand up when he's casting, but he's not very balanced or coordinated. The slight rocking almost causes him to pitch into the water.

Once he has the basics, I take the oars in hand and start directing the boat as it rides the current. I pull into a few well-known spots where he's almost guaranteed to get a hit, and by the third riffle he casts into, he surprisingly does as I instruct and pulls the tip of the rod up hard when he feels a trout snag the fly.

I talk him through the mechanics.

Keep the tip up.

Reel it in.

Keep reeling.

Tip up so there's tension. If you lower it, he can jump off the hook.

All right. Hold steady. Let me get my net.

And sure as shit… I swear he almost squeals when I offer to let him hold the fish briefly before I release it back into the water. With his nose wrinkled, he says, "No, thank you. They look terribly slimy."

No shit, Sherlock.

As we continue downstream, Magnus makes some more casts, but then he seemingly gets bored and says, "I think I'll take a break."

After setting the pole down, he kicks his legs out, crosses them, and says, "So, how long have you been a member of The Silo?"

"Going on about a year now," I say as I periodically look over my shoulder at the river since I'm sitting with my back to the direction we're headed. I use some small maneuvers with the oars to keep us in the center, which is guaranteed to get us to our destination much quicker than if I were going side to side to hit some popular fishing spots.

"And what do you think of my sweet Auralie?" he slyly asks.

I think about playing dumb or aloof, but despite what a shmuck I think this guy is, I don't think he's overly stupid. "She's extremely beautiful. Surely, you know that."

"I do indeed," he says. "She'll fetch a good price for sure."

"So it's true then," I push at him, because I know he's being intentionally coy to make me ask. "You're going to auction off her virginity?"

"That I am," he says like a proud peacock. "And I was wondering if you'd be so kind as to perhaps give me some inside scoop on some of the wealthier patrons there. Perhaps not just the wealthiest, but also those most inclined to have a proclivity toward virgins. While I'm not in an overall hurry to get this deal done, because I want to drive the price as high as possible, it would certainly make things more efficient if I can let those most likely to bid on her have a little bit of time with her first. Sort of an appetizer, so to speak."

My jaw locks and I want to tell him to go to hell, because no way in fuck do I want to help him perpetuate this travesty. I have no clue why Auralie feels like she needs to do this, but I know without a doubt she doesn't want to. But before I decline, his next words almost knock me on my ass.

"And if you'd be willing to give me some good tips, I'd be inclined to reward you," he says in a smooth voice. "With perhaps a little liaison with Auralie tonight?"

"Liaison?" I ask, my voice croaking with tightness.

"Well," he says with a giggle—and Jesus fuck, men are not meant to giggle. "You can't have her virginity, but you can do whatever else you want with her. Of course, it has to be in a viewing room so other patrons can see. She's still a very valuable commodity to me. Everything is about making that sale, you understand?"

"I get to be with her tonight?" I ask, terrified he's bullshitting me. I want her so bad, but I don't want any part of this deal, which means I'm equally terrified he's being serious.

"Tonight," he confirms. "You give me the inside scoop on those I should be focused on, and I'll start focusing on them *after* you have her tonight. Deal?"

I'm absolutely going to hell.

And I don't care.

"Deal."

Chapter 6
Auralie

T ODAY WAS UNBEARABLE. I spent most of it in my
room, trying to read a book but constantly distracted
by worries and unwelcome thoughts. The only bearable
part of the day was that Magnus was gone for a good
chunk of it, on a guided fly-fishing trip with Logan.

God… Logan.

He's been starring in the unwelcome thoughts all
day. I keep analyzing last night's events, replaying in my
mind every minute of interaction with Logan in that
back hallway.

His anger… he was so angry last night over me being
fed to the sharks and my disgust with the situation.

Perceptive. Even though I told him I was okay going
with Jacob into the Orgy Room, he saw the real truth in
my eyes. He knew I didn't want any part of that horrid
situation.

He was protective. Stepping in to manipulate the
situation to save me another painful humiliation at the
hands of stranger.

And regardless of how much you could tell he
loathed my situation, he looked at me in such a way as

no other man ever has. Yes, he wanted me physically in a way that made my heart pound and my girlie parts tingle, but he also wanted something else.

He wanted to accept this weird, silent connection we have, but even as he wanted to, I could tell he was both baffled by it and fearful as well.

As was I, because it was not something I could ever act on.

When I was not distracted by thoughts of Logan, I was plagued with worry and dread over the approaching evening. Magnus didn't truly buy that I was not feeling well last night, and the only reason he let it go as easily as he did was he felt it was a good tradeoff to meet Logan and get some insider information. In fact, he came back from his fishing trip today complaining of how slimy looking the one fish he caught was, but he was practically chittering like a happy squirrel that found a nut from the "abundance of information" that Logan provided him on The Silo patrons.

When he told me that over the dinner I reluctantly shared with him down in the kitchen, I wasn't sure what he meant. I'm not sure how I feel about the fact that Logan seems to be helping Magnus. This is at odds with the way I know Logan feels about the situation, unless I'm completely off base about him.

Regardless, the worries and unwelcome thoughts still plague me as I walk into The Silo with Magnus. He's dressed in his usual dark, custom-fitted suit that he currently prefers with a skinny-pant type of style that I find makes him look ludicrous. He did not pick out my wardrobe tonight, which alerted me to the fact that I probably wouldn't be wearing clothes once we got into The Silo. Because of this, I practiced deep breathing exercises I'd been taught once by a yoga instructor I dated briefly, putting on my "persona" of the shy virgin who is quietly, but with abject acceptance, meeting her fate. I know it titillates some of the patrons to watch Magnus ordering me around and for me to appear powerless to argue against him.

So tonight, I went middle of the road. I didn't pick one of the dozen or so dresses he'd bought for me that are sweet and sugary like I wore last night, but I didn't go for sexy either. I chose a shimmery blue dress that was fairly loose across the top. It had a neckline that ran straight across the top of my chest, but it was fitted from the ribs down. The hem came down to my knees with a modest slit up the back. I paired it with a pair of silver, pointed-toe pumps. It was sexy without being slutty, and it didn't make me look too old or too young. It made me feel… like me, and when Magnus didn't say anything about my choice, I considered it a very small victory to at least feel slightly normal before the abnormality of this whole fucked-up situation was going to start.

The inner core of The Silo is packed. I suspect because it's almost midnight on a Saturday. While The Silo was busy the last three times I was here, I expect just like any business, there's a slump during the workweek.

As soon as we clear the entrance hall, I immediately

hear grunts and moans coming from the glass-walled rooms that run the perimeter. When Magnus first told me about this "establishment," I simply couldn't wrap my mind around a sex club. My first visit here was spent mostly with my face burning hot—which lent credibility to my virginal status—and my jaw hanging wide open as I snuck glances at the wide variety of sex acts taking place.

Fortunately, Magnus does not keep me here long. He normally brings me out late to The Silo, parades me around for a bit, let's someone have a piece of me, and then ushers me back out again so that he can let the gossip mill run rampant when we're out of earshot. This is something I'm grateful for, because even though I don't consider myself a prude or overly sensitive, I'm still just having a hard time with the concept of so much public display of sexuality and lack of inhibition.

With his hand on my elbow, Magnus walks up to the bar and orders a white wine spritzer for himself and a bottled water for me. He hands my drink to me without a word. To my shock, he doesn't make any move to meander through the crowd, socializing and striking up conversations, all while making sure I'm on prominent display. Still, I don't let my guard down because I know this evening can only end with me getting humiliated in some way with some strange man.

I stand beside Magnus, shoulder to shoulder, and we just look out over the crowd. A few men come up to Magnus to make small talk, all done while eyeing me lewdly. But I'm surprised when Magnus remains slightly aloof. He'd normally delve into discussion on their backgrounds and what they did for a living so he could determine if they were worthy to potentially have a crack at me.

Tonight though, he merely listens politely and keeps the talk small and light, which now makes me wonder… is he not bothering anymore because Logan gave him all the information he needs?

Then another thought… perhaps Logan gave him such good intel that Magnus has already made a decision on who will buy me. And if that's the case, that means my time in Wyoming is coming to a short end. This makes me enormously happy to be close to the end game, but a bit disgruntled over this weird sense of loss that I won't see Logan anymore.

Ridiculous really, when you consider we've hardly interacted at all.

Except with our eyes.

And almost as if a magnet grabs ahold of me, my gaze is magically pulled to the entrance hallway almost directly across the room from where I stand.

And there is Logan, looking directly at me.

Damn, he looks amazing in his usual casual attire of worn jeans and a dark blue chambray shirt with the sleeves rolled up his powerful arms. He's wearing a pair of worn hiking boots on his feet and his hair is slightly damp from what I'm guessing was a recent shower.

My skin flushes warm from the way he watches me.

When he licks his lower lip, my knees almost buckle. My head goes absolutely dizzy when he starts walking toward me, and while I know I should feel nervous about the proprietary look upon his face and how Magnus may dislike that greatly, I can't seem to send him any sort of silent warning that he needs to back off.

In fact, I lift my chin and let the warm radiance of my focus upon him speak what I'd say to him if I had the power to speak my mind in this moment. *Yes, please… come and get me. Take me away from here.*

When Logan is but a few paces away from us, I feel Magnus stiffen up beside me. I don't have to look at him to know he has Logan's purposeful walk in his line of sight. I brace for a clash between these two men because I can tell that Logan is on his way over here right this second to take me out of here.

Instead, Logan's eyes slide over to Magnus and he gives a polite tip of his head. "Magnus, I came to collect what you promised."

I jolt at the rough timbre in his voice that's laced with bitter anger, but I look up to Magnus to see his reaction.

Because… collect what?

Magnus gives Logan a charming smile and places his hand on my lower back. With a tiny shove, he pushes me toward Logan and says, "Of course. Please enjoy, but remember the rules. Her virginity stays intact."

Logan doesn't even answer. He just takes my water from me, handing it carelessly to Magnus before taking my hand in his. My gut instinct is to pull away, but I'm so shocked by what's going on that I follow along meekly. I risk a look over my shoulder at Magnus as Logan winds his way through the patrons, but he's not even looking at me. He's already engaged in conversation with someone else.

When Logan turns right down the perimeter hallway, I finally come to my senses and pull hard against his momentum. My hand tears free from his grip as I say, "Wait a minute. What's going on here?"

Logan spins on me, his eyes flashing with a combination of undisguised lust and self-loathing for said lust. He doesn't answer me. Walking right into me, he pushes me back into the concrete staves. His hands come up to lay flat on the wall to either side of my head, and he bends his own down to put his nose inches from mine. "Magnus said I could have you tonight. As payment for my services today."

I lick my lips, which feel so dry from nerves, and I ask, "You mean for providing him inside information on the patrons here to best determine who's most likely to pay the biggest price?"

"Something like that," he mutters, his eyes dropping to my mouth.

A small thud of disappointment resounds in my chest that Logan would help to facilitate this mockery, especially since I know by the prior looks he's bestowed upon me that he's firmly against the proposition of auctioning me off. I want to push him away and tell him to go to hell, but he surprises me when he says, "I told him what he wanted to hear… not necessarily what was going to help him."

I blink in surprise. My eyes get soft with gratitude that even though I will, in fact, be auctioned off, probably fairly soon, Logan is still attempting to protect me. He sees my reaction and because we've become used to communicating through the nuances of facial expression, his eyes also soften and some of the bitterness fades away. "I had to be with you… at least once. I know it's never going to be in the way that I truly want, but I'll gratefully take anything at this point."

"I don't want to be doing this," I whisper, and I don't have to clarify what I mean. He knows I mean being sold like a piece of meat. He knows I'm not talking about standing toe to toe with him in this private hallway with the prospect of something quite sinfully carnal occurring between us.

"Fuck," he growls, his eyebrows knit together in frustration. "I don't want you to be doing this either, but I don't have the kind of bank to make a bid for you."

I shake my head quickly in denial he'd even think that. "No. I'd never want you to spend your money on me like that. I'm not worth—"

Logan's mouth presses to mine, effectively shutting up my self-deprecation. Surprisingly, his kiss is soft but short. When he pulls away, his voice is heavy with grievance. "This is it for us. Tonight. Right now."

I nod in sad understanding, hating my life so much.

My eyes drop from the weight of my dejection.

"I'm going to make this good for you, Auralie," he says quietly. My eyes snap up to his with astonishment. "We have to do it in a public room so others can watch, but I want you to try to ignore that and concentrate on me. I swear I'll make it good."

My heart squeezes hard, and then bursts outward, filling up with a warm sensation of comfort I've never felt before. I've always taken care of myself, even since I was a little kid, and to have Logan declare his devotion to my well-being is almost more than I can handle.

"Logan, I don't understand any of this…"

Placing his fingertip over my lips, he says, "We don't have time. Magnus is expecting us to appear soon, and we're not going to be able to say much in there, but know this… I'd make things different for you if I could."

My eyes mist up, and I have to blink them furiously to make them go away. As he pulls his finger away from my mouth, I manage to nod my understanding. "I wish things could be different."

Placing both of his large palms against my cheeks, he pulls me away from the wall and up slightly as he says, "First though… I want to kiss you. I mean really kiss you before we go in there. I want to kiss you in a way that would declare to everyone you belong to me, which I couldn't possibly do without pissing Magnus off. So I'm going to kiss you now, okay? And you will know it's the way I'll want to kiss you in there."

I can do nothing more than nod dumbly at his beautiful words before he's bringing his face to mine.

The first touch of his full lips are whisper soft, just a slight grazing back and forth across mine that makes my breath puff out in a contented sigh. Pressing in closer to me, he puts pressure against my mouth, and I open up to him. His head tilts and I mirror in the opposite direction. He gives me a soul-possessing kiss full of wet tongue and minty breath while his hands gently frame my face. It's a kiss for the ages, and it will never be forgotten by me. It's full of sweet romance. The way in which he moves against me suggests a rumbling inferno of passion barely contained. It's also full of regret and sadness, but mostly it's a painful reminder of the fact this is fleeting.

When Logan pulls away from me, his eyes peer into mine. I read what he's saying loud and clear, *Another time. Another place. I wonder what we could be together.*

"I know exactly what you mean," I tell him softly.

Chapter 7
Logan

JESUS FUCK... WHAT in the hell have I gotten myself into?

I have to restrain the urge to grab onto Auralie and bolt for the exit door. I'll take her to my camper, put that fucker in gear, and drive balls to the wall to get her away from Magnus.

Instead, I take her hand and lace my fingers through hers before leading her toward the Black Room. If I had any respect for either Auralie or myself, I wouldn't use her to get my rocks off this way. But I can't fucking help it. I'm a glutton for punishment because I would be far better served to walk away from her now and never know the pleasures I inherently know she'll bestow. Instead, I'm going to get a taste of what I know in the depths of my soul will be heaven, and it will ruin me that I won't be able to have more.

But just to make sure, before I turn the knob to the Black Room door, I ask, "You have to go through with this sale?"

My heart sinks when she nods. "I don't have a choice."

Thought so, because why else in the fuck would she even ever start down this path?

I let resolve take over my spine, stiffening it up before I push the door open and pull her inside. She gives a slight gasp as she sees the interior of The Silo from a very different angle. While the back wall is concrete, the outer wall is glass. You can see the other patrons milling about, engrossed in conversations or making out with each other. Some minor stuff always happens out there like dick sucks or fingering a girl to orgasm while sitting on one of the plush chairs. But the really good stuff always happens in one of these rooms.

I chose the Black Room because it's designed for a singular show with either a couple or at the most a threesome. There's a raised dais done in black lacquer with a huge king mattress on top, covered in black silk. Even the flooring is done in a shiny, black tile. I assume Bridger decorated the room this way so as to highlight the simplicity of the actions that would take place upon those silk sheets. He even made sure the only lighting in this room was a single overhead light that shines down like a spotlight onto the mattress.

Auralie stands frozen, staring out at the patrons who are starting to congregate at the glass now that the room has occupants. I walk up behind her, press my body into the backside of hers, and bring both of my hands around to cup her breasts over her dress. Dropping my head, I put my mouth near her ear and whisper, "Try to ignore them. Concentrate on me, okay?"

She nods and I squeeze the firm globes of her breasts, which are utterly fantastic. I mean, I knew they were because Magnus paraded her around naked one night, but feeling them—even with a clothing barrier—is beyond better than I could have imagined.

I'm stunned when Auralie reaches a hand back and rubs her palm over my growing erection before spinning in my arms. Her hands go to my belt, and she starts to work at it, but I bring my hands down to cover hers and bring them to a stop. "Uh-uh," I chastise her so softly that no one outside the glass would be able to hear me. "Not going to do this the way you sucked those other guy's cocks."

Her eyes snap up to mine, and her heart-shaped mouth pops open in surprise. She gasps when I reach around her back, find the zipper of her dress, and lower it down. When it reaches the base of her spine, I bring my fingertips to the collar and peel the material down over her shoulders, past her arms, and over her hips where it slithers to the floor. She stands before me in a nude strapless bra done in satin with matching panties that sit high on her hips, providing more than ample coverage of her crotch and ass. My fingers work the hooks at the back and the bra comes free, spilling out those fantastic tits with nipples already standing pebbled and ready for attention.

I massage her breasts with my hands briefly, and then lower my head to suck a nipple in my mouth. Auralie's hands fly to my head, her fingers digging into my hair briefly, but then just as quickly release me as if she doesn't want to show her reaction to my touch. This I understand because it would upset Magnus if she were to show favoritism to a customer, so I give her a pass on it and pull my mouth away from her puckered flesh.

"Get on the bed," I tell her as I step back and pull my shirt over my head. Auralie's eyes go wide, and she stares at my chest for a brief moment before letting them travel down my abs.

"The bed, Auralie," I gently remind her.

She turns and steps onto the lacquered dais, those high-heeled silver pumps making the toned muscles in her legs stretch and elongate. I can't help but stare at her ass as she places a knee on the bed and then crawls to the center before turning over and lying down.

I smile at her because she looks uncomfortable as hell, her legs stiff and her spine straight, casting furtive glances at the glass. Stepping onto the dais, I wrap my hands around her ankles and jerk her legs apart, causing her to gasp in surprise. I know Magnus is watching every bit of this to make sure I don't do anything that would "devalue" his little flower, but my back is to him and he can't see me grin down at Auralie as I crawl right up her body and press my aching cock down onto her pelvis. Even with her underwear on and my jeans, I can feel the heat our bodies generate.

Dropping my weight slightly, I lower my stomach and then my chest down onto her, putting my face right over hers. I want to kiss her again the way I did in the hallway, but I don't want Magnus to suspect there's anything more between Auralie and me than a man wanting to have a bit of a thrill.

So I take just a moment to whisper, so softly I know she can barely hear me. "Going to eat your pussy now, honey. And it's going to be intense. You're going to come like I suspect you never have before."

"Oh, God," she moans, her hips pressing off the mattress against me with a grinding motion.

I hiss through my teeth and quickly move back down her body, because I don't want to fucking come in my jeans. Pulling her underwear off, I drag them down her legs, tossing them over my shoulder. I don't even risk a glance back at the crowd I know is watching, and I'm briefly thankful I didn't see Jacob out there as he'd know Auralie lied to him yesterday about having her period by what I'm getting ready to do. Auralie's gaze drifts toward the glass, so I remind her, "Eyes only on me."

She obeys instantly so I reward her, dropping to my knees and pulling her body down to the edge of the mattress. She slides easily along the silk, and I get a good look at her waxed pussy as it gets closer to me. I'm not surprised by this, although I would have rather seen her more natural. I suspect, however, Magnus insisted on this to make her look as innocent as she's held out to be.

I run a fingertip over the soft, fleshy mound. While I'm sure having my fingers near this pussy makes Magnus extremely nervous, I drag it right down her slit where I'm utterly satisfied to find her already wet. Her entire body shudders.

I slide my gaze up Auralie's body and find her lifted up on her elbows, watching me with hazy, lustful eyes filled with fascination. Bending over, I bring her legs over my shoulders and move my hands up and over her stomach before using them to peel her wide open for me. She glistens. Her clit is so swollen it peeks out from her wet flesh. Bending over, I gently prod it with the end of my tongue, and Auralie's hips shoot off the bed as she moans. I press her back down, flick my tongue out again, but this time, I'm ready. I hold her down in place, but I'm not able to suppress the cry of pleasure that tears out of her. This I know the patrons out there heard. My dick starts pulsing in my pants I'm so turned on right now.

I want so badly to press my fingers inside of her, but that's a no-no, so I open my mouth and bring it down on her, giving her a long lick up her center before settling my lips right over her clit. Licking at her slowly, I prolong what I'm guessing might be torture the way she thrashes and calls out my name. I lazily rub circles around her swollen flesh, sometimes giving a little flutter of my tongue against her clit, but when I sense her getting close to an orgasm, I back off again. I could lie here all night and do this. Because Magnus gave me no time restrictions, I'm not in a hurry for this to end.

Over and over again, I lick and suck, sometimes pressing my finger on the little bundle of nerves and rolling it around. Auralie cries and begs, and when I finally risk a glance up at her, I find her watching me with almost anguish in her eyes. She opens her mouth and I expect her to beg me for release, but instead, she whispers in a low voice that won't carry past my ears, "Logan… let me do the same to you right now."

I rear slightly backward from the naked want in her voice. From knowing she wants her mouth on me the way I have mine on hers. I raise my eyebrows at her. *Are you sure?*

She answers back with a look so intense, I can't even doubt her meaning. *Yes. Now. In my mouth.*

I go a little dizzy from what she just communicated to me, but I gather my wits enough I'm able to stand up on the dais and shed the remainder of my clothes. Nothing I'm planning on doing is breaking any of Magnus' rules, but I'm so compelled to shove my cock in her mouth, merely because she really wants it there, that I'd do it even if he'd told me not to. Nothing's stopping this train now that it's left the station.

Auralie is back on her elbows again, watching me with keen eyes. I drop to my knees back on the mattress, my dick bobbing almost painfully. I take note of the flushed cheeks, tangled hair from her thrashing, and pebbled nipples, and I can't wait another minute. Flipping my body around, I lay on my side with my face at her hips, which puts hers near mine as she rolls to her side. I can't bear to look down at her, so I concentrate on getting my mouth back on that sweet pussy by taking her outer leg, picking it up, and maneuvering it onto my shoulder. I use the arm I'm lying on to snake around her back and press her toward me, using my tongue to prod through her wet folds and find the prize. When my tongue hits her clit, she jerks and moans. I fucking love that sound from her.

Then her hand is on my cock and I'm the one who jerks, which mashes my mouth to her harder. I hold my breath for a moment that lasts for years, and then I can feel her hot, wet mouth on me. I groan against her pussy. And fuck… she takes me so deep my balls start tingling.

I can't see a damn thing because I'm face first into some sweet eating, nose, lips, mouth, and tongue deep into her snatch, and I think it might even be better I can't see. Rather, I can imagine. Her cheeks hollowed out, her throat begging to be plowed. Her mouth so damn wet that she glides seamlessly up and down my shaft. She places a tentative hand to my balls and rolls them against her palm, and I feel the head of my dick bumping against the back of her mouth. Every time I put pressure on her clit, she moans, which vibrates against my aching shaft and shoots jolts of pleasure down to my nuts.

She's so fucking good at this, but I knew she would be.

I just knew it.

I'm so close to coming and the thought of her drinking me down starts sending me over the edge.

I don't want to leave her behind so I hit her clit hard with my tongue, flicking it quickly with increasing pressure.

Both of us are so far gone, our hips pumping against each other. My head bobs between her legs as she gyrates and I ram my cock in and out of her mouth, entering the top of her throat.

With a sudden heave of my body, I roll to my back, my arm around her, taking her with me so I'm on the bottom and she's on top. Her mouth never misses a stroke. I use both free hands now to pull her down so she's sitting on my face and my tongue is lashing at her pussy. Auralie is leaking all over my mouth and chin faster than I can lap it all up, and when I sense she's right on the edge, I do something deliciously dirty to her that's also not against Magnus' rules.

I reach a hand past her hip, over her lower spine, and push my fingers lightly down the crack of her ass. Pushing them past her tight hole, down to the base of her pussy where she's dripping wet, I rub my fingers around until they're soaked. Then back up again where I push the tip of my index finger right into her ass.

Auralie shrieks against my cock and then tilts her pelvis so she's grinding on my face, her entire body quaking as an orgasm rips through her. It causes my own to fire and I plant my feet on the mattress, punch my hips up, and start to unload what seems like buckets into her hot little mouth.

I groan my relief against her pussy, pull my index finger out to the tip, and push it back in. Auralie cries out again, but it's muffled because her mouth is full of cum and cock, still holding me so deep I can feel her throat swallowing against my overly sensitive head.

When she's given one last pull on my cock, she pulls her head back and I flop out of her. Her face falls and rests on my thigh as I pull my finger out of her ass, giving a slight push on her hips to lift off me. She's practically dead weight and I'm barely able to breathe, but I also don't want to lose the feeling of her against me.

So I roll both of us to the side again, slipping my arms around her waist and resting my cheek against her pelvis as I try to get my breathing under control.

Not once did I think about the crowd watching us, or if Magnus is pissed that was clearly a bit more than I'm sure he imagined happening, or even if Auralie's mortified we did that in front of all those people. I don't think of anything other than the fact that was my one and only crack at this gorgeous creature, and now I've got to figure out a way to move past this and put her out of my mind.

Chapter 8

Auralie

I PULL MAGNUS' rental Porsche into a parallel parking spot just one block off the town square, almost giddy with excitement to have the opportunity to explore Jackson. To say I was stunned this morning when Magnus woke me up at the crack of dawn was an understatement. He burst into my room, telling me that I needed to drive him to the airport as he had an emergency back in New York he had to handle.

There was no way I was going back with him because he wasn't about to waste money on a plane ticket when I wasn't necessary to him there, and he also didn't want me having any face-to-face contact with my father. When I asked him what the emergency was, my stomach dropped when he said with icy menace, "Your father apparently can't follow instructions. He's going to cause everything to crumble if I don't get there and settle things down."

Yeah, well, that's what you get, Magnus, when you get a two-bit hustler to run a long con that's completely out of his comfort zone.

I worried, of course, for my father. Magnus may at

most times project an air of civility and politeness about him, but that's just part of him staying in character. I've seen the nasty side that gets out of control with blistering anger. While Magnus Albright could never be compelled to violence as he might hurt his prissy, delicate hands, he has enough goons on his payroll that his messages are always imparted with brutal clarity as to his seriousness.

So Dad has screwed up apparently, and I'm worried for him, but I also have to remember that Magnus left me here and this game hasn't been played out to his conclusion. He's not going to do anything to my father that will send me running, so I'm just going to have to hope my dad didn't fuck things up too badly and that Magnus can fix whatever it is.

And then he can come back here, and we can get this finished. I can move on with my life then, which most definitely includes a plan to pay Magnus back for making me do this.

But for now, I'm stuck in the picturesque town of Jackson. Although I've been here a week, I haven't left the rented house I shared with Magnus except to go to The Silo. I was going stir crazy on top of plain old crazy because of this shit I've landed myself into, and now I'm going to spend a nice day just being a normal girl on a very abnormal vacation.

Over the next hour, I walk in and out of various shops, most of them geared toward visiting tourists. I spend twenty minutes alone in the studio of a photographer who specializes in native wildlife, wishing I had time to go explore Yellowstone. Maybe tomorrow, depending on how fast Magnus is coming back. I assume he'll call me at some point today and give me a tentative plan. Until then, he merely told me to stay out of trouble and to keep a low profile until he got back.

I walk a few blocks off the town square, passing by a tattoo shop and wishing I had the time or extra money to get one. It's always been a wish of mine, and I know exactly what I'd get.

A pair of rolling dice on my inner forearm.

My signature grift.

I pass a novelty T-shirt shop with product hanging in the window that says things like "Wyoming: Where Men Are Men and the Sheep Are Scared" or "I Support The Right to Keep and Bear Arms" with a picture of a grizzly holding a rifle.

Past a winter sporting store called Teton Ski and Snowboarding, which even though it's still fairly warm out, it seems to have a ton of people inside as I pass by.

To a shop specializing in cowboy boots—

"Auralie?" I hear from behind me.

Turning around, I freeze in place as I see Logan walking out of the ski shop carrying a small paper bag in his hand. His expression mirrors mine, I'm sure. *I never thought I'd see you again.*

This we both knew was a truth because Logan whispered it to me last night. While we were getting dressed after that incredible session in the Black Room, he said he wasn't going to come back into The Silo until after I was gone. It was both a sweet and sad sentiment, and I understood his thinking without even asking him why. I was also grateful he wouldn't come back, because I didn't want him to see me on my knees before another man, nor did I want him involved in this farce any longer.

"Hey," I respond in a quavering voice, shaking as he walks toward me.

"What are you doing here?" he asks, his head swiveling left and right, I'm betting looking for Magnus.

"He's not here," I tell him, and his eyes snap back to mine as his shoulders visibly drop into a relaxed posture. "He went to New York for a few days and left me back here."

The very second Logan comprehends that Magnus is gone and I'm here with no one to look over me, something flashes in his eyes that looks dark and dangerous and yet so alluring, a surge of adrenaline courses through me. I almost half expect him to grab me, pull me into a dark alley if such a thing existed in Jackson, and have his way with me.

Instead, he reaches out for my hand and says, "Come on. Let's go get some breakfast."

I don't hesitate. Don't even think to deny him. My hand lifts out and clasps his palm to palm because there's nothing else I'd rather do in this moment. He turns and leads me back in the same direction I had just come from. We walk side by side in silence as he maneuvers us past tourists who clog the sidewalks, across a busy street when the walk sign says we can go, and down another sidewalk, which puts us back on one of the main streets that border the Town Square.

He leads me with purpose. The long strides and the way he grips my hand strongly but gently tells me he's determined to get me someplace where we can sit down and talk.

Actually talk.

No more intent meanings hidden within the depths of our eyes.

While it was an excellent means to communicate when we couldn't actually converse, I'm looking forward to just hearing more of his deep voice that has just the sexiest of rumbles to it.

Logan leads me to a restaurant called "Frannie's" that looks like a log cabin. It has a flat, wide porch across the front with several rocking chairs where customers can rock away the time while they wait for a table. It's past the early breakfast rush, and there's no one waiting outside. Logan leads me in, nods at one of the waitresses, and pulls me through the restaurant to the back where there's a semi-private table in a corner by the kitchen. He only releases my hand to let me slide into my chair, and then he takes the one opposite me.

With quiet speculation, Logan just stares at me, as if he can't quite figure out what to do with me, except maybe feed me. I'm equally at a loss as to what to say, because talking about what happened between us last night could be extremely dangerous.

So I pick up the paper menu before me and start to

study it. I don't look up at Logan, although I can feel the weight of his stare, but I'm also so flustered to even be in his presence that I really can't see anything on the menu either.

"Why are you letting Magnus sell you off?" Logan asks quietly, and my eyes lift until they peer at him over the menu. His visage is troubled and stormy, and I can't have him incensed on my behalf. He could easily get me angry over the injustice of it all and convince me to run, and I just can't do that.

"How about we talk about something that doesn't have to do with The Silo?" I say quietly.

"So I can't tell you how unbelievable last night was?" he asks, his eyes turning practically golden to match the heat of his words. "Since that happened in The Silo?"

I squeeze my legs together and duck my head behind the menu again. My privacy from such an intimate question is short lived as his fingertips peek over the top and pull it down. I notice his fingers are rough and nicked with cuts and scars, a hazard, I would guess, of his job as a fly fisherman.

My eyes reluctantly go to his, and reluctantly only because I'm terrified of the way he makes me feel. "We really should forget about it."

"I'm pretty sure that's an impossibility on my part," he says dryly before leaning across the table so he can murmur. "And I know you can't either by the way you're squirming in your chair right now."

Damn.

I immediately plant my feet hard on the floor and make myself stay still. "Logan… maybe another time—"

"Okay, if we can't talk about The Silo or the amazing orgasms we gave each other last night, how about telling me a little about yourself? Where are you from?"

"Brooklyn," I say, blinking in surprise at the abrupt change of subject, but with a lingering tingle in my lower spine over the mention of the orgasms. Because last night was the singularly most amazing thing that has ever happened to me in my life. I knew the power of what an orgasm felt like, but it never felt like that before.

Never.

"Your whole life?" he asks to clarify.

"Yes. Born and raised. And you?" I ask politely, not really liking this stilted, demure conversation, but knowing we're both better off not venturing from this path.

"Chicago," he says with a shrug. "Although I've lived in quite a few places since then."

"Like where?"

He's prevented from answering when a waitress comes to our table and places coffee cups before us without even asking if we want some, although she does ask, "Want anything else other than coffee?"

Logan and I both shake our heads.

"Know what you want to order?" she asks.

Logan pushes his menu aside, clearly having eaten here before. "Three eggs over easy, hash browns, bacon—crisp, toast—white not wheat."

The waitress scribbles and then looks to me. "And you, honey?"

"I'll have the same," I tell her with a smile, not because that's the easiest thing to do but because that's the normal breakfast I would order, except sometimes I'd get sausage instead of bacon.

Seems our connection transcends to breakfast foods now.

"So, where else have you lived?" I ask again after the waitress leaves. I occupy my hands by adding a little milk and sweetener to my coffee, although Logan apparently drinks his black since he doesn't doctor his up, so I know there are ways in which we differ.

"Several places really," he says in a flat voice. "Texas. Spent a little time in Southern California. Then Washington and Oregon. Landed here a little over a year ago."

"And before you started traveling?" I ask, my elbows resting on the table and my coffee cup held before me with both hands.

"I was in Chicago working a dead-end job," he says, and the flatness in his voice goes so monotone, it's almost difficult to distinguish the words from one another. There's so much antipathy for whatever his life was in Chicago, that it's clear it's not a subject he wishes to discuss.

So I remain quiet and take a sip of my coffee.

"What did you do in New York?" he asks, attempting but failing miserably at the generalized conversation you might try if you were out on a first date. But we are well beyond that. Logan had his mouth on my clit last night, and I let him come down my throat.

I shrug, playing it vague and loose with the real truth. "My father does some apartment management-type stuff, and I help him out with that. But I was in the process of looking at some local colleges I could go to."

"For what?" he prods, his coffee remaining untouched.

I shrug again. "I don't know. Not sure what I want to be when I grow up, but I figured I needed to get started, right?"

"Depends," he says neutrally. "How old are you?"

I don't even hesitate in my lie. "Twenty."

He lowers his head slightly and curses under his breath. "Fuck." I can tell this displeases him. I'm not sure why, because I know Magnus has propagated the gossip grapevine at The Silo with my "age" and my sexual status—"virgin". It's common knowledge to everyone, so this shouldn't be a surprise.

"I would have thought you were older," he says to clarify.

"Why's that?" I ask, my head tilted.

"You just have a wisdom about you that I can't quite explain. I find most of the younger women I meet to be flighty… unsettled. And here you are, in a pretty untenable situation, and yet, you handle it with a solid backbone. You're a strong woman, Auralie, and most twenty-year-olds don't recognize that within themselves."

I hate that he's so close to the mark, but he's right.

Growing up the way I did made me street smart and gave me wisdom I didn't ask for at a very early age. But I could say that whether I was fifteen, twenty, or twenty-five years of age. I've been more mature than my age for as long as I can remember.

"So I ask again," he says, his voice going hard and demanding. "Why is a woman as strong as you doing this?"

Emotions war within me. I'm pleased and warmed he cares enough about me to ask, but also affronted that he's judging my actions. We may have some sort of connection that can't quite be explained at this point, but he has no right to be piqued by my choices because he could never understand my motivation.

It's with irritation I snap at him. "You mean debasing myself by sucking unknown men's' dicks and letting another stranger eat me out in front of a crowd of sexual deviants?"

He jerks back with true surprise on his face, before clarifying in a voice low and rumbling with dissatisfaction over my answer. "I'll let the stranger comment pass. I'll also let it pass that you failed to mention I made you come harder than I guarantee you ever have in your life. And if you enjoyed what you and I did, that was in no way debasing yourself. Plenty of people get off on that type of thing, and there is nothing wrong if you enjoyed it. So, again… I'd really like to know why a woman such as yourself—who is strong, confident, and smart—feels the need to do this? And I want to know this because I want to know if I can help get you out of this situation."

I immediately shake my head. There is no way I am involving a good man in my very bad and fucked-up circumstances. "You can't help."

"Perhaps I can—"

"Logan," I say with a firm voice. "Leave it alone. If you can't do that, then I'm out of here."

And I don't want to be out of here, I tell him with a pointed look. *I like your company and looking at you and listening to your voice, and hell... even silence is golden between us. So please... don't make me leave.*

His jaw locks tight. I can see the irritation flash in his eyes, along with frustration and some unfulfilled need, but he only holds that for a moment before every bit of it clears out and there's nothing but understanding left.

"Okay," he says softly. "I won't ask you why you're doing this, but just know... if you want to try to figure another way out, I'm ready to help you do it."

I know I just shut him down tight a second ago, but I can't help it when my mouth opens, my vocal chords engage, and a single whispered and needful word comes out, "Why?"

Logan finally picks up his coffee, blows across the top, and takes a sip while looking at me over the rim. When he sets it back down, he says, "Because we're tethered."

"Excuse me?" I ask, not in a tart, offended way, but in an I'm-completely-confused way.

"From the moment you and I first locked eyes on

each other, there was an understanding of sorts between us. I don't know the how or the why something like that happens between two people, and fuck… we spent three days communicating through looks and body language, but you can't deny it, Auralie… you and I have something that ties us together, and I'm not sure what it is. But it was absolutely confirmed after the way we consumed each other last night."

God, and I know it too. I felt it from the very first time we beheld each other. Call it metaphysical or just a product of my underused imagination, but there is a connection there that I've never experienced with another human being in my life.

"You with me?" Logan asks quietly.

I nod, getting ready to speak the words back to him, but the waitress arrives with our food. The intimate connection is broken as we both lean back a bit so she can set the plates down. After she leaves, Logan picks up his utensils. While he busies himself pulling his eggs over onto his hash browns and cutting them all up together— same as I like to do—he says casually, "I've got a fishing trip this afternoon, but I'll pick you up at six tonight. I'm taking you out to dinner."

I just blink at him, my own utensils in hand and poised to mix eggs and potatoes together. There's not one part of me that enjoys being bossed around, and I've gone most of my life not ever having to withstand that, but for some reason, I like the way he just told me that's what we were doing tonight.

So I just nod and smile, then I pull my eggs on top of my hash browns.

Fuck you, Magnus. I'm doing this for me.

Chapter 9
Logan

W E WALK INTO the Blue Lion, my hand on Auralie's lower back as I guide her in. It's strange… seeing her in normal clothing. By normal, she's wearing a pair of white skinny jeans with black flats, a graphic t-shirt, and a black, blazer-type jacket. The clothing's not overly expensive, but it is stylish, at least from what I can remember of my days immersed back in a life filled with style and culture.

I have to keep mentally barking at my dick to stay down—not that I didn't need that same advice when she was dressed all virginally sweet in The Silo, but for some reason tonight… the way she looks like a normal, beautiful young woman makes her all the more attractive to my senses.

It makes me wish for something I hadn't thought possible in my lonely existence.

I also know this is a fool's quest, but I can't fucking help myself from wanting to be around her when I can. I can't even have the promise of fucking her after dinner tonight, but it just doesn't seem to matter.

I'm helplessly drawn to her like a moth to flame.

A hummingbird to sugar water.

A bear to honey.

And what-the-fuck-ever other cliché you can think of that describes an irresistible need to have something—it's what I have right now. It's why I never once hesitated when Magnus offered me a deal to exchange information for a night with Auralie. It's also why I didn't bother going to Bridger for advice because even though I was being selfish and taking something I wanted, it was eating at my gut a little to get involved with her. And Bridger could always be counted on for good advice.

The problem is that I didn't want to hear Bridger's good advice because it would prevent me from being with Auralie, so I stayed away from him.

It would be an absolute understatement to say I've been obsessing about Auralie since last night. That utterly fucking amazing sixty-nine session in the Black Room, where a woman has never tasted better to me and my cock has never shot off like that. And I'm not going to lie… the fact it was being done in front of all those other men who wanted that same crack at her but would never have it the way I had it last night made it all the better.

While The Blue Lion isn't an overly fancy place as I'm wearing jeans and a nice shirt and that doesn't offend their dress policy, it is a bit pricey and this is taking a chunk out of my wallet. This says something as I live pretty much hand to mouth, and I might be eating cheese and crackers for a while to compensate, but I wanted to do something "normal" with Auralie. Everything between us so far has been so mystifying; it naturally calls upon the senses to deny it as being real in any form or fashion.

Perhaps tonight… I can manage to de-mystify this connection we have. Maybe I can shed a light that would reveal this girl to be nothing more than a hot way to get a nut.

Or terrifyingly, it might reveal we really do have something that could be both magical and real.

Whatever.

The waitress leads us through the restaurant and to the outdoor deck that holds about ten tables. I requested outdoor seating as it was an unseasonably warm day, and I knew the evening would be mild enough. Once we're seated, a waiter appears with a flourish and asks for our drink orders. I order a local microbrew, but Auralie shakes her head and just asks for water.

After the waiter leaves, I ask, "Don't drink?"

"I'm only twenty," she reminds me.

"Plenty of people still order drinks… have fake ID's," I counter.

She looks across the table at me, looking angelic from the glow of the crystal-encased candle in the center, and shakes her head. "My mom was an alcoholic. Drank herself to death. Always been afraid, I guess, that the gene ran in me. I never wanted to take the chance."

I manage not to wince at the mixture of pain and determination in her voice, but I ask, "How old were you?"

"Ten," she says with a bitter smile. "Been just Dad and me since."

"That must have been tough."

Her smile grows fond. "My dad did the best he could. We survived it together. But what about your parents? And do you have any siblings?"

My stomach tightens, and I realize what a dumbass I am. I invited this woman out to a romantic dinner, hoping to figure out what there was going on between us, and never once did I think she'd turn an eye toward wanting to know about me. I'd gotten so good over the years at keeping a barrier up and making it clear my private life was private, that I'd not had to field a personal question in a long time.

I swallow against the guilt over my half-baked truths. "No siblings. My mom and dad are still back in Chicago, but we don't talk much."

Well, we don't talk at all.

Ever.

Not in two years even though they tried and tried to reach out to me with unanswered phone calls. I finally changed my number and that effectively stopped that. While stopping contact with them helped to alleviate my guilt that they were trying to help a son who couldn't be helped, I was now weighted with guilt that I was hurting them by not talking.

Seems hurting people is what I do best.

Auralie picks up her menu, I think a bit rebuffed by

my curt answer, and my mind spins trying to figure a way to get some normal conversation going without pushing it in a direction that puts a spotlight on me. But then movement from another table three over catches my attention, and I see Rand and Cat standing up to leave the restaurant. I take in the fact that their meals are half eaten and they appear to be leaving early.

Cat looks upset. She hurries through the double glass doors and to the left, down to where I know the restrooms are. My eyes go back to Rand. I find him staring at me. With a quick, curious glance to Auralie, his gaze comes back to me. He walks our way. Auralie looks up at him in surprise when he comes to a stop by our table.

"Hey man," I say, reaching my hand out for him to shake.

"Just on our way out," Rand says in what sounds like glum resignation. "Thought I'd stop by."

My eyes slide over to the doors that Cat just ran through, and I ask, "She okay?"

Rand brushes a hand through his long, blond hair before blowing out a breath. "Yeah… she's still a bit rattled, I think."

I nod in understanding. While it was just five short days ago that I had that amazing fuck session with Rand and Cat, it was the night before last that someone attacked Cat outside of Rand's apartment. I heard this from Bridger. While I had a brief conversation with Rand that night to assure she was okay, I haven't talked to him since.

Which also makes me realize…

I haven't had sex since that night with Rand and Cat. Sure… I'd had all kinds of amazing oral with Auralie last night, and a mediocre blow job the night Auralie sucked another man's dick, but I haven't fucked another woman—or man—since my time with Rand and Cat five days ago. I've been content to go home and get my rocks off while thinking about Auralie while I masturbate.

So fucking weird.

Rand's gaze cuts down to Auralie and back to me with a pointed look.

"Oh, fuck," I mutter and give an apologetic smile to Auralie. "I'm sorry. Auralie… this is my buddy, Rand. Rand, this is Auralie."

Rand breaks out in a big smile, one that says he's immensely happy to see his friend out on a date with a normal girl. He reaches a hand out to Auralie. When she takes it, he asks, "Are you local, Auralie, or here on vacation?"

I open my mouth to jump in with some immediate lie to help cover Auralie's reason for being in Wyoming because Rand hasn't been to The Silo in a while and has no clue about her.

But she beats me to the punch. "I'm actually just here temporarily visiting."

"Oh, and how did you two meet?" Rand asks her, still beaming that curious smile of happiness.

Auralie looks a little unsure of what to say, so instead, she says, "Um…"

She looks to me with a helpless gaze. I shoot her back one that says, *It's okay. This guy is solid.*

I look up to Rand and say, "We met at The Silo."

I look back to Auralie. I can tell she's a bit tense to have revealed that, so I try to reassure her. "Rand's a member. Cat too."

She still looks tense, so I stretch a leg out under the table and slide it up against hers in nothing more than a press of reassurance. She relaxes slightly, but then tenses again when Rand says, "Oh… wait. Are you the virgin who—?"

"What the fuck do you know about that?" I growl in a low voice.

Rand looks chagrined and says in a lower voice, "Sorry… Bridger told me about her a few days ago."

Auralie's head drops down, and even though it's dim and I can't really tell, I think she's embarrassed. This really bugs me. So I turn to Rand and say, "Listen… nice seeing you and all, but—"

He doesn't need the hint. "Yeah man… sorry. Good seeing you, and Auralie, very nice to meet you. My buddy, Logan here, is a good man."

Auralie looks up and gives him a polite smile, but it's guarded. "Nice meeting you too, Rand."

"Tell Cat I said hello," I say as an afterthought, and Rand nods his head.

As he walks away, I watch his retreating back for a moment and realize something that's very interesting. Usually when I'm in Rand's presence, I will often think of sex. Not just because he and I have fucked and sucked each other, but because we have had numerous women we've shared over the past year. He's a good friend, yes, but most of our encounters revolve around fucking, and that's because I use sex as a drug and so I have it a lot. So naturally, whenever I was around Rand, it would only seem to reason that I'd think about sex.

And Cat… who couldn't think of sex when she was around?

But when I saw her just a bit ago, and talking now to Rand, I didn't think of sex once during my conversation with him. Didn't have a stirring in my pants. No matter how hot our encounter was last week, and I'm sure they'd probably be up for that again, I didn't have any desire to be with the two of them.

For now, they merely felt like good friends.

"So, he's a friend of yours?" Auralie asks softly, and my head swivels to face her.

"Yeah, really good friend," I say, which is sort of true. Well, good as in as long as we keep things simple, we're good. He doesn't know shit about me. No one here does.

"Did you meet him through The Silo?"

The waiter returns with our drinks and asks if we're ready to order, but I decline and tell him we need more time. Neither of us has even looked at the menu, and I'm in no rush for this evening to end.

When he leaves, I answer her question. "Rand and I both got part-time jobs at The Wicked Horse around the same time to supplement our full-time jobs. We got to know Bridger. He eventually let us in on the secret club behind The Wicked Horse and offered us jobs there as Fantasy Makers."

"You get paid to… to… have sex?" she asks hesitantly.

"No," I say with admonishment but temper it with a quick grin. "That would be prostitution. But we do get a free membership. Bridger even gives out 'quarterly bonuses' to the Wicked Horse employees who… shall we say… make the other full-paying members happy."

"So you *are* getting paid for sex," she points out but her face is still questioning. It's asking, *What motivates you to do that?*

So I enlighten her. "I don't do it for the money although it's nice and it helps pay the bills, and frankly, I don't do a lot of fantasies there so I don't make a lot of money. I just take advantage of my membership, and I use it a lot."

She just stares at me.

"I do it because I like the kinky sex," I clarify further, and wait to see how she takes that.

"I've seen a lot of weird things go on in that building that I never even knew were possible," she murmurs, and I don't mistake the sensual heat in her voice.

I can tell she's both put off and attracted to the debauchery that she's seen. It makes my dick start to swell at the thought that perhaps we share that in common too. Because while I love sex, even just normal, missionary, fuck-pussy-until-you-get-off sex, I also get off on the perversion of the things that happen in The Silo. Never even blinked an eye the first time I fucked Rand—my first guy. I wanted to be different and drown my misery in the new and exciting world of unrestrained sexual play.

"Anything you saw that you liked in particular?" I ask, my voice husky without meaning it to be.

She drops her eyes in only the way a virgin would when an experienced man asks what turns her on. This strangely does not turn me on. The one thing that makes my attraction to Auralie very weird is that I like my women experienced, bold, and adventurous. Those are not words synonymous with virgin.

"I like watching other people have sex," she says in almost a whisper.

"It's living porn," I agree with an encouraging smile.

"It's still shocking to me."

Not so much to me. Most times now in The Silo, I'm not even really paying attention to what's going on. My mission is simple, and that's to find an interesting way to have a release. I'm almost numb to the experience.

Except last night.

An amazing performance in front of the entire club last night with a woman who made me hornier than I've ever been in my life. I'd recreate what we did last night, every night for the rest of my foreseeable future, and be happy with it.

"Can I ask you a question, Logan?" Auralie asks.

I have to blink to orient myself back to the present

and this beautiful woman who is having dinner with me, not sucking my cock. "Sure."

"You truly don't do it for the money? Just because you like 'kinky' sex?"

Well, isn't she persistent? Still, I hedge because she's pushing too close at my personal boundaries. "What's not to love about kinky sex?"

"I don't buy it," she says with a shake of her head, her long, black hair falling over her shoulders. "I watch the people in there, and something drives them. It's more than just feeling good or carefree. It's more than just being a libertine. I mean, the men who want a virgin… they want that because it represents something rare and precious that they'll likely never get another crack at. It's like someone who collects rare antiques or works of art. There are bragging rights and inflation of ego. Every person in there wants something, and they are being driven by something personal to want it. I want to know what drives you."

I stare at her, my heart thundering so hard in my chest that it feels like it will punch through bone and flesh and race right out of the restaurant without me. She's asking me the one question that would explain everything about my life in the last two years, and it's not something I discuss with anyone.

Ever.

I take a deep breath, will my pulse to calm down, and try to tactfully decline her curiosity into the reasons Logan McKay is the way he is. Besides, she hasn't offered up any of her secrets to me, and even if she did… I'd still never tell her. I'm not prepared to suffer "the look" that I would invariably get. Not ready to destroy what little bit of attraction and connection she has to me.

So I lie to her… yet again, and I try to shock her at the same time so that she gets misdirected. "I'm just a very sexual man, Auralie and that's all there is to it. I like sex, and I like variety. I'm adventurous. I like trying everything, and The Silo is the perfect place to do so. It's just as simple as that."

"How adventurous?" she asks, eyes wide with almost a childlike curiosity, and that totally makes my dick twitch. Any further conversation along these lines, and I'm going to have to pull her out of here and do something about it. Maybe drag her in the bathroom and have her suck my dick since she's getting me riled up.

So instead, I pick up my menu as I say, "How about we figure out what we want to order, and maybe keep the sex questions down to a minimum? There's only so much I can handle with you sitting across from me looking as sweet as I remember you tasting last night."

Her eyes go round and a small gasp slides past those lips that I never did even get to see on my dick last night. I could only imagine them since my face was full of pussy.

I grin at her and open my menu, lowering my gaze to check out the salad choices as a starter.

Chapter 10
Auralie

THE REST OF dinner was relatively… normal.

I mean, as normal as could be for a girl posing as a virgin for money, who lets another man dictate whose dick she can suck and who put on an oral sex show for a crowd of strangers.

There's no doubt that Logan and I are doing an awful lot of lying to each other. Because we have this weird extra-perception going on with each other, and can have entire conversations with mere looks, we both know we've skirted the truth with each other on multiple occasions.

While I've refused to talk about my reasons for being in The Silo, and so Logan can only guess as to those, he knows I'm being evasive when he's asked about my background. Likewise, I know there's something twisted in his past that has driven him to a place where he takes solace in anonymous, kinky sex. We're hiding things from one another, but somehow, it seems to be okay right in this very moment. We know our time together is limited, so we seem to be okay with the partial truths and banal conversation regarding world events and funny stories from our lives that don't impact the house of cards we've built so far.

But overall, dinner was enjoyable. It was not a hardship to spend a few hours with an amazingly gorgeous man who made me feel like I swallowed butterflies or something. It's a feeling I've never had before with a man.

Granted, grifting is not conducive to relationships. When you live moment to moment in one con or another, you build a wall around your very human nature so that you never let your guard slip. Grifters are notoriously unromantic creatures, shifty and sly. We can't open our hearts up to be stolen because we're too busy doing the stealing.

It's not to say I'm without experience though.

I've dated here and there, usually people from my world, but we're territorial and competitive, and always looking for a way to one-up the other. So yeah… meaningless dates and even more meaningless conversation. Nothing more than a way to step outside of my structured little world, blow off some steam, and accept something for just a moment that feels good even if it's completely manufactured.

Logan pulls his beat-up old truck into the driveway of the rented cabin outside of Jackson. He'd picked me up here a few hours ago. I'd come out the door and met him before he even made it to the porch. I didn't want to feel compelled to invite him in and give him a tour of a home that meant nothing to me.

But now… as he cuts the engine off, which rumbles and sputters once before going dead, I wonder if I should invite him in now. We diligently avoided the topic of sex for the rest of our meal, but it didn't mean we weren't thinking about it. I would have images of last night pop into my head at the most inopportune times, causing my panties to get wet. Logan seemed to squirm at times in his chair, and once he reached down to adjust himself.

Just the two of us sitting across from each other at dinner with simple memories of the previous night, and we were both turned on.

Will we repeat it tonight?

I know I'm game, but I wonder if he is as he was clear last night that it was a onetime only thing.

"I'm going to offer to walk you to the door," Logan says into the quiet truck cab. I turn my gaze to him because something about the rumble in his voice causes me to go on alert. "And if you accept, I'm not stopping when I get to the door. I'm coming in with you."

"I can't—" I start to put him off, because I need him to know that sex is out of the question. I can't blow this elaborate set up just because I want to feel him inside of me.

He shakes his head, cutting me off. "I'll leave your pussy alone. But that's all I'm promising."

A violent shudder runs up my spine, producing a full-body shiver. Every detail of last night pulses in my mind. Things he did to me that I have only imagined in my sexiest dreams, and things he did to me I'd never imagined.

His finger in my ass…

Another shiver.

"Okay," I say in a rush. For a split moment, I think Logan looks almost disappointed. As if he wanted me to decline him so we could say goodbye right this minute and try to move on from each other, because we're only making the addiction worse by feeding it.

But then, just as quickly, his eyes start to shimmer with an almost fevered need, and I know he's going to wreck me even better than he did the first time.

"LAST NIGHT," LOGAN asks me in between soft kisses down my belly. "First time a man's gone down on you?"

"Mmmm. Hmmmm," I manage to purr from the back of my throat as his lips trail along the waistband of my panties. It was the one and only time I'd had a man do something like that to me, and it was more incredible than anything I could imagine. My orgasm was definitely bigger, brighter, and longer than any I'd ever given myself with my own fingers. It's like Logan knew my body better than I did.

"Tell me how it felt?" he whispers as he uses his hands to drag my panties down, peppering my legs with kisses as he goes along. "My mouth on you. What was that like?"

"Warm," I say, gasping as he spreads my legs wide and crawls in between them.

"What else?"

"Electric," I moan as he glides his fingers over the bare skin of my pussy.

Two thumbs at my swollen lips, and he peels them apart, making me both self-conscious and apparently wanton as my hips start to move. My body flushes warm all over. When he bends over and rolls his tongue in a circle around my clit, I cry out. "More."

"It felt 'more'?" he asks teasingly, and I lift my head up from the bed to see him smiling at me lecherously.

"Give me more," I clarify.

Well, it's actually a demand.

"Mmmmm," he ponders thoughtfully. "Giving me orders. I like that. What else do you want me to do?"

My pulse starts hammering with the possibilities, but while I'm not without some experience, I'm without the kind of experience that would ever give me confidence. So I mumble, "Do what you did last night."

"Uh-uh," Logan chastises. "Specifics. Tell me specifically what you want."

I heave with a frustrated grunt, rotating my hips again to try to get his attention there, but when he just stares at me expectantly, I finally tell him, "I want your mouth on my clit."

He nods with a smile. "What else?"

"I want you to suck it," I say, my voice more firm and with a tiny bit of authority that sounds weird. He apparently likes it because his eyes go dark with appreciation. So I add on, "Hard. I want you to suck it hard."

"Christ," he mutters and rears up, his hands swiftly pulling his shirt over his head and then whipping his belt open. I watch in fascination as he unzips his jeans and pushes them down slightly, pulling his swollen cock out from its confines.

He gives me a sheepish grin as he strokes himself a few times. "Had to get my dick out. It was getting strangled because your dirty talk was making it so hard."

I give a feminine chuckle and try to provoke him further, because I have just found out that turning Logan on is turning *me* on. "And your fingers… I know you can't breach… well, you can maybe stick one in a little bit while you're eating me out."

"Holy Jesus fuck, Auralie," he groans, stroking his dick harder. "No. I get anywhere near the inside of that pussy and I'm not stopping. But I'll finger fuck your ass again if you want."

Oh, God.

I swear if words could cause a mini orgasm, I think I just had one by the savage shudder that rippled through me. With my breath practically frozen in my lungs, I say, "Logan… I want you to do whatever you want to me. Whatever you think I can take?"

The last comes out almost like a question.

His hand freezes on his cock and he tilts his head at me for a discerning moment before he tells me, "Baby… I know you don't have much experience, but I think you could take whatever I handed you. You've got the backbone for it."

Oh, geez. Another ripple runs through me as an ache forms between my legs. "Then do it," I whisper.

Logan's eyes narrow at the challenge in my voice, and I expect him to fall on me like a starving man at a buffet. Instead, I give a tiny shriek as he pushes off the bed and pulls me with him.

"What are you—?" I start to ask, but then he's sitting on the edge of the mattress and spinning me so my stomach comes down over his legs. Suddenly, I'm staring at the carpet. He rests a large, warm palm on my butt and strokes it, and oh… that feels so nice.

Then it's gone. Within a nanosecond, it's back with a resounding slap to my skin. I cry out, "Shit," but then his hand is stroking the spot warmed by his palm, and I moan at how good that feels.

"Knew you'd like that," Logan practically purrs at me. "So I'll tell you how we're going to start…"

The threat in his voice is unmistakable, and I know there's going to be a sting to whatever he does to me. But I can't deny I want that more than anything because I know he'll ultimately make me soar above the stars when it's all said and done.

Logan nudges my legs open a bit before tentatively sticking his fingertips to my wet opening. He drags his fingers through to test my reaction so far, and says, "I'm going to spank your ass. I'm even going to give a few well-aimed slaps at your pussy, because I know a sweet girl like you has never had her pussy slapped. I'm going to do that until you're dripping, and when you're wet enough, I'm going to drag that sweetness up to your ass. When it's slick, I'm going to use at least two fingers on you back there… maybe three. I'm going to get you so worked up that you're going to beg me to fuck your ass, but I won't do it. We'll leave that cherry too, but then I'm going to flip you over and make you come with my mouth on your clit and my fingers in your ass. Sound good?"

One last giant, seismic shudder quakes my entire body. All I can do is nod in abject capitulation mixed with dizzy anticipation.

"Good girl," he says just before he brings his hand down on my ass again.

EVERYTHING FROM MY waist down is tingling. Ass, clit, butt cheeks. Hell, even my toes are still curled and prickling after what Logan just did to me. But I don't let it distract me as Logan silently crawls off the bed to shed the remainder of his clothes. He knows he's next. I have a lot to give him to make up for what he just gave me.

The man has no personal boundaries when it comes to my body, and he's touched and tasted parts of me that I'll never know myself. And he was right. I was begging for his cock in my ass, but he only gave a dark laugh when I did. True to his promise, he flipped me over and made me come with his mouth while I ground down on his fingers that were deep inside my tightest spot.

"Get on the bed," I tell Logan with a nod toward my

pretty, western-themed comforter that's all sorts of disheveled.

He doesn't grin at my tart ways or give me a comical rejoinder. Instead, he crawls back over me, fitting his entire naked body against mine, and presses his mouth to me. Logan gives me a blistering kiss that starts to make my core ache again, but then he's pulling away before rolling to my side and onto his back.

His cock is gorgeous. While I haven't had much up-close experience—my prior encounters being fumbles in the dark and the two men in The Silo being quickly finished with my eyes closed—I am not going to pass up an opportunity here.

Logan's body is beautiful. Tan, hard, and muscled with hair over his chest and right below his belly button leading down to his pelvis. He's into grooming as his pubic hair is trimmed tight and his balls are hairless, which makes me wonder if guys wax down there. I'd never been waxed before until Magnus dragged me out here, but he told me it was necessary.

It was awful and hurt like a son of a bitch. After my hair grows back in, I'm never doing that again. I'll shave and make sure I'm trimmed, but I'm never having hot wax slathered on my pubes and then ripped violently out again.

Nope.

Never.

But back to Logan's body, more importantly, his cock.

I come up to my knees as I study it. Logan is lying on his back with his hands behind his head. He's pretty big. Bigger than any other I've had. Solid, straight, and dusky colored, with a fascinating vein running up the underside that I think I'll trace with my tongue.

"Said you never had a man go down on you before you came to The Silo," he says in a voice that sounds like warm honey, causing my eyes to cut from his dick to his face. "Ever sucked a man's cock before The Silo?"

It's a truth I can give him. "Yes. A few times."

Because I had. His name was August, but he went by "Gus." We ran a few scams together in our late teens. I guess I sort of fashioned myself in love with him, even though deep down, I knew con artists could never really love. I wasn't about to give up my virginity at just sixteen years of age, but I did want to please him so I gave him what he wanted. He made fumbling efforts to get me off with his fingers, which didn't work more often than it did. Definitely not a mutually satisfying relationship, but really… we did our best work on the streets making money in the only way we knew how.

By taking it from others.

"You okay?" Logan asks, and I noticed he's come to his elbows, his eyes laced with a bit of worry over my contemplative mood.

"Sure," I say with a tremulous smile. "Was just thinking the other times… they weren't good."

"Oh," he says, tone flat.

But I hurry to clarify. "Except last night. Last night

was very, very good."

He smiles at me. It's a smile I've never seen from him before. Completely open without one thing hidden in his meaning, fully reaching his eyes and causing two beautiful dimples to appear on his face. It's a smile that tells me he's very happy I enjoyed what I did to him last night.

"I'd like a repeat," he says with a low rumble of need.

I give him a sexy smile before I turn and bend over him. Putting my hand around the base of his dick, I squeeze tight and descend over the mushroom-tipped head, noticing it is leaking clear fluid from the top just before it touches my tongue. Logan lets out a loud sigh of relief, but then his hand goes to my head. He pulls my hair back away from my face and mutters, "Want to see your mouth on me."

I pull up on him, tighten my lips on the head, and cut my eyes sideways to him. He's watching me in fascination, his eyes glowing more green than anything with gold flecks sparkling. I go down on him and he groans, his hand tightening in my hair to hold it back so he doesn't miss a thing.

Because I want him to feel as good as I did, I set a moderate pace as I bob up and down, flattening my tongue on the underside of his dick and alternately pumping him with my hand. Logan doesn't say anything, but his breathing becomes labored and harsh. Every few strokes, I'll catch a glimpse of his face, which is etched with full-blown lust and pleasure.

This makes me happy, that I'm making him feel so

good, so I double my efforts and really go to town on him, sometimes going a little too exuberantly and causing myself to almost gag. I'm so into what I'm doing it takes me a moment to realize he's pulling on my hair and saying, "Hold up, Auralie," in a rough voice.

I pull off him, involuntarily dabbing at the corners of my mouth where a bit of saliva has pooled. His face is stormy, and he looks a bit angry.

"Did I do something wrong?" I ask hesitantly, a feeling of gray despair starting to overcome me.

"Fuck no," he says harshly as his hand loosens in my hair. "You're doing that a little too good, and I'm not going to last."

"Oh," I say in wonder that I had the power to bring this vibrant and highly experienced man to completion so soon.

"Do me a favor?" he asks with a soft smile, his hand now stroking my hair. "Use just your hands on me, okay?"

"My hands?" I ask, dumbfounded.

"Just your hands," he affirms. "You can use your fingers too… if you're feeling really adventurous."

My fingers?

Where would I put my—?

Oh. My fingers.

My eyes slide down to his cock. Logan spreads his legs a little, giving me a better picture of what lays beyond.

A quiver of excitement flutters through me. I slide

my fingertips over his balls, down past them to the area just behind.

"My fingers, huh?" I ask, my eyes gleaming with the challenge.

Logan swallows hard and nods. With a voice so roughened by desire, he practically croaks. "Yeah… your fingers."

"I can do that," I tell him wickedly, and I have to wonder… if Logan and I were to actually have real sex with penetration, how could it ever be more thrilling than this right here?

I probably wouldn't survive it.

Chapter 11
Logan

IT'S BEEN AN utterly perfect morning and I've only been awake a few minutes, but it's perfect because Auralie is spooned into my body.

It only complements the utterly perfect night I'd had with her, the sweet, virginal temptress who sucks dick like a sexual goddess.

And yes… she ultimately ended up sucking my dick again, but only after she'd gotten me off with her hand and fingers alone. While she's clearly inexperienced, she is not without adventure. She let me talk her through the mechanics of massaging my prostate with her finger while she jacked me off. I came so hard, my jizz actually hit at the base of my collarbone it'd shot so far up my body, and I roared like a fucking grizzly bear.

We both got cleaned up. I took a piss. Then we dozed after she settled into my arms.

I woke up a few hours later with her mouth on my cock, taking what she wanted and being assured I'd gladly give it. Of course, I shredded her pussy with my tongue after. I have to admit, my name coming out of her throat as she orgasmed was very nice indeed.

After that, we slept hard. I only woke up one more time around three in the morning by a violent thunderstorm that had rolled through. I listened to the rain pelting the roof and the rumble of thunder, seeing flashes of lightning, and I did it all while I held a woman in my arms that I had become completely obsessed with.

Not once as I laid there did I think it in any way felt uncomfortable. I couldn't quite remember the last time I'd held a woman in my arms, and a quick inventory of my memories says not once in the last two years. And prior to that with Donna doesn't count. Nothing prior to my life on the road counts anymore.

When my alarm on my phone went off at six AM, I rolled away from Auralie to shut it off and saw that I had a text from today's fishing charter. It was sent a few hours ago and only said, *Need to cancel. Will we get refund on deposit?*

No, fucknut. You do not get a refund. I have a business to run.

I quickly send a return text. *No refund.*

I didn't expect to get an argument back. My clients today were two clearly wealthy college boys here on summer vacation. They apparently had more money than they knew what to do with. When they booked me yesterday through Teton Ski and Snowboard—which isn't just a winter sports store obviously—the owner, Jake Gearhart, told me they'd been partying when they stumbled in and he wasn't quite sure they would even show up.

Again, it didn't matter. That was the purpose of a non-refundable fifty-percent deposit on the trip. In my line of business, you couldn't just reschedule a missed charter at the drop of a dime. I don't make a lot of money doing this. After Jake takes a small commission for booking the trip, I'm lucky if I clear a hundred bucks on each four-hour trip. I also pack snacks and water for my customers, as well as supply the tackle, which is not inexpensive. During the high season, I can do two trips a day. So on a good week, I can make about twelve-hundred, which is good bank. The problem is you have cancellations either from dicks like these guys or weather, and in a bad week, I could make as little as three hundred. Still, it's more than enough for my solitary existence living in a camping trailer, so I don't go without.

So while it sucked losing out on the dough, there was an upside in that I was free today. I had a beautiful woman, who intrigued me greatly and made me feel absolutely amazing to be near her, right beside me and at my disposal. Besides, at least I have an afternoon trip scheduled. Jake told me these were two really wealthy men and would be tipping well.

Putting my phone aside, I roll back over and bring my arm over Auralie's waist, pressing in tight to her backside and bringing my mouth to her shoulder where I kiss it.

"Auralie," I whisper, and she snuggles into me tighter.

"Auralie," I whisper again. Dragging my hand down her stomach, right to her mound, I press a finger just above where her clit lays nestled in her warm flesh.

Her hips gyrate against me, and my cock starts getting hard.

"What?" she mumbles sleepily.

I move my mouth to her ear, bringing my hand back up to lay flat on her stomach. She sighs in frustration. Smiling, I tell her, "Get up. I'm going to take you fishing."

IT'S SO MUCH fun watching Auralie fish, and she's a fucking natural at it too. I spent a few minutes on the bank with her going over casting techniques, and then loaded her into the boat. I made sure she slathered on sun block because I didn't want to see her pale skin reddened by anything but the palm of my hand, and I gave her a fishing hat I had in one of the storage bins. It flared out wide and had a strap she could tighten under her chin.

Then I set us off down the river, watching as she was able to catch fish after fish with just a natural affinity for when to pull up on the rod tip at the moment the trout was breaking the surface of the water to grab the dry fly that floated there. It really is all about timing and instinct. She had a natural intuition about it all that made me proud.

By mid-morning, I pulled the boat over to the far

bank that had a fairly well shaded patch of thick grass. I pulled out some bottled water and some convenience store muffins I bought after we picked the boat up from the campsite. Auralie's greatly intrigued that I live in a camper, and she tried to pepper me with questions as to what it was like. I answered them as best I could, but there wasn't much to it really. It's just… a humble life and I'm satisfied with it.

After I drop the weighted anchor, I help Auralie to jump down, noting proudly she is not worried about getting her tennis shoes wet. I spread a blanket on the grass and we sit down in the shade, watching other boaters as they float by. Some are drift boats like mine with guides teaching tourists how to fish, and others are just lazy tubers floating down in groups while drinking beer. While the Snake River does have portions that have Class IV and V rapids, this section of the river is slow with only a few gurgling riffles that do nothing more than sway the boat.

"It's so beautiful here," Auralie says as she sits cross-legged and picks at a blade of grass near the edge of the blanket. "It almost doesn't seem real."

"I know," I tell her in agreement. "I've been here a year. Sometimes, I'll be on the river and I'll come around a bend. I'll see a butte I've seen hundreds of times before, and it still takes my breath away."

"Are you happy here?" she asks, and I sense that her question has a deeper meaning. It's not been hard for her to figure out that I'm solitary and private. She knows I have no relationship with my parents and my friendships with people revolve around a sex club.

"I'm happier here than anywhere I've been in the past two years," I tell her carefully, happy to give her a truth.

"Happier than where you were prior to two years ago?" she inquires, and I feel myself shutting down. But I don't want to retreat from her.

Not wholly.

But I don't want to give more of myself to her either.

So I use a tactic that worked well last night.

I redirect.

"I'd be very happy right now if you did me a favor," I murmur as my eyes cut out briefly to a drift boat with three occupants going by. It's being guided by Cash Holstead, one of the few local guides here. I know everyone on this river, and most of us are not native to Wyoming. The main reason I came here and how I was easily able to get a job as a fishing guide, which is just not something you can do without experience, is because I worked at Yellowstone all four years I did undergrad. I learned how to fish in the summers, and my father and I would come out for hunting trips in the winter. I had plenty of transferrable skills to be able to get work in this area. While I was probably competent to take a hunting trip out in the non-fishing months, I preferred to make money either taking on bartending jobs or sometimes guided-snowmobile trips.

"What favor do you want?" Auralie asks me naively,

as she surely missed the heat in my tone.

"Put your hand down your pants… get yourself off while I watch," I tell her with a challenging grin.

"What?" she exclaims and sits up straight. "No."

Mission accomplished. She forgot all about her very personal question to me, and the thought of watching her finger herself is thrilling, especially out here in the open.

"Yes," I insist. "Come on. Live a little."

Auralie narrows her eyes at me before she flat out busts me. "You're deflecting a personal question, Logan. Not very nice."

And yeah… that does make me feel guilty that I can't give her what she wants. I should admit defeat and tell her she's right. I should be a gentleman and change the subject.

But fuck… now I really want to see her get herself off. I love watching my shy little virgin come out of her shell and experience the ultimate high of sexual pleasure.

So I compromise. "I'll answer your question if you promise to get yourself off out here… right now… so I can watch."

Auralie rolls her eyes. "We're out in the open, Logan."

"Not really," I point out. "We're in a little alcove. People on the river can't see us until they're exactly parallel. Most of them floating by haven't even looked over this way."

She looks to her right and her brows furrow when

she realizes I am correct; she can't even see the river to her right because of trees and bushes that jut out past us from the alcove we're in.

"And we'll switch positions," I tell her. "I'll put myself between you and the river."

"You'll answer my question?" she asks for clarification.

"Yes."

Her eyes dart to the right again before moving back down to the left, possibly taking note that the current is swift and people are moving past us at a good clip. She is probably also recalling that not many boats or tubes have gone by in the last half hour. Maybe only four total, so there are many minutes in between where there's complete privacy.

She finally looks back to me and says, "Okay. I'll do it. But first, I want to know if you're happier now than you were two years ago before you began your travels?"

I don't even bother trying to suck in a breath of fortitude. If I did, it might actually give me too much pause and cause me to lie to her. So I go ahead and let out the truth as best as I can relay it without giving away why I feel that way. "There were moments where I was happier, but there were moments that were the worst I've ever felt in my life. As such, I try not to think of my life before my travels. It's easier to try to forget all of it."

"Oh," Auralie breathes out.

The sympathy in her gaze nearly undoes me. I can't stand to have her look at me that way because I have the absolutely insane urge to lay my head on her lap and pour out all the pain I keep locked up tight inside.

I shake my head, force fleeting images of operating tables and flatlined EKG machines out of my head, and I call forth the one way in which I know Auralie can bring me peace.

"Hand down your pants, baby," I say roughly, my eyes going down to the button on her khaki shorts as I scoot over on the blanket to put myself between her and the river.

She doesn't move or even say anything for a moment, and I refuse to meet her eyes, terrified she'll push me for more. But I won't give it. I answered the question, and I did it truthfully too.

Finally, she swings her legs out from her Indian style of sitting and lays down on her right side, facing me. I go ahead and mirror her movement, lying down on my left side, with only about two feet separating us. Because my shoulders are broad and I'm much bigger than she is, I think I've got her relatively shielded.

At least until they get past us. If some boater happened to look back, they'd get a nice surprise.

The prospect of strangers watching doesn't make me feel guilty in the slightest. I've always loved the excitement of voyeurism, both as the watcher and the watched.

Auralie takes a deep breath. With one hand, she manages to undo her button and zipper. I'm surprised when she even pushes the waistband down a little to give herself more room. She slides her fingers into her underwear, and they disappear from sight. My eyes are pinned on her crotch, her hand moving under the pink silk of her panties. I know when she touches her clit because she gasps and her hips jerk.

That's so fucking sexy that I feel it straight through to my own nuts. I bring my hand over to rub at my crotch, not relieving anything in the slightest, only creating a deeper ache.

"Fuck," I curse. My hand goes to the zipper on my cargo shorts. In a flash, I have my cock out. I risk a glance up at Auralie, whose eyes are now pinned on my hand jacking my dick. Her cheeks are pink and her lips wet from repeatedly licking at them.

"Feel good?" I ask her hoarsely, and her eyes slide from my cock to my face. She merely nods with a feminine grunt as she rubs at her clit and her hips start bucking.

"God, baby… that's so hot watching you do that," I praise her, and then I push at her. "Rub harder. I want you to come."

Auralie's hand flies against her pussy, the movements having dragged her panties down so I get little peeps of her wet and swollen clit.

"Imagine it's my tongue on you," I murmur to her, my hand stroking and squeezing my cock. Pre-cum oozes from the top to help lubricate my palm.

"Oh, God," Auralie moans. Her hand is practically vibrating it's moving so fast. Then she stiffens, throws her head back, and moans, "Oh, God… Logan… I'm coming."

And fuck, it's so goddamn beautiful my eyes almost hurt watching her fall to pieces with dappled sun and shadow falling across her.

And I think I'm dying, my need for release causing my dick to ache and my nuts to pulse with frustration. Oh, and to have her mouth back on me again.

I release my cock and scoot up on the blanket a few feet at the same time, my hand going to the back of Auralie's head. Her eyes are glazed as she pulls her hand out of her pants, and she doesn't resist when I pull her face toward my hips.

"Open up, Auralie," I tell her, pulling her closer to my shaft.

"Logan," she whispers, but she still doesn't pull back against me. "Someone might see."

"Good," I growl at her. With one hand on her head and the other on my cock to hold it steady for her mouth, I tell her, "Open that pretty mouth, honey. Take it in deep."

"Oh, God," she moans, but her mouth opens wide. That first touch of her tongue on the head of my dick, I can't help it. I grunt like a fucking caveman and slam my hips forward, filling her up. Auralie makes a slight gagging noise, and I mutter "sorry" as I pull back a little. I force myself to hold still.

To let her set the pace.

To let her finish me off the way she wants.

And then her hand is on my hip and she's pushing

me to my back. She surges up and bends over my dick, caught up in the lust of the moment perhaps, or maybe just not giving a fuck the way I don't give a fuck if we're seen. No one would recognize her. The most that would happen is some other guys would recognize my boat and give me shit about it later.

But whatever.

I can't see Auralie's gorgeous mouth working me as her dark hair falls all around to shield her face. All I can see is her bobbing head and feel the hot, wet, sucking pull of her mouth, which causes my nuts to start to tighten and my blood to boil.

I tilt my head, look downriver, and see a boat in the distance that was probably going by the minute she rolled me on my back. Three men are in the boat, two fishing, one rowing, all three now currently staring at us. I lift my hand up and give a "thumbs-up" signal. One of the guys holds his thumb up high in the air back at me in salute.

And oh, yeah… Auralie's hand is now rubbing my balls. I think about her finger in my ass last night, and my fingers in her ass, and how bad I wanted to fuck it, and how much I want that hot pussy on my cock with her under me or me riding her from behind, or fuck… the best of all… her riding me reverse cowboy.

I think of the million different ways I want this woman, and I can't hold it back anymore.

I erupt in her mouth and call out her name as she sucks every drop I give her right down her throat.

Chapter 12
Auralie

I STEP OUT of the shower, wrapping the towel around me and tucking it in tight. Another is wrapped turban style around my long, wet hair. I feel refreshed from a long nap I took this afternoon and sparkling clean from my shower. Drifting down the Snake River under the bright sun, casting the line hundreds of times, reeling in fish and sucking Logan's dick... I was worn out when he dropped me off around noon with a quick kiss as he walked me to the door and promised he'd be back to get me around six PM. We haven't made full plans, but he suggested perhaps going out to his campsite and cooking something simple like hot dogs over a fire or perhaps he'd bring a pizza and we'd watch a movie. I'm personally hoping for the campfire because I've never eaten hot dogs cooked over one before.

Hell, I've never been camping before.

Or fishing.

Or had oral sex outdoors for the entire world to see.

My face should be burning hot right now for that last one, because I've become the type of woman who Auralie Foster just doesn't recognize anymore. That's not to say it's a bad thing… these changes or perhaps they're awakenings in my sexuality. I'm also powerless to fight these newfound desires because Logan blows through me like the force of a hurricane, completely overwhelming me and battering down what faint resistance I try to keep toward him.

He's getting harder to resist, and I'm extremely worried about tonight when we're alone. The more time I spend with him, the more I want to ditch my responsibilities.

Will I have the power to say no to something more? Or worse yet… will I beg for him to give me something more, despite how careless that would be of me?

My phone rings from where I left it on the dresser in my room, so I scurry across the hall from the bathroom to grab it. I see Magnus' name on the screen briefly before my finger is "accepting" the call. I've been a bit worried he hasn't called me to let me know when he's coming back, and while I seriously doubt it's today, because that would have given him mere hours to handle whatever problem my dad caused, I can't rule that out either. The man is completely unpredictable.

"Hello Magnus," I say with what I hope is a pleasant tone to my voice.

Why I'm worried about being pleasant is beyond me, as I've made no bones about the fact I despise him? Maybe it's subconscious guilt that I'm carrying on with a man who could ruin all of our plans, or maybe it's merely because I'm feeling so great after an amazing few hours with Logan and one tremendous orgasm.

"What did you do today?" he asks in an equally cordial tone.

I never once consider telling him the truth because he doesn't deserve it. "Stayed around the cabin. Read a book. Watched some TV. Took a nap. The usual lazy stuff. When are you coming back?"

He's silent a moment before he says, "Maybe tomorrow. Maybe day after. Not sure."

I grit my teeth. He's doing that on purpose to keep me off balance and ensure I'm a good girl, not knowing if he'll catch me doing something that will void his obligation to me to keep my dad free from harm.

Sadistic prick.

"Okay," I say like I'm nonplussed. "Just let me know when your flight will be in and I'll pick you up. Now, I just got out of the shower and I'm dripping everywhere so I'll talk to you later."

"You're going to The Silo tonight," he says briskly, not biting at my push to get him off the phone because I just can't stand to hear his sanctimonious voice.

"What?" I ask in disbelief.

"I want you to make an appearance tonight. Don't want the potential customers getting cold feet or forgetting how hot the little prize is."

"And what exactly do you want me to do there?" I ask through gritted teeth, not making any pretext I don't like this plan. I don't like it because it interferes with my normal plans. It also puts me in danger of another man touching me, which I don't want anyone to do but Logan.

"The usual… pick someone new and give him a blow job. Make it nice. Put on a show," he says as if he's talking about an ordinary day of business.

"Any particular preference as to who I should pick?" I ask sarcastically.

It goes right over his head. "Not really. Just someone new who hasn't touched you. Put on a show and make it good, then we'll concentrate on the few people I've narrowed it down to when I return."

God, I hate him.

Hate him, hate him, hate him.

My brain immediately starts whirring, trying to come up with something that will get me out of this. He'll never buy another illness. Perhaps I can just make up something—

"And Auralie?" He breaks into my manic thoughts.

"Yes?"

"I want proof. Have someone take a picture and text it to me," he says, and I can hear the triumph in his voice.

I take a deep breath, fight off the overwhelming urge to hyperventilate, and try to ask my next question as subserviently as possible. "Is my dad okay?"

"He's fine," he says crisply. "For the time being anyway."

"Anything else?" I ask, my voice hoarse with fury because I'm rising to his bait.

"That will be all," he says pleasantly. "I'll see you soon."

He disconnects the call on me, and I have to resist the urge to throw my phone across the room. I also resist the urge to call my father and curse at him for getting us in this mess. For even stepping foot into Magnus Albright's world all those years ago, and dragging me right along with him.

And I was almost free of it all. I told my father I was out. I told Magnus I was out. I would have told Gus I was out if Gus was still in the game, but no one had seen hide or hair of him in three months, and this scared the shit out of me because he had been working for Magnus. The word on the street was he double-crossed Magnus and *poof*—he was just gone.

It's why I wanted out. The further you got sucked in, the bigger the con, the more chance of getting caught. Magnus didn't like mistakes, and he was brutal in his reinforcement of said dislike. I was afraid I'd one day just *poof*—be gone—if I messed up.

Two months ago, I was almost out.

Until I wasn't.

"Dad," I called out as I pushed open our apartment door, my head bowed down over the mail I'd picked up from our mailbox in the dingy, poorly lit lobby of our building. "I'm home."

"So I can see," someone who was not my dad said.

My head popped up, my eyes immediately narrowing on Magnus sitting on our couch, one leg elegantly crossed over another. He had on his classic, dark-tailored suit and his dishwater-blond hair gelled over to the side.

My eyes immediately took in other people in our small living room, and my eyes snapped to my father sitting in his old, ratty recliner. I looked just like him… black hair and crystal blue eyes, except the main difference I saw now was that he was sporting a split lip and a black eye. One of Magnus' goons stood behind my dad, and he actually popped his knuckles as he leered at me.

"Are you okay?" I asked my dad.

"Yeah," he mumbled. "Apparently, I've fucked up though."

My eye roll said everything, directing my silent question to Magnus with raised eyebrows. What now?

Magnus shifted on the couch, laying one arm across the back as he looked at me with a smile. "Seems your dad was skimming the top off my cream."

My stomach lurched.

My dad tried to stand up from the recliner as he proclaimed his innocence. "I wasn't, Magnus. I swear it. My bookkeeping just got a little out of whack."

The big goon put a hand to Dad's shoulder and shoved him back down in this chair.

Goddamn, Dad, I thought.

There was no doubt in my mind that it wasn't a simple math screw up. My dad was a wizard at juggling a dozen different cons and keeping the money straight. He had been doing it for years for Magnus and hadn't ever made a mistake. No, he took that money intentionally and I knew why.

So I could pay tuition when I enrolled in a community college this week.

"How much?" I asked Magnus, because if this wasn't made right and done soon, Magnus was going to do far worse to my dad than a split lip and a black eye. "I'll get it for you."

"You're darn right you will," Magnus said irritably. "And I've got the perfect con that will net us a small fortune. It'll more than cover your dad's obligation to me, plus a 'reasonable' penalty for his shoddy bookwork. There will even be a little bonus for you. More than enough to help you with some college."

"I don't want any of the money," I growled, not even bothering to get the details on the con he wanted me to help him with. "I said I'm out. I'm only doing this one job, and then I'm done. But I want your promise right now if I do this, you'll leave my dad alone and he'll be safe."

Magnus smiled an evil smile at me, and I should have taken that as a hint of what was to come.

I should have bothered with the details of the con before I committed, because I would have never agreed to this if I'd known how low I'd have to stoop to pull it off.

Oh, who the fuck am I kidding? I would have done anything to protect my dad. He may have been a wayward man, and he may have raised me on the hustle, but he provided a roof over my head and more love than I could handle when my mom died, even foregoing his own grief to make sure I was as happy as possible.

Yeah… this con isn't a choice for me. My dad's life

depends on it, and so I'll see it through to the end.

LOGAN KNOCKS AGAIN on the cabin door. I shuffle with dread toward it as I know without a doubt he's not going to like what I need to tell him. Hell, I'm not going to like it either, but I need to pull my big-girl panties up and focus back on the end game.

When I swing the door open, Logan almost takes my breath away. He'd recently showered as his hair is still damp along his neckline, and whatever soap he uses smells crisp and fresh. He's wearing his usual "Logan" clothes of jeans and a casual shirt—this time plaid flannel with sleeves rolled to mid-forearm—along with a pair of camel-colored hiking boots.

And he stands there in the sexiest of poses with one hand holding onto the doorframe and the other shoved in his pocket. He's big and looming, and his eyes sparkle with excitement to see me.

Then they drift down, taking in what I'm wearing, and his jaw goes rock hard.

For you see, I'm wearing what I'm thinking of as my "Auralie Virgin" clothes. Tonight's ensemble is a floaty white skirt with lace edges that comes down to my ankles, along with a sky-blue blouse that sits demurely at my shoulders and cinches at my waist with a chiffon belt. My hair is tousled and then wrapped in a loose bun I'm wearing at the side of my neck with a few wispy tendrils pulled lose.

I have no makeup on other than a little lip gloss, and I can read the thunderous expression in Logan's eyes without him needing to say a word to me. *You are not fucking going to The Silo tonight!*

"I have to," I say flatly, choosing to use words because communicating with my eyes is too personal. I have to figure a way to build a barrier up between us.

I turn and walk back into the cabin, heading into the kitchen to get my purse off the counter where I'd left it earlier today after Logan dropped me off from the fishing trip.

"Absolutely not," Logan says from behind me.

Close behind me.

I spin on him. "You can't tell me what I can and can't do."

He's so close he runs right into me, his hands going to my arms to hold me upright so I don't go crashing to the ground. But he uses my momentum to his advantage, walking me backward into the kitchen and right into the refrigerator, which sways backward a few inches before righting itself.

"You are not going there by yourself—"

"Fine," I snap at him, because I'm feeling every bit of frustration that he is. "You can come and watch then."

"Jesus fucking Christ," he yells as he releases me, spins away, and places his hands on top of his head. He looks upward to the ceiling as if it has all the answers, and then my heart breaks a little when he turns to face me with pleading eyes. "No, Auralie. Tell him you're sick again. I can't bear to watch you—you—"

"I know," I say softly as I push off from the fridge and walk to him. I lay a hand on his chest, feel the wild gallop his heart, and try to make this easier on him. "I don't want that either, but Magnus will never accept my excuse of being sick. You have to know I don't want to do this."

"Then don't go," he says as his hand comes to mine, and I can't handle how lost he sounds at this moment. This man and me… we've known each other barely a week, and yet something has forged tight between us. It's my fault for letting it bloom and develop, and I should have never let him get this deep with me.

I thought I was safe though, because while I'm holding much back from Logan, he's doing the same to me. We may have a connection, but we really don't truly know each other. Not the bad stuff anyway.

I pull my hand away and take a step back. With a firm voice, I tell him, "Logan… I don't want to do this, but trust me when I say I have to go through with this. I literally don't have a choice in this matter—"

"How do you know?" he interjects with his arms thrown out to the side. "How do you know unless you let me in on—?"

"I've involved you too much as it is," I tell him with quiet confidence because this is a truth beyond all truths. "I should have never let it go this far. But you are going to have to let me go and let me do what I have to do. As I said, there's no choice and you're just going to have to accept that."

"Fuck," he mutters and scrubs his hands through his hair again, his eyes cutting across the kitchen… not really looking at anything but clearly trying to think of something.

Anything.

He spins on me. "What does Magnus want you to do tonight?"

I shrug. "A show. He wants me to put on a show."

"Then I'll—"

"He said it has to be with someone new," I cut him off, watching his face crumble. My voice quavers a bit. "Said he wants picture proof."

"Goddamn, I want to kick that motherfucker's ass," Logan growls, but his eyes look at me with grim determination. "But I have an idea. Go upstairs and change out of that shit."

"But—"

"Just do it," Logan barks at me, and if it weren't for the frustration and almost near panic in his voice, I'd balk at someone talking to me like that.

But I don't hesitate because if Logan has an idea that will save me from having to put another man's dick in my mouth, and still let me put on a show for Magnus' liking, then I'm all for it. I turn around and scramble toward the staircase, mentally putting together a new wardrobe outfit.

Chapter 13

Logan

JEALOUS.

I'm goddamned jealous.

An emotion I don't have in me.

Fuck... I never even got jealous if another man looked at Donna in an unseemly manner. I was such a cocky, egotistical son of a bitch in those days that it never once crossed my mind I should be jealous. That Donna might look back. I mean, she never did. Not that I know of, but still... I never once even had the humble grace to think a woman would want anyone else but me.

And now, here I am about ready to commit violence at the thought of Auralie even walking in that Silo. Forget about her sucking strange cock... I don't even want those fuckers to have their eyes on her.

That's how fucking green this jealousy is.

And I don't have any good way out of this if Auralie truly believes she has to go through with it. She doesn't need to convince me how distasteful this is. I see it in her eyes and the way she nervously fidgets beside me in my truck as we head to The Silo. I could also hear it in her tone of voice, how very sorry she was to be doing this to me. I read it loud and clear in her expression that this was an emotionless job she had to do and she was by God going to do it, despite how badly it might make either one of us feel. Whatever her obligation is, it's something that runs deeper than whatever feelings she might have developed for me, and goddamn fuck it all to hell… even that makes me jealous.

But I do have something of an idea that might alleviate a bit of stress off Auralie, and possibly off me. It's not optimal, but I think it's something I could live with.

I think.

Maybe.

Fuck… I don't know.

"YOU WANT ME to do what?" Bridger asks, his eyebrows practically crawling onto the top of his head.

"I want you to let Auralie suck your dick," I say again, my eyes cutting to the office door where Bridger sits behind his desk. I left Auralie out in the hallway, preferring to lay this shit out to Bridger in private.

"Has the bright sun reflecting off the Snake River baked your fucking brain?" he asks me with narrowed eyes.

I disregard his snarky tone and pin him with a glare. If he's as adept at reading me as Auralie is, he'll understand I'll kick his motherfucking ass if he doesn't stop fucking with me.

But still, I guess I owe the dude some context.

Taking a deep breath, I let it out and say, "Okay. Hear me out. You see… I've been seeing Auralie—"

"Dude, if you popped that cherry, you've probably put her in danger," Bridger cuts in darkly. "That Magnus asshole is bad news."

I shake my head and hold my hand up. "I didn't have sex with her. Well, no penetration, but we've… well… we've been fooling around."

Bridger leans back in his chair, crosses his arms over his chest, and skeptically cocks an eyebrow at me.

"Okay, fine," I grumble. "We've been spending time together, and we have this… I don't know… there's a connection that I can't explain. I've never felt it with anyone, and so I'm intrigued by it, but it also scares the fuck out of me, you know—"

I don't give him an opportunity to even nod in agreement with me.

"—but the thing is, she's got herself into some bad shit. She does not want to be involved in this… whatever the fuck this is with Magnus selling off her virginity. She sure as fuck doesn't want to be sucking other men's cocks or parading around naked like Magnus' little pet. And man, Bridger… that selling off your virginity… that's fucked up. Giving that up should be special, to someone who cares about you… not some fucking high bidder."

"Someone like you," Bridger says with a knowing grin.

"Exactly," I say from more of a reactionary place rather than from within the boundaries of reality. So I start to backpedal. "Well, no… that's not what I'm saying. I mean, yeah… if she wanted to gift that to me, sure… but it shouldn't be in some seedy sex club."

Bridger's face darkens.

"Sorry," I mutter. "Your place isn't seedy, and you know I love it."

"Really?" he says sarcastically. "Because I haven't seen you fuck someone in here in almost a full week."

"That's beside the point," I snap at him.

"No," Bridger says calmly. "That's the exact point. I think what you're trying to say is that Auralie's in a bad spot, she can't get out of it, you care for her, and you need some help tonight."

My breath comes out in one long rush of relief.

He totally gets me.

"Yes," I say as I walk up to his desk, put my palms on it, and lean in closer. "Magnus is back home in New York, taking care of some business. He demanded she come in here and put on a show, meaning he wants her to bestow a hot cock suck on someone. Can't be me. Woolf, Cain, and Rand are out of the question now that they've gotten tied down. You're the only other one I trust."

"Trust to do what?" Bridger asks. "You know not a member in here would hurt her."

"It's not that," I grumble, my fingers going back to scrape along the back of my neck, which is knotted with tension.

"Not to enjoy it?" he asks quietly. "Because I'm sorry, Logan. She sucks my cock, I'm going to enjoy it."

"No," I growl, frustrated it has to be this way and beyond pissed he's making me say this. "I know you'll enjoy it and that's fine. But I trust you to feel bad about what it's doing to me."

Bridger is a tough son of a bitch 98.3% of the time. But that other 1.7%, he can surprise you with uncharacteristic displays of caring and compassion. Like right now… his eyes get a little bit soft as he takes in my most embarrassing confession and merely nods at me.

"Take Auralie over to The Silo," he says as he nods toward the door. "I'll be over in about ten minutes."

I sigh out a breath of relief. Again, this is not an optimal solution, but it's the only one I have. I turn toward the door.

"And Logan," Bridger says in a low voice.

I turn back around to look at him, my face trying to appear grateful for what he's doing but still feeling sick inside.

"You know this is only putting off the inevitable for one more day, right?" he asks.

I nod. "Yeah. I get that."

"Then you get your shit sorted tonight," he tells me sagely. "You either get her to let you help her or you get the fuck gone. Go find some pussy and fuck it hard, but you walk away after tonight. Magnus is a bad dude. You're going to put her at risk if you keep up with this jealous bullshit when you may not have any right to be so."

I curse under my breath. "Understood."

"And buddy," Bridger says in a far gentler voice. "I know you're here for a reason. I know something drove you to Wyoming and The Silo and that you get something from all this. I suspect it lets you exist as best you know how. But you can't find happiness in this place. Not for the long haul anyway."

My stomach tightens and I stare at him through hard eyes, refusing to give any credence to his very spot-on assessment of me. I've not shared that piece of me with anyone, and it sure as fuck won't be him.

"You can't outrun your demons," Bridger says meaningfully, completely at ease in giving me advice I don't want or need. "You can't outrun them because they're inside of you, not behind you. Until you confront that shit, you'll never lose them."

This takes me aback, not because he's being nosy as fuck into my life by his uncanny insight, but because his voice holds something more than just a friend giving out a piece of unsolicited advice. It sounds as if he might know a little something about running from demons.

I've always found Bridger to be coolly aloof and guarded with most everyone except his buddy, Woolf, who used to own The Silo with him. Figured something made him that way. It's not until this moment when I realize by the tone of his voice, that whatever it is that has made him a very strange man, it's something that's caused him great pain.

Maybe even a pain as great as mine?

I shake my head to clear it, but I still can't help but ask. "That work for you? Have you made peace with your demons?"

It's an impertinent question to the man who essentially keeps me employed as a Fantasy Maker, and I half expect him to kick me the fuck out of his office.

But instead, he gives me a wry smile and shakes his head. "Nah, man. I keep those fuckers around intentionally as reminders of what I'll never go through again."

I don't even know what to say to that, but on some level, I recognize the reasoning. It's why I keep myself reserved from relationships and friendships. Because if you don't have anything of value to lose, it can't hurt you down the road.

"Thanks for the help," I tell him quietly as I turn toward the door. "I'll see you over at The Silo."

Bridger's silent as I walk out, and I find Auralie waiting there for me, looking far more beautiful and normal in a simple black dress that is cut to reveal a tiny amount of cleavage and black, strappy heels. She still has a clean, fresh face, but at least she doesn't look twelve, which will probably disappoint those that come to gawk at her tonight.

Sucking Bridger's dick.

Goddamn, I hate this, but it's the only play I have.

Auralie's chewing on her lower lip when I open the door. It pops free, glistening wet. I want to chew on it some more, but instead, I walk up to her and take her hand in mine.

"I've set it up for Bridger to help us," I tell her with my mouth near her ear because the country music filtering down the hall from The Wicked Horse is cutting into our privacy.

She pulls back and looks at me. "You want me to— with Bridger?"

"Yes," I tell her, and then fudge a little on my motivation. "He won't hurt you, and I don't trust any of those other douches."

She seems to accept that. and I'm glad because I sure as fuck am not about to admit to her the way I did to Bridger that it's going to kill me to see her lips wrapped around a dick that is not mine.

"Let's go," I tell her as I pull on her hand and we hit the exit door. This puts us out right at a stone path that leads to The Silo sitting just a stone's throw. "Bridger's going to come over in about ten minutes. I want you to go in, wander around, and mingle. It's not going to be overly crowded since it's so early, but flirt and hit on some men or something."

Christ, it pains me to tell her to do that.

It's going to hurt like a motherfucker when I watch her actually do that.

"Logan," Auralie says with a tug on my hand. I stop and turn to look at her. "You should go."

"I'm staying," I grit out.

"You need to forget me," she says in a small voice, but her face says it all. *I couldn't ever, ever forget you. I wish we could just run, run, run and never look back.*

"Couldn't forget you," I mutter back to her in affirmation of all the things she just said with her eyes.

"But tomorrow," she continues on, stepping into me and placing her hands on my shoulders. "I'm going to have to be right back here again. Probably with Magnus. It's going to happen one way or the—"

My mouth descends on hers because I don't want her to finish that thought. I don't want to hear about inevitability. I want to focus on right this moment. Tonight, after she gets Bridger off with her mouth—can't stand that fucking thought either—I want to take her back to the cabin and do as many wicked things to her as I can without compromising her virginity. I want to do this for hours, let it turn into days, and let the future that would lead her to kneel at another man's feet never arrive.

Auralie leans into my kiss, her hands going to clasp at each other behind my neck. She moans against my tongue, and the smell of her sweet perfume makes me dizzy.

Reluctantly, I pull away and give her a little push toward The Silo. "Go on in. I'll be in soon."

She nods at me and walks away, and yeah… I stare at her swaying ass that I'd love to tap one day if I had the time to build her up to that. I wait until she disappears inside, waiting about five more minutes before I walk in. Bridger should be soon on my heels and then we'll get this travesty of a show over with for the night.

When I clear the hall into the main area of The Silo,

I see Auralie standing at the bar talking to one of the members. Nondescript dude, doesn't come in often. Don't know much about him, but it doesn't matter. He won't be touching her tonight.

I walk over to one of the black leather couches that sits perpendicular to the glass rooms. From there, I can watch the action in one of said rooms if I want, although they're empty at this early hour, or I can swivel my head and watch Auralie.

With Bridger.

Fuck, my stomach hurts.

As if on cue, Bridger appears from the entrance hall, his eyes scanning the entirety of the room, although he passes right over me. There are only a handful of people in here. Two bartenders, Auralie and the man she's talking to, as well as perhaps another five people sitting at the bar. Add Bridger and me and that's only eleven total, which will at least help to cut down on Auralie's humiliation, no matter if her sucking Bridger's dick makes me feel slightly better, she wants no part of anyone's dick but mine.

"Everyone, let me have your attention," Bridger says with an authoritative boom.

I sit straight up from my pouting slouch, completely stunned he's going to really make a spectacle of what he and Auralie are about to do.

Auralie's face is even more pale than normal, her lips almost white. Her eyes cut to me with worry, but we both look back to Bridger when he says, "I've just gotten a call from the fire department. We had our yearly inspection, and they found some burned electrical. Unfortunately, until that can get fixed, they've ordered us to close down immediately. I'm really sorry, but I'm going to have to ask everyone to leave. Hopefully, we'll be opened back up by tomorrow."

My jaw hangs wide open as I watch Bridger shuffle the patrons out while the bartenders start packing away their wares. I look at Auralie, who is saying goodbye to the man she was talking to, and then back to Bridger as he starts to walk toward me.

I stand from the couch, unprepared for how jello-like my legs feel from the shock of reprieve I was just given.

Not Auralie.

No, Bridger gave that reprieve to *me* so that I wouldn't have to suffer watching my girl take his cock.

My girl?

Well, yeah… I think so.

Fuck. I have no clue what to do now.

"It's just for tonight," Bridger says in a low voice as his eyes cut briefly to Auralie, who is walking our way. It drops an octave lower when he says, "I mean it… figure your shit out tonight or get the fuck gone and don't look back at her. You hear me?"

"Loud and clear," I tell him as I turn and hold my hand out to Auralie.

I have some work to do tonight.

Chapter 14
Auralie

"MAGNUS CAN'T BE mad," Logan says as soon as he has me in his truck and we're pulling out of the parking lot. "Text him and tell him The Silo is closed down."

"Okay," I say, pulling my phone out of the little clutch I brought.

I shoot off a quick text. *The Silo is closed down tonight. Burned wires. Fire department shut it down.*

"I can't believe he did that," I say in wonder to Logan. "He must be a really good friend."

"Yeah," Logan mutters in agreement, but he doesn't say anything more. While I know he's relieved that we've been given a day's reprieve, I also know he's already worrying about tomorrow. If I were strong and really wanted to spare both of us more pain, I'd be a brave girl and turn him away when he drops me off at my cabin. I should cut the string quickly and decisively, and yes… even cruelly if I have to, and let him be free from my bullshit.

Because this man does not deserve my shitty life, nor does he deserve to be burdened with my lies and bad deeds that have probably earned me a one-way ticket to Hell.

My phone chimes, and I look down at Magnus' return text. *You better not be lying to me to get out of this.*

My fingers fly over the screen as I respond. *Call Bridger if you don't believe me. He's the one that just came in an announced it.*

His response is just as fast. *You're at The Silo now? It's not even 7PM. Far too early for you to have gone and put on a good show to the biggest crowd.*

"Oh, for fuck's sake," I growl at my phone and pull up my screen, punching Magnus' number. Logan's head turns to look at me and I shoot him an irritated eye roll, which he knows is not meant for him but for another.

Magnus answers right away. "You were supposed to go late tonight. I told you I wanted a show. There couldn't have been anyone there this early."

"Jesus, Magnus," I say in irritation. "What does it matter? It wasn't going to happen anyway since it just got closed down. One way to look at it is if I'd have gotten there a bit earlier, I could have probably sucked a cock and made some inroads for you."

He makes a disgusted sound on the line. "Do you have to be so crass?"

"You got to be fucking kidding me?" I ask with astonishment, my voice rising higher and higher. "Crass? Crass? You're pimping my body out for money… and you call me crass?"

"It's a job, Auralie," he says smoothly. "Nothing more than that."

My eyes cut over to Logan, who is thankfully only privy to my end of the conversation. I can't bear for him to know I'm doing this for something as base as money. "I'm hanging up now, Magnus," I say tiredly. "Any idea when you're coming back?"

"Day after tomorrow," he snipes at me. "And be ready to get back to work. I want to up our efforts."

"Fine," I snap. "I'll be ready to suck dick when you command."

"Auralie," he chastises me, but I hit the disconnect button and throw my phone on the seat beside me.

"I don't understand why you align yourself with such a douche," Logan accuses.

I turn to look at him, but not before I realize I have no clue where we are as I take in unfamiliar scenery as the sun hangs low over the horizon.

"Where are we going?" I ask curiously.

"To my place," he says. "We'll cook some hot dogs like I promised, because I figured you'd be more into that than a pizza and a movie. Then we're going to discuss the real reason you align yourself with a douche like that."

I give a tired sigh. "Logan… I'm not going to —"

"Just fucking stop, Auralie," Logan barks at me. "I'm tired of you hiding stuff from me."

I stare at him, my jaw hanging wide open. "That's sort of the pot calling the kettle black."

That effectively shuts him up because he knows I'm right, and I find it more than telling that he didn't offer to trade quid pro quo. I tell him something, and then he tells me something.

It's not going to work that way for Logan McKay apparently, because he stays stonily silent the rest of the drive.

So by the time we pull into his campsite—which admittedly is adorable—I'm beyond pissed and ready for a fight.

LOGAN GETS OUT of his truck the minute it turns off, stomping up to his trailer. I have half a mind to get out and walk out of this little campground to hitch a ride back to Jackson, but I'm just as angry as he is and I want to have it out. I need to purge and get it out.

I get out of his truck, slamming the door behind me, and take in the little blue and white camper he just disappeared into. It can't be more than fifteen feet long. Clearly, it's old as it's sporting rust spots where the sides are riveted together and the paint is flaking. The rest of his campsite is neat and tidy with a picnic table, a fire pit that's currently dead and cold, as well as a canvas-folding chair sitting in front of the pit. I imagine Logan out here, drinking a beer and pondering the flames in his solitary life.

Walking up to the trailer, I hear slamming around inside. I hesitantly enter, only to find him angrily getting dinner ready. My brief scan of the interior shows it's sparsely decorated and minimalist in all other ways. To my right is a tiny bathroom and I can see inside as the door is half-open. It's so small that it's nothing more than a shower stall with a toilet. To my immediate left is a small counter with a two-burner stove. Opposite that, a refrigerator about half the size of a normal one. Past that, at the rear of the camper, is a bed that runs perpendicular. Twisted sheets and blankets tell me that Logan can be a restless sleeper.

He opens the refrigerator, pulls out a pack of hot dogs, and slams it shut. Throwing the hot dogs on a counter unceremoniously, he reaches into a cabinet above the sink and pulls out a pack of hot dog buns. He slams the cabinet shut just as hard and I wince.

"Beating up your trailer isn't going to make you feel any better," I say simply.

He shoots me a glare that clearly says, *You're not helping matters, Auralie.*

Good. Because I don't want to help. I want to rail against the unfairness of it all. "You know, Logan," I say sarcastically. "You're not the only one who hates this situation."

"Oh, really?" he asks snidely as he turns on me. In a condescending voice, he says, "Because it looks to me like you just want to sit back and let Magnus shit all over you. You apparently don't hate it that much or you'd be working with me to try to figure a way out of whatever fucked-up mess you got yourself into."

"It's not that simple," I yell at him in frustration.

He leans into me, gets right in my face, and yells

back. "It is too that fucking simple. You tell me the problem, and I help you make it go away. Then you don't have to suck any dick but mine."

He pulls away and gives me a sly smile. "That is… unless you like it."

I gasp and rear backward, knowing he truly didn't mean that but still letting myself be hurt by his words even as I see immediate contrition in his eyes. "You insufferable, pigheaded lout. I have no clue what I ever saw in you."

"Well, that says a lot," he says caustically. "Coming from someone who has their head stuck up their ass."

"You asshole," I seethe.

"Bitch," he counters.

"Ooooohhhhh," I scream out in frustration, turning toward the spring-hinged door that slammed shut behind me not two minutes ago. "I'm leaving."

"Like fuck you are," he snarls and leaps at me. With one hand on my upper arm, he spins me and then jerks me to him so my body goes slamming into the hard, muscled planes of his. My hands immediately go to his chest to push away, but he slaps one big hand on my butt and the other to my upper back, pulling me in tight until I'm pressed up against his entire frame.

It is not lost on me he has an erection the size of a rocket ship pressing into me, and I have no doubt in my mind he'd find me as wet as an oasis. Still, that's beside the point, and I try to wriggle out of his hold.

"Let me go," I grit out and consider kicking him in

the nuts, but no… no way I could harm those precious jewels.

He responds with a brutal kiss, forcing my mouth open and shoving his tongue in deep. Mine immediately meets his and twists against him. I turn my head, open my mouth wider, and suck his kiss down like I'll starve to death without it.

Logan turns us, slams me back into the refrigerator so he has some leverage, and grinds his cock against me. A bag of potato chips falls down and glances off his shoulder, and not once does he let up on the kiss.

I try again to shove him off me, not because I really want him gone, but because now we seem to be in some sort of hate-foreplay and it's actually quite thrilling.

Logan doesn't take kindly to me trying to push him away, so his hands go to my upper arms and he spins me again, so fast I go dizzy. Pushing me down the very short hallway past the sink and stove, to the mussed up bed, he gives me a good shove toward it. My knees catch the mattress and I go falling onto my butt. I try to bounce right back up, but he's on top of me, one arm under my ass where he lifts me up and throws me further up the bed, my head actually grazing against the end wall.

He doesn't even apologize for his rough treatment, but leaps right back off me and tears my sandals off my feet.

I gasp when he flips me over so forcefully, the wind is knocked out of my lungs, but I wouldn't have been able to breathe anyway because he's jerking the zipper down the back of my dress. I become muddled with lust over his brutally forceful ways.

Logan's breathing is harsh and I can feel energy, venom, frustration, and passion pouring off him in waves. He pulls my dress past my shoulders, reaching in front of me and sliding his hands between my collarbone and the mattress to help jerk it down. It comes along inches at a time, and he curses that it's not coming off as quick as he'd like. At one point, he pulls so hard to get it past my hips that I hear the stitches ripping. That must excite him, because he starts pulling at it harder.

And then my dress is gone and I'm lying facedown on his bed with nothing on but some black lace panties. I didn't need a bra with the dress as it had a thick lining so I could go without.

Logan's gone, and, for a moment, I wonder what he's doing. I hear his boots thud, hitting the floor, and I rise up a little to look over my shoulder at him. He's glaring down at me, his bare chest heaving as he works at his jeans.

He snarls at me as he starts to push his jeans and boxers down his long legs. "Lose the panties or I'll rip them off you."

For some odd reason, my chest actually swells with elation over the words, because what I truly know is that yes… he's angry at the situation, but he also wants me so badly right now, he's on the verge of losing control.

That causes a gush of wetness to soak my panties, and I have the temerity to say, "Guess you'll have to rip them off."

He pauses for a brief moment, one leg out of his jeans, the other almost completely out, and looks at me with narrowed eyes. "Going to fire that ass up."

More wetness seeps out of me.

Logan kicks his pants off and flies at me. I expect a palm to come crashing down on my ass, because I very much like it when he spanks me, but he surprises me by flipping me over instead, only to do exactly as he promised.

My panties are gone in a nanosecond and flying over his shoulder where I see them land on one of the stove burners.

God, I hope we don't burn the place down.

Logan practically slithers up my body. I luxuriate in the feel of his coarse chest hair brushing along my stomach and over my breasts. He gives me a swift, hard kiss that causes our teeth to knock together, then he grabs my lower lip and tugs on it to the point of pain before it pops free.

Looking down at me with burning eyes, he says, "Going to eat this pussy. Make you come really hard. Then I'm going to ask you to tell me the truth. If you don't, going to eat you again. Make you come again. Going to wear your stubborn ass down until you tell me what I need to know. In between, I might fuck your mouth, but before this night is over, Auralie, I'm going to know all there is."

Oh, God.

Why did that threat just have to sound like the best thing that will ever happen to me in my life? And why does my heart flop over and then flutter madly because he cares so much about me, that he's almost driven beyond reason to get to the bottom of my dilemma?

I try to push that away, merely responding by cocking an eyebrow at him and spreading my legs a little. Up until now, Logan had been holding the bottom part of his body off me, but in response to my invitation, he lowers his pelvis. I feel the hot, hard length of him press right over my pussy with the tip of his cock resting just above my pelvis bone.

He grinds a little against me and mutters, "God, I want to fuck you so bad, baby. You just don't know."

My pussy absolutely floods over his words, which are said in a low, sexy rumble.

Oh, yes, I do know. He has no clue how very close I am to just opening my legs… spreading them a little further and letting him slide right in. But the only reason I don't is because I still possess enough self-control that's fueled by a burning desire for Logan not to get sucked into this any further.

Because Logan has already laid out what his nefarious plans are—interrogation tactics that equate to something like waterboarding by orgasms—he moves back down my body and puts his mouth where my money is.

And oh, Lord.

I'll never get used to how good that feels. The softness of his lips that he will sometimes purse tight around my clit, or the rough way he licks at it. Or when he'll even flirt with sticking the tip of his tongue inside of me, knowing that's it's not really a breach of my "virginity," but still be respectful of it all the same.

"Yes," I moan as he works me feverishly, because he has something to prove. One of us is breaking tonight.

My hands go to Logan's head, my fingers slipping in and then curling so I hold him tight. I press him down onto me, something he loves because he gives an appreciative growl, and I let him gorge himself on me.

Higher, and higher, and higher he drives me.

He's brutal about it. Determined. A little vindictive in how fast he's getting me there. I have a feeling he's not going to stop after just one and ask me to tell him the truth. I think he's going to go in for an immediate second, and the knowledge of how important this is to him… how important I have become to him… it hits me straight in the middle of my core, causing my orgasm to ripple and spread.

"Logan," I cry out, my hands gripping his head tighter.

He lifts his mouth just the tiniest bit so I can understand him. Talking with his lips against my wet flesh, he says, "That's it, baby. I want you to feel good. Does that feel good? Memorize that feeling because I'm going to do it all over again."

I gasp and moan, writhe against him. He finally lifts up and surprises me by crawling back up my body, once again lowering his cock to my sopping wet pussy, where he just presses the length down over me and holds still.

His mouth comes to mine, and I taste myself when he kisses me softly before looking into my eyes. "Tell me how I can fix this."

I shake my head, barely coherent to what he's saying. Because fuck… I still have little aftershocks of orgasm running up my spine and my pussy is still involuntarily clenching… begging for something more.

"Tell me," Logan demands again. This time, he does the unthinkable. He flexes his hips so the length of his dick slides along my wetness, back and forth.

"Oh God, Logan, don't," I beg him with a cry of surprised pleasure. My hips automatically lift up for him to give me more.

"Come on, Auralie," he growls, his face hovering over my mine. "Quit fucking around and tell me so we can set this shit straight."

I start to shake my head, but he's having none of it, intent on rattling and confusing me at every turn. His hips flex again. This time, the length of his cock pushes through my swollen lips, running right over my uber-sensitive clit.

My cry is strangled this time as I undulate under him, almost every bit of sanity having left my mind.

"Christ, you're wet," Logan says. He rears up off me, holding himself up with just one palm braced flat on the mattress at my ribs. With his other hand, he pushes my leg out, opening myself to him, and then he grabs his cock.

I watch in shock and wonder as he brings the tip right to my opening and slowly rubs it through the wetness there. In a strangled voice, he says, "Goddamn, I want to fuck you so bad that it hurts."

This bold statement is not new to me, but the level of pain in his voice hits me deeply. I also can't seem to concentrate because the tip of his dick then comes to my clit, circles, and then goes back to my slit where he starts to rub it faster.

"Logan," I whisper… a simple plea to… what?

Stop?

Fuck me?

Logan lifts his beautiful face and locks his eyes with me, still rubbing the tip of his cock all over me, but mainly in between my wet, swollen lips. "Auralie… you shouldn't give your virginity to just anyone. It should be given to someone special. Someone who cares about you."

I can't think. He's rubbing that beautiful big cock between my legs, and I can't think.

"You deserve special," he murmurs, his eyes dropping briefly to watch what he's doing, and then… oh damn… he thumps his cock a few times on my clit before he brings it down and starts guiding it back through my opening.

"Auralie," he says softly as he lifts his eyes back to mine. "Don't waste what's special about you."

And God… I can't take it anymore.

I can't take the way he feels between my legs or the

desire and care in his eyes. I can't stand his words telling me I deserve more than my shitty, fucked-up mess, and I most certainly can't stand the devotion to his claim that he will help me out of this.

Mostly, I cannot stand wondering what it would be like to be with this man in every sense of the word. I want him everywhere in me, on me, over me, under me. I want him inside every part of me.

"I'm not a virgin," I blurt out. I'm not prepared to see the shock register on Logan's face over the first lie that's been revealed to him. I hold my breath, thinking he might push up off the bed and leave me. Probably not only disgusted by this ugly untruth, but also by the fact that I'm not the virgin he desired.

But instead, I'm the one who is surprised when he groans, "Thank fuck," before tilting his pelvis and thrusting right into me.

With one solid push, he slides all the way in, and my eyes sting from the tiny bite of pain his girth produces as I stretch to accommodate him.

One push and he's connected to me in a way that should never feel this good, and yet I know it only feels this good because it's Logan.

"You on the Pill?" he growls as he holds absolutely still inside of me.

I nod, dragging my lower lip in between my teeth and biting down hard.

"Good," he mutters as he peers down at me. "Because I'm going to fuck you hard, and I'm going to come deep inside this pussy. After that, you've got a lot of explaining to do, understand?"

"Yes," I whisper and then wrap my hands behind his neck. "Now fuck me already."

Chapter 15

Logan

I AM PISSED.

Beyond pissed.

But don't get me wrong. I am not pissed she's not a virgin. I'm actually fucking relieved. Partly because I didn't want to hurt her, but mainly because it was the permission I needed to claim this pussy the way I've been wanting.

Which she's getting ready to find out will be done in a hard, deep, and rough manner.

I want her too much to go about it gently, and besides… I am pissed she held this information from me. I could have been fucking her sooner.

Tentatively, I slide my cock out of her. I do it slowly, not for her benefit but rather to gauge just how good it's going to feel and how fast I'm going to blow.

And f-u-u-u-u-u-ck.

My eyes involuntarily close because that feels way too good, and I sink slowly back into her tight, wet cunt. So goddamn good.

Never felt anything like it.

I'm not going to last, so my mission is to make sure

it's as good for her so I don't leave her in my wake.

Opening my eyes, I find her staring at me with hazy eyes and her mouth parted as she pants heavily. "I want you to come hard, Auralie."

She nods. She wants it too.

"I'm going to hit you fast and hard, so I need you to get there with me, okay?"

"Okay," she whispers, and then licks her lips.

So fucking sexy.

I pull my cock out again slowly, and I have to smile as her eyes roll in the back of her head. Sliding out all the way to the tip, I punch my hips forward… hard.

I slam back into her, bottoming out, and her eyes fly back open as she cries out in surprise. Bringing my elbow under one of her knees, I spread her a little wider for me.

Pulling out, I ask through clenched teeth, "Did that hurt?"

She shakes her head, and I'm guessing the power of speech may be gone for her. Which is fine. We communicate quite well without it.

"Good," I praise her. "Because not sure I could stop even if it did."

Slam.

Back in deep and her back arches off the mattress with such force, I'm slightly lifted.

"Fuck yeah," I growl as I realize my baby can take every inch of me as hard as I want to give it to her.

I pull out again, thrusting in deeply with a groan of utter satisfaction.

Out and in.

Harder and rougher than I thought I would originally go, but Auralie pants the words, "yes" every time, and it's driving me crazy to pound as deeply as I can go. So I can pummel my imprint into her so she never forgets who this pussy belongs to.

Christ, she feels good. Wet and hot, and damn… so tight as her muscles contract around me.

My breathing hitches as I race toward a release that I'm pretty sure is going to wreck me completely. "How you doing, baby?" I grunt in between thrusts.

"G-o-o-o-o-d," she stammers, eyes still closed tight as I tunnel in and out of her mercilessly.

"Sorry you lied to me?" I ask her through gritted teeth.

Her eyes fly open and her lips quirk slightly.

"Think it's funny, do you?" I ask, my eyes flashing with the promise of retribution for her impertinence, and I admit… I get momentarily sidetracked as I note her breasts jiggling all over the place because I'm fucking her so hard.

Back to the task at hand. "Think it's funny… making me suffer… making me obsesses about this pussy? Holding it out there for me to fantasize about?"

She doesn't answer me, but I see lines at the corners of her eyes start to form as she tries desperately not to smile and miserably fails to look contrite.

I pull all the way out of her, feeling triumphant when she cries out in protest, then I'm flipping her over roughly. She lands with a slight ooooph and I kick her legs apart, put my hands to her hips, and drag that gorgeous ass into the air. Reaching down, I grab my cock, line it up to her wet opening, and just as I slam in, I bring my other hand down hard on her ass cheek. The crack resonates sharply throughout the little trailer. When my hand pulls back, I smile at the red imprint left behind.

Auralie shrieks when I smack that ass again. "Think it's funny?"

I think I hear her snicker. She slams backward on my cock, forcing me to groan, so I smack her again, and I swear to fuck, I feel wetness gush all around my cock.

My baby likes this a lot, and if she's pleased, I'm pleased.

I give her three more slaps, each one just as hard. Each time, Auralie chants, "Yes, yes, yes".

The next time I crack my palm down, Auralie's back bows. She throws her head back, those long, black locks fanning over her back and she cries out, "Oh, Logan… I'm coming."

No need to tell me. I can feel her rippling all around me. This right here… never felt that before.

This urges me to go faster, and I start lurching into her body as I get dizzy with the need to come. I'm grunting on every thrust, barely have any oxygen left in my lungs, and yet I don't want this to end. I want to come, but I don't want to at the same time.

Choice is taken out of my hands though when Auralie takes over and starts pulling herself off my cock and slamming back against me. This causes me to go so deep, I can feel the head of my cock knocking against something inside of her. I force myself to stop, hold my hips still, and with my hands lightly on Auralie's hips just to hold her steady, I let her fuck me to completion.

Watching her throw herself mercilessly onto my cock before pulling herself back off, groaning and hissing out curse words, I'm so fucking turned on right now I might stroke out.

"That's my cock I'm fucking right now," Auralie mutters as she impales herself over and over again, and I'm so stunned by her dirty talk, especially when just minutes ago I thought she was a virgin, that my body decides to give it up.

I start to come as she tries to pull off me again, so I hold her hips tight to me and groan with utter abandon and relief, "Coming, baby. Oh, yeah… my girl fucked her cock and I'm coming so goddamn hard."

I unload jets of cum into her body, streaming hot and filling her tight channel until I can feel it oozing out as I hold myself planted deep. Auralie moans and whispers, "Yes. That's it, baby."

A huge aftershock of pleasure ripples up my spine, maybe a second orgasm. I groan because I can't not groan it feels so good, and yeah… that's never happened before either.

When I've stopped… when I don't think I have anymore, I pull out of her slowly and take my still-hard cock in hand. It's super sensitive but I wrap my hand around it, stroke upward, and squeeze the head, pulling forth more cum from the slit. I lean forward, rub the pearly liquid right over the fiery handprint that's going to be there for some time to come, and I muse out loud, "Not going to take me long to recharge, babe. But first, we need to talk."

Auralie flops to her stomach on the mattress and gives me an audible groan of dread.

I look back to the handprint practically shining like a neon light at me and feel a measure of satisfaction. Now it's time for me to hear what the fuck is really happening so I can fix this shit and have this for myself with nothing to interfere.

RELUCTANTLY, I DON'T force Auralie to talk right away. We haven't had dinner, and I did promise her hot dogs over an open campfire. It only takes about fifteen minutes for me to get a fire going as I keep a ready supply of dried wood under a tarp. I pull another canvas folding chair out of the storage locker in the back of my truck.

Auralie and I sit side by side, the sun having gone down. The dark sky is filled with low-hanging stars. We put the hot dogs on thin, green branches that I'd whittled the ends into points, and we roast them in silence.

I'm a patient man as she eats two and drinks a bottle of Coke to chase it down. I eat four and drink a beer, but when that's done, I stand up from my chair slightly to pick it up and turn it to face her.

"Now tell me… all of it," I demand as I sit back down.

I almost hope she hesitates because I would love nothing more than to drag her ass back to bed, spank it lava red, and fuck some obedience into her.

But she launches into her story without any qualms. She knows I need the entirety of it because she already exposed her big lie.

"I'm a grifter," are her first words, and I can't say this surprises me. The minute I learned she wasn't a virgin, I knew it was a con, but still…

"Unbelievable," I muse, intrigued as I'd never met one. At least, I don't think I have.

"Well, I used to be. Was raised to be one from an early age," she says with a wry smile.

"Wait a minute," I butt in. "How old are you?"

"Twenty-five," she says with some shame in her eyes. "I'm sorry I lied to you."

"Because a twenty-five-year-old virgin isn't believable," I conclude, and again, I'm oddly more relieved than pissed. Somehow, an eight-year age difference is more palatable than a thirteen-year one.

"Right," she says and then continues. "My parents were both con artists, so it's all I knew. I told you before, my mom died when I was ten, but it's not like she was a great role model. It was just my dad and me. His name is Mickey, by the way, and we just did what we had to do to survive."

I can't help it. I'm fucking fascinated. "I don't understand. I mean… what does a con artist do? Did your dad have a job? You said he did apartment management. Did you work? Or is all you do is scam money? Christ… did you even go to school?"

She laughs at me. In the firelight, she's never looked more beautiful. "We weren't homeless, and yes… I went to school. But grifting is a hard life, and it's not a rich one. Well, unless you do it on the level that Magnus does."

"You can tell me about him later." I wave an impatient hand because I want to know every tiny detail of this little criminal's life. I can't figure out if I'm appalled or slightly titillated by the cunning she obviously possesses. "Tell me what your life was like growing up."

Auralie plays with the lip of her empty Coke bottle. If I were a gentleman, I'd offer to get her another, but I am not and I don't because I want to hear her story.

She blows a puff of breath out and looks at me. "I was rolling trick dice in alleyways when I was nine. By the time I was twelve, I could run a flawless change-raising scam and none would be the wiser."

"Change raising?" I ask confused.

"It's a typical street short con. I go up to someone and ask if they have change for a ten. The con runs by passing bills or change back and forth, confusing the person as to what's going on. I'd walk away with twenty."

I whistle low through my teeth, and I'm very confused. I am truly appalled and yet oddly fascinated at the same time, but it's kind of hard to place blame on her. She was a child.

"As I got older, the cons got a little more complex. Still short, as I didn't have the means to run a long con, but my friend Gus and I would often run a mugging scam."

I raise my eyebrows, but before I can ask what that means, she provides me the answer.

"I'd see a woman walking, always a tourist and a dumb one at that, who didn't keep a good grip on her purse. I'd sneak up, snatch her purse, and run."

"Holy shit," I say in shock that she'd resort to common thievery.

"Calm down, Officer," she mocks me with a wave of her hand. "My friend, Gus, would "play" the Good Samaritan and give chase. I'd duck down a quick alley; he'd catch up to me and wrestle me for the purse. I'd be "overpowered" and then I'd take off running so I didn't get caught, gladly giving up the purse. He'd return it to the tourist, who would be so grateful she'd give him money for his help."

"You're fucking kidding me?" I ask, totally in shock that this sweet woman could be so devious.

"When I got older—became an adult—I did things that would disgust you," she says softly, her gaze finally falling.

Even though my stomach turns at the thought of

what she might reveal, I reach across the expanse between us and take her hand in mine. "I assure you, nothing you can say will disgust me. I'd already figured you were conning someone out of money for fake virginity."

She gives me a sad smile, and with a small voice says, "I'd go into a bar and find a lonely looking guy with a wedding ring…"

I have to swallow hard to suppress the growl that wants to come out.

"I'd flirt… get him interested. If he were local, I'd flirt harder. He'd have a few drinks and get bold, and then we'd make plans to go to a hotel together, because even though he loved his wife, he was still hot and horny for a young girl he met in a bar."

She stops, plays with the bottle some more, and I realize she's embarrassed.

"Go on, Auralie," I tell her gently. "Let me hear it."

"We'd go outside… wait for a cab, and I'd let him kiss me. I'd get him in a compromising position, and then Gus would come up on us and start taking pictures. The mark would notice and get upset, asking Gus what he was doing. Gus would admit to being hired by the man's wife who suspected he was cheating—"

"But the wife really didn't?" I ask for clarification.

"No," she says with a wry smile. "I was just really good at picking marks who I knew had probably cheated on their wives and so it would not seem out of character for the wife to have hired an investigator."

God, that's fucking insidious.

"At any rate, inevitably, the man would offer Gus "more money than the wife paid" in exchange for the pictures. One time we got five hundred in exchange for the SD card in the camera."

"Damn," I say in wonder, as I had no clue this shit went on. I mean, why would I? My life in Chicago was charmed. "And you did this every day?"

She shrugs noncommittally, I think perhaps feeling she's said too much and has put me off. So I try to get her back on track to something that would be easier to talk about. "You said you were looking at going to college?"

"Yes," she says with a quavering voice. "I told my dad and Magnus I wanted out. Dad let me happily go. Magnus wasn't so easy to convince, but he ultimately agreed."

"How does Magnus fit into your life?" I ask.

"Well, that's an interesting story," she tells me, "but I'd like another Coke first."

Chapter 16
Auralie

I DO NOT get another Coke first.

Logan puts the fire out and takes me back into the trailer where he fucks me again. Well, actually, he has *me* fuck *him*, rolling to his back and having me straddle him.

"Ride me, Auralie," he commands with glittering eyes.

And I do.

I sink down onto that gorgeous cock, and I ride him until both of us are gasping and shaking and practically seizing it's so good. After I come and he comes and our breath regulates—he's still planted inside of me although I feel him starting to go soft because I don't feel as full—he says something that surprises me.

"We fucked up." His warm palms resting on my thighs are meant to feel reassuring, but his words are chastising.

"What do you mean?" I ask fearfully, feeling the weight of catastrophe hanging over us.

"We had unprotected sex," he mutters. With eyes locked on me somberly, he adds, "I never do stupid shit like that. Twice now... out of control with you and taking risks that are just plain idiotic."

I can't tell if he's pissed at himself, me, or both of us, but I hesitantly say, "Logan… I've never been tested, but I've never had unprotected sex before either, so I'm confident I'm safe. But I'd be lying to you if I said I was out of control like you and didn't think about it. Because I did think about it… when I told you I wasn't a virgin, I figured you'd be fucking me pretty quickly. I did nothing to slow this down. I let you slide into me without a worry."

Logan swallows as he understands what I'm trying to say. "You trusted I wouldn't expose you to anything."

"Yes," I whispered. "I trusted you."

And I did.

Apparently, he trusts me, even though I've proven myself to be a liar and exposed myself as someone who routinely cheats in life. But he trusts me because he says as he lifts me off his dick and rolls me to his side, "Then we're good. We'll keep fucking without condoms, because I have to say, baby… that was fucking amazing."

I giggle and nod, very happy with this mutual understanding, but then something occurs to me. Logan goes to The Silo, and he does so to fuck random women. Does this mean he's giving that up? Or will he continue to do that but just wear condoms with other women?

The thought of him being with someone else causes my chest to constrict painfully, and yet I really can't say anything about it because I have a con to pull off. That means I'll be back in The Silo soon with random dick down my throat.

That thought causes nausea to well up inside of me.

"Okay, tell me about Magnus," Logan says as he leans up briefly in the bed to pull the sheets and blanket up over us. He lies back down on his side facing me and waits patiently for me to put this all together.

"Probably about ten years ago, my father went to work for Magnus," I say, telling him how it all started. "And by work for him, I mean he helped Magnus pull off some longer cons, and yes… he made more money than he was doing on his own. We were struggling, trying to make enough money to survive. By that time, my dad had been living that life so long, he had no real work experience. I wasn't able to do much with going to school. Going to work for Magnus, who had what seemed like a bazillion cons just waiting to be tapped, just seemed like the natural thing to do. It was like money growing on trees for us."

"You said your dad did apartment management," Logan points out, and yes, I did tell him that at dinner that first night we went out.

I give him a wry grimace. "Yeah… that wasn't exactly true. He managed an apartment scam."

"Oh-kay," he says slowly with a disbelieving shake to his head. "I'm going in. What does that mean?"

"He'd take an ad out on like Craig's List, and list an apartment for rent. Take first and last month's deposits. When the people show up to move in, they find out that the apartment is not for rent and is, in fact, owned by someone else."

"Jesus," he mutters in astonishment. "The stupidity of people sometimes. Did you ever feel guilt for what you were doing?"

"Sometimes," I tell him simply while holding his stare without an embarrassed lowering of my eyes. "Sometimes not. It was my way of life. It was how I helped pay things like the electric bill and put food on the table. It's all I knew."

Logan looks at me in such a way… almost as if he's terribly sad for the way I've lived my life. I think he's conveying to me, *I have to wonder what you could have become had you been taught a value's-based way to lead your life.*

I answer him out loud. "I wonder all the time what I could have been."

He gives me a soft smile, leaning in to kiss me gently before pulling back. "I still don't get what Magnus could do for your dad that he couldn't do for himself?"

"Magnus could pull off more complex stuff… that requires set up and time, usually other people involved. It also has a better payout. For example, Magnus had a pretty big mystery shopping con going. He'd send a fraudulent check to a mystery shopper, enough to buy a nice item, but more than the price of said item. Mystery shopper deposits the check. Part of the mystery shopper's agreement is that they had to return the difference by wire immediately upon purchase and they were being timed on responsiveness. This ensured the mystery shopper would purchase the item quickly and then wire the difference back."

"Money gets wired and picked up," he hazards a guess, "before the fraudulent check bounces."

"Yup," I say in a matter-of-fact tone. "Magnus had my dad manage those more complex cons. He's always been good with numbers and multi-tasking. It was almost like a management position for Magnus. And when I say manage those cons, I mean Magnus had hundreds of grifters working for him all over the city. They paid him commissions, and he got rich from their labor with none of the risk."

"And your dad oversaw all the cons being run and tallied the money for Magnus?" he sums it up.

"Yeah… that's what he was supposed to do," I affirm bitterly, and that leads us up to what brought me into his life.

"What did your dad do?"

I shift my body, curl my arm under the pillow where my head is resting, and tilt my head so I can maintain eye contact with him. "I mentioned I wanted out. I was tired of that type of life, and, unlike my dad, I was still young enough I could do something different. I wanted to go to college, but I had no clue what I wanted to be. I just knew I didn't want to scrape by with that type of life."

"You said they both agreed to let you out."

I nod. "My dad very happily, actually proud I wanted to go to college. Magnus wasn't so happy because I was good at what I did, but he had plenty of people working for him. I was just getting ready to enroll in college when I came home to the apartment I shared with Dad and found Magnus and one of his goons there with my dad. Apparently, my dad's books weren't quite adding up, and Magnus assumed he stole from him."

"Did he?" he asks.

"Yeah… later told me he skimmed just enough to help me with tuition. But he was so good at moving and hiding money, and cooking the spreadsheets to reflect what he wanted, Magnus really couldn't pinpoint it so he couldn't know for sure my dad stole from him."

"But I'm guessing he wasn't letting it go," he surmises.

"Nope. Wasn't letting it pass. My dad got roughed up, and I immediately offered to make it up to Magnus. I walked right into his trap."

"His trap?"

"He had this con already cooked up," I explain as I shift my legs, which causes my shin to brush against his. His eyes darken just from that slight touch, and tingles shoot up my spine in response.

While Logan's eyes say, *I want to fuck you again*, I try to ignore it so I can finish my explanation. "Magnus found out about this club and was going to sell off a fake virgin. He needed someone who looked young, sweet, and virginal to serve as shill."

"Did he even know your dad took money or was it a stab in the dark?" he asks in wonder.

"I think it was a stab in the dark," I murmur glumly, but I'm very impressed that Logan's sort of got Magnus figured out a bit. "But I wasn't about to take the chance."

"Chance with what?"

"That my dad would go *poof*," I say simply.

"Excuse me?"

"My friend, Gus… the one who ran scams with me on the street? Well, he skimmed money off the top before he paid Magnus his share, and *poof*… he just disappeared."

He blinks at me in surprise. "You're saying Magnus killed him?"

I laugh darkly and try to keep the venom in my voice to a minimum. "Magnus doesn't have the balls to do his own dirty work, but yes… I'm saying Magnus ordered it. He has plenty of muscle who will gladly carry out those orders."

"And you think he'd kill your dad?" he asks, understanding my need to see this con through to the end in one bright, clarifying moment.

"I do," I whisper. "I think he'd do it. Oddly, I think he'd hate it, but he'd do it. At least, that was his very clear threat to me if I don't hold up my end of the bargain."

Logan's silent for a moment, trying to digest what I've told him, but it's really pretty simple in my opinion. My father's life is at stake, and I'm willing to perpetuate a pretty big fraud to ensure he remains safe.

"It's the only reason I'd ever get on my knees and suck a stranger off, Logan," I say apologetically, because while I know I'm a rotten person for doing this, I don't want him to be disappointed in my choices. His eyes jerk to mine, and I hate that they're holding pain for me. "I'm not that type of girl. I might have done a hell of a lot of cheating and lying in my life, but I've never peddled my body like that. I hope you believe me."

He doesn't speak but rather reacts. His arms shoot out and wrap around me, pulling me in close to him. My face settles in the crook of his neck, and one of his large hands comes to the back of my head to hold me there. "Hey… don't even go there. I know exactly what type of girl you are, and you're a survivor. Nothing more."

"I'm sorry I lied to you," I mumble against him, my lips gliding over his skin. "I never wanted to do that."

"I get it," he reassures me, and sadly, I know one reason he gets it is because he's hidden things from me. But that's a discussion for another time.

We lay silent for a few moments, but then he asks, "How exactly were you going to get past the fact you are, in fact, not a virgin?"

"Simple," I say softly. "Magnus has fake medical records proclaiming my hymen's intact, and I'm merely going to drug the mark before we can get to the sex part. By the time he wakes up, Magnus and I will be long gone from Wyoming."

"Someone losing that type of money will come after you both," he points out darkly.

Pulling back so he can see my face, I give him censuring look and ask, "You really think his name is Magnus Albright? He'll never be found because he's a shadow and he goes by many names."

"Jesus fuck," he grumbles as he pushes himself up and pull his arms away from me. Logan holds himself up on one elbow and looks down at me, his other hand coming up to push some hair off my face. "I don't even fucking know your last name. I've fucked the shit out of you, going to do that again and again, and I don't know your last name."

Sadness fills me up, and I shrug. "You don't know any of the last names of the women you fuck from The Silo, I'm guessing."

He winces and I know that cut deep.

Bending down, he drags his lips across mine and cups his palm to my face. "Yeah, but the difference is I want to know yours. Want to know every damn thing about you, and even things you don't know about yourself."

I blink at him, astonished by the fervor in his tone, yet still on guard as he's asking something that a good con artist never gives up.

"What's your last name, baby?" he pushes at me, and I have no control over my reaction. I've got years and years ingrained in me to hold myself aloof from personal attachments, and I know my eyes go a bit frosty.

"It's never a good idea for someone like me to give my full name," I say coolly.

He jerks in surprise over my refusal, and then narrows his eyes at me. "You still have my cum puddled warm inside of you, but you don't trust me enough to tell me your last name?"

I hold silent.

And then he understands why, commanding me. "You are not going through with this con."

"I have to," I say with a sigh of regret. "My dad's life is at stake."

"We'll find another way to get you both out of this," he responds resolutely as he leans back over me, putting his hand down on the mattress beside my ribs so I'm caged in.

He's displaying his dominance over me, in a classic alpha move to get me to come to heel.

"You are absolutely not going back into The Silo to suck cock unless it's my cock," he adds on with a grunt.

Caveman.

"There is no other way," I say in exasperation. "My dad can't just walk away. He knows no other type of life. No other way to support himself. This is it for him. He's stuck in that world. He's stuck working for Magnus. If I want my dad to live, I have to pull this off and ensure Magnus gets his money."

I'm not prepared for what he says next. "I'll put in the winning bid."

And I can read the look on his face clearly, and it makes me wince. *Why not? Wouldn't be the first time I'd bought pussy.*

"Are you fucking out of your mind?" I snap at him, putting my hands to his chest to try to push him away from me. "You couldn't possibly have that type of money."

He gives me a condescending laugh. "What are you going to fetch? A hundred thousand? Five hundred thousand?"

I roll my eyes at him, but remind him resolutely. "It's more than a fly fisherman can afford."

He doesn't debate this with me, but instead says with utter confidence, "I'll figure something out, but you are not going through with this."

"Yes. I. Am," I punctuate through gritted teeth. "My father is all I have in this world, and there's not a damn thing you can do to stop me from doing what's necessary to make sure I don't lose him. You have no idea the type of man Magnus is, and—"

Logan moves so suddenly, I can't do anything but suck in my breath in shock.

Throwing his leg over me, he moves to straddle my chest but holds his weight off me. His legs have me pinned at my upper arms. He puts his palms on the pillow beside my head before hunching over and putting that beautiful face all up in my space.

"Tired of listening to you tell me we can't fix this another way," he growls at me. "Tired of you thinking you're going to go back in that Silo and let another man touch you."

"Get off—"

"Tired of listening to you period," he says with a grin. He flexes his hips so that his dick, which is now brutally hard, brushes against my lips.

My eyes flare wide with surprise, but I restrain myself from opening my mouth to take him in. It's what I really want to do, but, instead, I give him a loathsome glare that doesn't come close to hitting the mark because he laughs at me.

"Open up, Auralie," he whispers with a grin, pushing the tip of his cock against my closed lips. "Let me fill that pretty mouth up."

Lust sizzles in Logan's eyes and I feel myself falling prey to it, but I refuse to give in. Besides, something about arguing with him and the hard fucking that occurs because of it is too good to pass up. So I remain stubborn. "This doesn't change—"

The minute my mouth opens, he pushes forward and fills my mouth with his cock, stopping before he butts against the back of my throat. I suck against him reactively, and he groans his approval. My mouth is stretched wide and I'm rendered speechless—which I think he likes very much at this moment—and God help me, but that excites the hell out of me.

I can't talk, but I let him know what I'm thinking in this very moment. My eyes level warmly on his. *I'm going to let you fuck my mouth, Logan, but this conversation isn't over by a long shot.*

He grins at me. Rising up on his knees a bit for better leverage, he begins a slow pumping in and out of my mouth. Once he rises, I note my hands are free so I bring them up and sink my nails into his ass—hard.

"Fuck that hurts," he complains, but he doesn't miss a stroke. And then he smiles down at me almost evilly. "But that's okay... I'm only going to fuck your mouth for a few minutes... just enough to get your jaw sore. Then I'm going to flip you over and tan your backside for even doubting that I can get us out of this mess."

I moan against his cock, not knowing if it's because I'm turned on by what he just said or that he cares enough about me to help me through this.

Chapter 17

Logan

I'M IN THE *viewing room again, my eyes already adjusted to the bright light. Doctors are shoulder to shoulder as they hunch over the operating table. My body leans left, and then right… just can't fucking see. I know I should know who's on that table, but it's just escaping me.*

I look to my right, immediately frustrated the faces are blurred and unrecognizable. I turn to my left, expecting the same, but instead, I meet a pair of crystal-blue eyes smiling at me sadly.

Auralie.

I stare at her, confused as to why she's here. How in the hell did she even get admitted? I look over her shoulder at the long row of people sitting to her left, but they're all blurred as well. I can tell, however, that they're all facing forward and watching the procedure down below.

With great effort, and because I'm afraid I'll miss something important, I tear my eyes away from Auralie and look through the glass to the doctors below.

The whoosh of the respirator is expected, as is the beeping from the EKG monitor. I still can't see a fucking thing though as to what they're doing, but a few words filter up through the speakers mounted in the corners of the viewing room.

"… I can't locate the bleeder. Can I get some more suction?"

"…BP's fifty over forty… heartrate 120… she's in hemorrhagic shock…"

Icy prickles cause my hair to stand up, and my heart starts beating rapidly. My ears strain to hear more because I still can't see shit below.

"…hang another unit of O-Neg."

"…she's had three already…"

"…can I get some fucking suction here…"

The doctors move only nominally, still huddled over the table. For as dire as the situation seems, no one seems to be doing much to the patient before them. It's driving me nuts I can't get a glimpse… then maybe I could….

What?

In desperation, I turn to my left. Auralie is still looking at me sadly.

"Can you see anything from where you're sitting?" I ask her desperately.

She gives a slow shake of her head, and I curse at the fates.

I start to turn back. Perhaps I'll get out of my chair and beat on the glass… tell those motherfuckers to move…

A warm hand presses down on my thigh, and I feel Auralie's delicate fingers press into the muscle there. I turn back to look at her, and she leans in to whisper, "You should fuck me, Logan."

"Excuse me?" I ask, my head turning so I can get a quick

glance back to the operating table. Still completely obscured. I look back to her. "What did you say?"

Her hand slides up my leg, and it feels hot. I mean, really hot, as if it's lighting the skin under my pants on fire. I want to turn to look back at the procedure below because I'm afraid I'll miss something, yet I can't seem to tear my eyes away from her hand that's creeping steadily up my leg.

"Logan," she murmurs, and I slide my eyes up to meet hers. She gives me an encouraging look. "You really should fuck me."

Before I can even answer, and before I can take another quick peek into the surgical room, her small hand covers my crotch and she squeezes what I'm surprised to find out is a hard-on I'm sporting.

Talk about inappropriate.

My hand comes up to cover hers with the intent to remove it, as I have far more important things to do right now. But the minute my palm touches the back of her hand, I find myself pressing her hand down on me harder and forcing her fingers to curl around the outline of my erection.

I groan and lift my hips up, because fuck… that feels so damn good.

I should probably undo my belt… get my zipper down.

"…we're losing her…" I hear someone yell, and my head snaps toward the glass.

"Logan… I need you inside me," Auralie murmurs, squeezing my cock. I use my hand to make hers start to jack me through my jeans, even as my eyes remain pinned helplessly on the doctors below.

"…blood pressure's falling…"

"I want you deep inside me, Logan."

"…she's gone into cardiac arrest…"

"Baby… I can make this all go away if you just fuck me…"

A long, slow beep from the EKG monitor.

"No," I cry out to the doctors below.

"Logan," I hear as someone shakes my shoulder hard. "Come on, honey. Wake up for me."

My eyes snap open, and I immediately recognize the interior of my trailer.

I know I'm on my bed.

I also know that is Auralie's soft body sitting in the bed next to me with her hand on my shoulder.

I'm covered in a thin sheen of sweat. My heart is pounding pretty hard, and I'm keenly aware I have a raging hard-on.

"Are you okay?" Auralie asks in a tremulous voice. "I think you were having a nightmare."

I turn my head, but I can't make out her facial features in the gloom. I can tell by the tone of her voice she's wigged out.

For fuck's sake… I'm wigged out too, because that was the same old dream that was seemingly mixed with something else. It's still with me, causing pulsing images of the viewing room, the operating table, the hunched-over doctors to all flash before me.

Gritting my teeth, I grab Auralie's hand and put it to my cock. I make her curl her fingers around and stroke it a few times, then remove my hand and let her take over.

She does so without question and I give a relieved groan, my mind instantly focusing only on the pleasure she gives me.

"Were you having a nightmare?" she presses me tentatively as my cock fucks her hand and my hips start thrusting into her grasp.

I don't answer but instead roll over her, forcing her to lie back on the bed. She loses her grip on me, and I immediately see the operating room again in my head. My hand reaches out blindly to the window ledge above my bed, desperately seeking the bottle of lube I keep up there. I knock over my alarm clock, fumble over my phone, and finally latch onto it.

The doctor on the end... he starts to turn to let me see the table.

Coming up on my knees in between her legs, I flip the cap and pour a hefty amount into my palm before using my thumb to latch it shut. The bottle falls forgotten. My lubed palm goes to my dick where I coat it thoroughly.

"Logan?" Auralie whispers in confusion.

A small body on the table... covered in a sheet.

I fall onto Auralie, her legs spreading for me automatically, and I shove my cock into her with a grunt.

She gasps, her entire body stiffening from my invasion, but I'm immediately filled with a warm peace. Her pussy is gripping my dick in such a way that everything else just becomes moot as I start fucking her.

Leaning my head down, I kiss her softly as my hips

pump away the misery before whispering to her, "Sorry, baby. Just needed you badly."

She answers me with a moan and her hands to my ass, urging me to go deeper. I fuck her so thoroughly that we both come quickly. As I orgasm, I can barely remember my own name much less a stupid dream.

Yeah… that's the stuff that nightmare demolition is made of.

I CRASHED HARD after I fucked Auralie post nightmare. Banished those god-awful memories good because the only dreams I had after that were of fucking Auralie again, which ensured I woke up with a hard-on and feeling horny but oddly refreshed. Downside was that I didn't have time to act on my instincts to have her again, but instead, slipped out of bed and quietly put my clothes on. It was barely six AM, but I always wake up early because that's normally when my workday starts out on the river.

After leaving a note for Auralie on the mattress beside her, I crept out of the trailer and got in my truck.

The minute I hit Highway 191, I dial Bridger, wincing slightly when it's clear I woke him up and also clear he's not happy about it.

"This better be good," he growls into the phone, his voice clogged with sleep and irritation.

"It's Logan," I told him succinctly, and so he would understand the urgency I boil the circumstances down to the most dramatic facts. "I've got to talk to you now about Magnus. He's a con artist, and Auralie is being blackmailed."

"What the fuck?" Bridger grumbles but his voice is clearer. "Where are you?"

"On my way to see you," I tell him. "Can we meet at your office?"

"Come to my house," he says.

I blink in surprise, but I don't question. I've never been invited there before. No one I know from The Silo has, except Woolf, but he warrants the exception since he's Bridger's best friend. "Know where it is?"

"No clue," I admit.

He gives me directions. I'm not surprised to find his house sits on Double J property, which is owned by Woolf. I have no clue exactly how big the Double J is, but I know the parent company, JennCo, has over three hundred thousand acres spread over three states. The Double J is first and foremost a cattle ranch—largest in the nation—but it also surreptitiously leases a small tract of land to Bridger upon which The Wicked Horse and The Silo sit. But interestingly, his house sits about as far from the Wicked Horse and The Silo as possible, actually putting it closer to the city limits of Jackson. Rather than taking me almost forty-five minutes to make the trip, it will only take me about fifteen.

Bridger meets me at the door wearing a pair of loose, black track pants and a white t-shirt. His hair is sticking up all over the place, and he has a cup of coffee in hand.

As he closes the door behind me, he walks into the kitchen and I follow.

Bridger's house is really nice and that surprises me. Not that he can't afford "really nice," but it's just that outside of his red Corvette, Bridger never really seems to be moved by money. I know he makes a shit-pot full between the bar and sex club, but he never flaunts it. He doesn't wear super expensive clothes, preferring jeans and cowboy boots, and he never takes vacations.

While his house is nice, it's not ostentatious like Woolf's. I'm guessing about three-thousand square feet, built in the classic western cabin theme with pine logs and large, rectangular windows that look out over the Teton Mountains. The mountain range is so large and sweeping, there are not many places on the Double J where you can't see the beauty of it.

The kitchen is state of the art with granite counters, custom cabinetry, and high-end appliances. Bridger silently pours me a cup of coffee from one side of a kitchen island, pushing it across to me with a nod toward one of the high-backed stools done in wrought iron and reclaimed wood.

I park my ass on one and pull the coffee toward me, grateful for it since I didn't bother to make any before I left. Didn't want to chance waking up Auralie.

"So spill it," Bridger says gruffly.

"Magnus is a con artist and Auralie's dad works for him. He skimmed some money, pissed Magnus off, and now Magnus is using Auralie as repayment to run a con at The Silo." I think that was about as succinct as I can make it.

"And you know this how?" Bridger asks, not because he doesn't trust my word, but he's angling to know what my connection to Auralie is.

So I tell him with brutal honesty. "She's not a virgin. I fucked her after she admitted it to me, and I plan on fucking her for the foreseeable future. She laid the entire story out to me last night."

Bridger cocks an eyebrow at me, and there's no mistaking the skepticism in his tone. "Logan… hate to point this out because I'm getting clearly that you like this woman, but she's playing the part really well; she didn't seem too averse to sucking dick."

I get what he's inferring. That Auralie is as much into the con as Magnus is, and to some extent, that's true. She was all in when it came to portraying the innocent virgin, and she didn't seem reluctant at all to get on her knees to suck strange dick.

He's doubting her endgame.

So, I have to be brutally honest with him. "She was raised by a grifter father to be a grifter herself. That has been her life up until recently when she got out. Was going to enroll in college. She's only doing this because Magnus will kill her father if she doesn't run this con with him. She's getting nothing out of this but her father's life."

"Fuck," Bridger mutters and leans onto the counter, his forearms flat and hands clasped to support his weight.

"So if she doesn't go through with this, her dad's in trouble."

I nod stiffly, because that is the real bone of contention I have with Auralie right now. She's determined to see this through to protect her dad, and I'm determined that she not step foot in The Silo again.

Which brings about a startling thought.

Am I willing to do the same thing? Am I willing to give The Silo up if I could have Auralie to myself?

I have no fucking idea, but my gut instinct tells me I could be wholly satisfied with what she gives me.

I think.

No real fucking clue, but that's not what my immediate worry is right now. It's trying to figure out how I get Auralie out of this mess so the only dick she touches is mine. Her dad isn't even my real priority, but I know he has to be a consideration because unless his safety can be guaranteed, Auralie will be on her knees tonight—and not before me.

This was a calculated risk coming to Bridger. My ultimate hope is that he may have an idea on what to do. Maybe we can reverse con Magnus somehow. Maybe Bridger can pull a fire code violation that closes The Silo down for the next six months, which I get is really unlikely, but I hold out hope.

Mostly, though, I'm revealing this shit to Bridger because I know the minute I spilled the beans on the fraud being perpetrated in his place of business, he was never, ever going to let it go any further. I know Bridger's initial reaction will be to kick Magnus' ass and kick him out of the club. My risk in bringing Bridger in on this is if he reacts swiftly and does something like that, Auralie's dad will be at risk and Auralie will never forgive my rash actions.

I am hoping beyond hope that Bridger will put his trademark calm, reasoning, and brilliant mind to task to help me figure out what to do.

"How was this supposed to be pulled off if she's not a virgin?" Bridger asks.

"She was supposed to drug whoever purchased her before they had sex. She and Magnus would slip away with the money."

Bridger growls and his face goes thunderous. I hastily remind him. "Remember… she's only doing this to protect her dad."

"I get that," he snaps at me. "Doesn't mean I like the plan or that your girl is involved in a scheme to dupe one of my customers."

"Just," I start off by saying but my throat gets clogged. I don't beg and this is as close to it as I'll come. "Just… can you figure out a way to help her?"

Bridger lets out a huff of frustrated breath. "When is Magnus coming back from New York?"

"Tomorrow."

"Any idea when he expects to make the sale?" he asks.

"No," I admit with annoyance. "He's kept Auralie in the dark on everything."

"Here's the thing," Bridger says as he pushes up off

the counter to a straightened position. "Any type of idea to reverse con him is not going to work as Auralie's dad will pay for it."

"Agreed. But what if we just spread the word to those thinking to bid that it's a con—"

Bridger shakes his head and glares at me. "We are not letting this cat out of the bag. I don't want my customers knowing that shit is going on in my club. It will damage the trust people have in the safety of it."

"So we have to bring Magnus down in a way that makes it so he can't harm Auralie or her dad in the future," I conclude.

"You can't murder him," Bridger says, and it makes me realize how menacing my tone just was. But he's not serious. He knows I wouldn't do that.

Or would I?

What would I do to keep Auralie all to myself and never let another man touch her?

I'm amazed at myself that I'm even considering these options seeing as how I never thought I'd ever be proprietary over a woman again. Never contemplated having a relationship again.

Guess I've changed, but the real question is, what have I changed into?

"Is he expecting her to go to The Silo tonight?" Bridger asks, and I blink to chase away my thoughts about murder and commitment.

"No clue." Although in my heart of hearts, I'm positive he'll tell her to go. The question is will I let her?

"Well, I can't close down another night," Bridger says with that look in his eyes that says don't even bother to ask. "So you best be prepared to let your girl do what she needs to do until we can figure something out. I have an idea, but it's not going to happen overnight."

I grimace but nod. I know even as brilliant as Bridger is, he's not going to fix this shit in a matter of hours. Not even sure he can fix this at all.

Which means I need to prepare myself to accept a few truths.

Auralie is going to be pissed as hell I told Bridger all of this.

Bridger is not going to let this fraud run its course, although he'll let it temporarily play out until we can figure something out.

The sale of Auralie's "virginity" is not going to take place, which means Magnus is going to get screwed over. This means that Auralie's dad could go *poof*.

Which means there's a good chance Auralie's going to hate me at some point.

Chapter 18
Auralie

I LEAN MY head against the passenger window of Logan's truck and watch the scenery roll by with a satisfied smile on my face. I'm exhausted as we've been driving around Grand Teton National Park all day, taking in magnificent lakes, crystal clear streams, snow-capped mountains, and meadows filled with wildflowers.

I had mentioned that day on the river with Logan that I wished I'd had time to see Yellowstone while I was here. We had a free day today—although I suspect Logan's day wasn't really free and he'd cancelled his trips for the day to spend it with me—and he told me he was going to take me to see "some things". This ultimately did not mean Yellowstone, which was at first disappointing to me because hello—Old Faithful—but now, as the day is nearing its end, I'm quite pleased with everything I've experienced today.

It started with Logan waking me up with take-out breakfast from a wonderful place he called "The Bunnery". He picked up some gooey chocolate croissants, bagels, and bear claws, which could not possibly all be eaten by both of us, and carried them into the tiny trailer where I was sleeping hard. The sounds of him banging around in the kitchen not five feet from where I was sleeping woke me up, and I stared at him with bleary eyes as he made coffee.

So sweet, the way he'd slipped out early while I slept and went into town to get breakfast. Just as sweet when he told me we were spending the day sightseeing. All of this was made infinitely sweeter by the fact he did it less than twelve hours after me admitting to being a fraud, a liar, and a cheat to him. All terrible qualities that he's apparently chosen to overlook.

We did not make it up north to Yellowstone, but rather took some time exploring the Bridger-Teton National Forest, which is 3.4 million acres that sits in between Jackson and Yellowstone. And while I can't speak for the grandeur of Yellowstone, and truly, the only thing I know about Yellowstone is that it boasts the fame of Old Faithful, I truly can't imagine more beauty than what I saw today.

Logan and I took a four-mile hike around String Lake, which is shallow, and the water so pure from glacial runoff that the water is a crystal blue. The hike brought us out to a clearing where we got a magnificent view of Cathedral Group, which is made up of Teewinot Mountain, Grand Teton, and Mt. Owen, said mountains with deep green trees at the base, and gray, craggy rocks thousands and thousands of feet up with snow still glistening at the peaks even though we were in late summer.

My favorite place by far was Oxbow Bend, with the Snake River spread lazy and curving with Mount Moran rising up behind the smooth waters. The sun was perfectly hanging with not a cloud in the sky, and Mount Moran's mirror image was reflected on the river. I couldn't even fathom the beauty of it, my mind almost refusing to believe that something so perfect could exist. I think Logan said something to the effect that it was one of the most photographed places in Wyoming, but then my attention got distracted by a family of otters playing along the riverbank and I was laughing at their antics.

I only became aware of my surroundings when I heard Logan laughing along with me, and I turned to face him in wonder. Granted, I haven't known the man all that long and yes, we clearly have a deep connection, but in that moment, I realized there was so much I didn't know because his genuine laugh was a surprise to me. While I've seen him smile and chuckle and even look amused, I had not heard him genuinely laugh until that moment. It amazed me as much as it made me sad that I'm guessing said emotion is a rarity with him.

And now as we make our way back toward Jackson, exhaustion starts to take over because despite how magnificent today was seeing all the grandeur of this beautiful state, there was almost no acknowledgment between the two of us of how fucked-up our situation was.

No discussion about my sordid past as a grifter, or that I came into Logan's life on a pure lie, or that I was still intent on perpetuating a fraud. No discussion about the amazing sex we had the first time, and then the time after, and the time after that. Most certainly, we didn't discuss what happened in the wee morning hours when Logan was clearly having a nightmare, and I couldn't get him to wake up at first. He mumbled in his sleep, but I heard pain-filled words such as "no" and "please help her," and he was thrashing slightly.

Finally, with some rough shaking and repeatedly calling out to him, he came out of it.

And then he did something that I'm not sure if it repulsed me or turned me on. He came out of a nightmare that was clearly causing him distress with a hard-as-steel erection, and, without a lick of foreplay or even a kiss from him, he poured lube on his dick and thrust it into me so hard, tears stung my eyes.

Granted, the sting only lasted a second, and then wow… the way Logan fucked me after was beyond words could even describe, but it was better than all the other times we'd been together. I think it was better—to me at least—because Logan needed me in a way that I've never been needed before. I could tell there was something I was giving him, and something he required and hadn't succeeded in attaining before, and that did nothing more than cement the bond that was already pretty mystically strong to begin with.

He didn't explain his actions. After he came inside me, he held me tight and we fell back asleep.

"One more thing I want to show you," Logan says

and I lift my head from the window to look at him. He slows his truck and takes a right turn down a gravel and dirt road that's narrow and lined to the edge with thick chokeberry and hawthorn bushes. "This is Moose-Wilson Road and will bring us out near Teton Village."

"Not well traveled, is it?" I ask with interest as I sense we are headed into some unchartered territory given the rough nature of the road and the wilderness encroaching right up to it.

"Actually, it is," Logan says to the contrary and points out his driver's side window. "This road is about eight miles long, but it's one of the best places to see moose in this area. There are wetlands on this side of the road… a lot of moose around in there."

"But I can't see anything," I say as I turn in my seat to get a better look, but the thick vegetation only opens up in patchy areas to provide brief glances of wet, marshy-looking land beyond.

"I'll drive slow. If you see something, I'll stop, but there are a few open places with some small ponds where we can usually see something."

We're silent as the truck bumps along. My eyes search for the elusive moose out of Logan's window. My eyes keep straying from the scenery beyond him to his face, which is in profile to me. He wasn't wrong… the road is actually quite busy as we pass several other vehicles, all driving slow with heads practically hanging out the window as they look for wildlife.

Logan's face is just as beautiful in profile as he is full

on. I can better appreciate the lines that make him so masculine as I take in the almost cocky natural arch to his eyebrow and strong jawline that sits above corded neck muscle made strong by his job. His cheekbones sit high with a slight hollowing underneath, but the angles are sharp so he doesn't look pretty but handsome.

Even last night, with the moonlight filtering into the gloom of the trailer, when Logan was fucking me in almost a furious attempt to banish his nightmare, his face was harsh but beautiful at the same time. Such an enigma.

So much mystery around him.

"What were you dreaming about last night?" I blurt out suddenly, and Logan's head snaps my way in surprise. His eyes are dark but inscrutable. "You were really distressed."

"I don't remember," he says so quickly but without any emotion. I instantly know he's lying. His face turns back to look out the windshield.

I'm not sure what compels me to fight him on this, but I'm guessing it has something to do with the fact that I opened up to him about something that was terrible and embarrassing. I almost expect the same back from him, I guess. "I think you do."

That strong, hard jaw locks, and it causes a muscle right at the hinge to thump. I swear I almost hear his teeth grind, not in an effort to prevent himself from divulging to me, but because my question irritates him. He remains stubbornly silent.

"Logan," I say carefully, all thoughts of moose sightings forgotten. "You can tell me anything. I've told you the worst about me, and it didn't send you running. You need to trust the same about me."

He doesn't respond, eyes remaining locked on the road in front of him and knuckles turning slightly white.

So I push, trying to be gently reassuring that I'm here for him. "I know I felt so much better once I told you what was going on with me. I bet you'd also—"

"Nothing will make me feel better about my past," Logan snaps at me, his head turning just enough to pin me with a hard look before turning back. Then, after he takes in a breath, he lets it out with a sigh, his voice losing a bit of the frost. "Look... I left my former life behind, and I don't think about it. It's done, and it doesn't define me anymore."

Oh, but it does, Logan. Surely you can see that because it's as clear as day to me.

Yet, I hold those thoughts. Logan doesn't want or need me to tell him that whatever has happened to him in the past is directly responsible for the fact that he's emotionally closed off right this moment, or that he's clearly not left it behind because it plagues him at night in the form of nightmares. I suspect this man has tried very hard to push the bad down into a place that is not easily accessible, preferring to ignore rather than address.

This bugs me to a certain degree because clearly we've shown trust in each other on more than one occasion. Neither one of us doubted the other that we could have unprotected sex based on just our assertions to each other that we were clean and I was on the Pill. Most importantly, I trusted him enough to admit I was in the process of pulling off a very serious crime, and yet he gives me nothing in return.

Except orgasms but those alone cannot sustain the bond we formed. In fact, him refusing to open up after I have will fracture that bond.

However, I also don't need answers from him right this moment. I asked because I was curious, and I offered to take on his burdens because I want to help him. But those are not things I need to have for myself but rather want to give to him. If he's not ready for that, I can afford patience. Granted… things are still going to move forward to sell my "virginity" as far as I'm concerned, but I'm hopeful that perhaps once that's done, Logan and I can continue to see where this goes.

There's no rule I need to go back to New York. I can go to college anywhere, really.

I know it's silly to look that far in advance, but even though this man is irritated with me and his lips are sealed firmly shut against my curiosities, I'm still very much aware that we have something that, despite being new, is deep-rooted and abiding. So I can wait and hope that one day Logan will open up to me the way I have with him.

It's absolutely something I can put off.

But there is one thing we do need to talk about, and I can't let him put me off anymore. Anytime I've brought it up today, he's distracted me by pointing out something interesting in the landscape or sneaking a kiss or changing the subject.

Seeing as how it's early evening and we'll be back to Jackson soon, we do indeed have to talk about this.

"I think it might be best if you don't go to The Silo tonight," I say hesitantly.

While I note that Logan's knuckles go white again against the steering wheel, his voice is relatively calm but no doubt set in stone when he answers, "I'm going with you."

"You do realize—"

"That you're probably going to have to do something that will drive me fucking nuts and make me possibly angrier than I can remember being in recent memory?" he finishes my thought.

Because yes… there was a text from Magnus this morning that said he'd talked to Bridger, confirmed The Silo would be open for business tonight, and that he expected me to be there.

I was going back on display tonight. No matter how much I hated it or Logan hated it, another man was going to touch me tonight. The thought was utterly repulsive to me because while I can usually do an adequate job of slipping into an acting role to pull off the con, the mere fact that I've developed a personal relationship with someone stuck deep within this world I've infiltrated is making it hard for me. I can't even begin to imagine what Logan's feeling, knowing that while I may say I don't have a choice to walk in that round building tonight, I actually could refuse to do it. I could choose to put Logan's mind at ease and not let another man touch me, but I will not choose that. I can't put my dad at risk, and so perhaps… this is the end of us?

"I'm sorry," I tell him quietly, turning back in my seat to face forward and looking down at my hands clutched in my lap. I have no desire to look for moose anymore. "I'm not sure if this helps, but I'm going to hate every second I'm in there tonight, but I have to do this."

Logan's hand reaches over and takes mine. "I know. I don't blame you for doing this. I get why you're doing it. You and I can both hate it though."

"So maybe you should stay away—" I offer again.

"Bridger," Logan says, as if that one word solves all my problems.

"Bridger?" I ask in confusion.

Logan turns to look at me. I swear I might even see a little guilt in his eyes, and this confuses me even more. But before I can even analyze what I might have seen, his mouth flattens into grim determination and he says, "Bridger will handle… be with you tonight."

"And I'm guessing there's not going to be another fire code reprieve, right?"

He shakes his head and his voice is strained when he says, "No. Club is staying open."

"So tonight, Bridger," I say with a shaky voice, not in the least mollified that Logan trusts Bridger. I don't know this man, and he's still a stranger to me. "But tomorrow night…"

I let that hang heavy on the air, wishing that Logan would fill in the rest of that sentence.

Tomorrow night… we run.

Tomorrow night… you do what you have to do and I'll live with it.

Tomorrow night… Magnus will drop dead of a sudden heart attack and you'll be free.

Tomorrow night… I won't come to the Silo and watch you work your con.

He says nothing though, and instead picks up his phone resting on the seat beside him. As he drives slowly down the gravel road, moose and beautiful scenery forgotten by both of us, he taps the screen a few times with his thumb and peers at it. When he doesn't see what he clearly wants to see, he mutters a curse under his breath and throws the phone back down.

I have no clue what type of message he's waiting to receive, or if it will make him feel better when he gets it, but right now, I can feel the tension vibrating off him in pulsing waves. I feel terrible as I know this is hard on him. It's just as hard on me.

The difference, I'm afraid, is that I intend to push past this and hopefully leave the memories of this far behind. I'm getting the feeling though that Logan isn't going to let this go, despite the fact he seems to have left a big chunk of his past in the rearview mirror without looking back at it again.

Chapter 19

Logan

M Y SKIN TINGLES all over as Auralie follows Bridger out of my line of sight to the perimeter hall. When I met with him early this morning, after he assured me he'd put some thought into a solution, we had to have the talk about what would happen tonight. While I don't think Bridger was overly happy about it, he agreed to take Auralie in hand tonight per Magnus' demand. He promised he'd do what he could to keep the sensationalism of whatever he had planned to a minimum despite Magnus' demand that Auralie put on a show. I made sure he understood that while a part of her knew this was a "job" and she was "acting," that it was still humiliating to her.

And now it's out of my hands and Bridger's going to have his hands—possibly his mouth—on her. Worse yet, she's going to most likely have her mouth on him, as Magnus is all about Auralie showing the clientele that although she may be virgin, she very much knows how to give pleasure and won't be a cold lay.

A bark of unbidden laughter bubbles up in my chest, but I suppress it down. Auralie's as far from a cold lay as humanly possible. I have done so many perverted things in the name of unfettered sexual abandon that the Silo affords, it's unimaginable that a sweet, ordinary girl like Auralie could light my fire the way she has.

But she absolutely has, and I can't even imagine anything sexier or more fulfilling than what she gives me. And we haven't even cracked the tip of the iceberg yet. We haven't even begun to explore all the dirty things I want to do to her, and I want her to do to me.

Bridger being with Auralie shouldn't bother me. I've shared women with him before. Fuck... wasn't all that long ago that Bridger teamed up with Rand and me, and along with Cain, all four of us guys tag-teamed Cain's woman, Sloane. It was hot as fuck. I enjoyed watching Bridger work her over after Rand and I had fucked her.

But now I'm not sure how I feel about him having Auralie, even if it's only in the oral sense. Bridger is an absolute joy to watch with a woman. Never seen a man more in command or more intent on his mission. And one of the reasons it's amazing to watch him is because he doesn't do it often.

Oh, he fucks often, but it's usually in the privacy of his office. Only on rare occasions does he play in The Silo, and that's usually to only hand out pain to a select few members that pay big money for his handy skills with a whip. He would never use that on Auralie, but it doesn't mean he wouldn't use his palm on her.

And fuck... thought of that makes my cock start to wake up. I guess I'm not as averse to her being with

Bridger as I thought I would be.

I can do this.

I can handle this. I'll watch Bridger make this as good as he can for her, then I'm going to take her back to my place and fuck her as many times as I can before the sun comes up and I have to turn her back over into Magnus' care.

The thought curdles my stomach.

The door to the room that Bridger normally uses to dole out his special brand of pain opens, and he leads Auralie in. Her throat moves, and I know she's swallowing down against her nerves. The Silo's packed and the minute people become aware that Bridger's going to play, they start to congregate near the glass windows. I want to shove them all away as it's bad enough someone else is touching her, but to have all the buzzards circling to watch makes me want to do serious violence.

So I spin away from the spectacle getting ready to start and walk my way to the bar. I don't intend to turn my back on Auralie and Bridger permanently, but I do want to put some space in between and slug down a bourbon—or two—for fortification.

I'm surprised when I see Cat sitting up at the bar by herself. A quick perusal of the room confirms… Rand's not here. I find this strange because after our threesome a week ago, I could have sworn those two were well on their way to monogamy-ville and that I'd never see either one of them in here again.

I head her way and take the stool next to her, which

is empty because everyone is meandering closer to the room holding Bridger and Auralie. A quick glance back shows Auralie standing there with her hands clasped before her, head bowed in nervousness as Bridger goes over to a floor-to-ceiling black and chrome cabinet that houses "implements". No clue what the fuck he's up to, but I'm sure Magnus will get the show he wants. Despite how much I'm dreading watching her with another man, I'd be lying if I didn't say I was a little turned on by the prospect too. I'm curious as to how pliant Auralie's sexual boundaries are given the fact that she knows I'm somewhat okay with this interlude she's getting ready to have with Bridger.

Cat turns to look at me when I sit down. A bartender walks up—a new girl I've never seen before—and normally when I first see fresh pussy in this club, I'm figuring out the fastest way to tap it, but oddly… no desire to do so.

"What's up, Cat?" I ask just to be polite and conversational, because that's what you do when you've tapped her boyfriend's ass while he was tapping her.

She gives me a wan smile and turns back to her glass of wine. "Hi, Logan."

"Meeting Rand here?" I ask and then tell the hovering bartender. "Maker's Mark, neat."

"He was just here," she says softly… sadly. "Now he's not."

There's no mistaking the tone in her voice. Something's happened to these budding lovebirds. While I'd normally not care enough to delve, I don't like the idea at all of either of them failing at happiness. "What's going on?"

She shrugs, and even the shrug isn't so much antipathy as it is desolation. "It's just not going to work between us. He's being stubborn about it so I had to make him see…"

Oh, hell no. I lean in to her and whisper harshly, "You are *not* here to fuck around on him, are you?"

"No," she says softly. "But he thinks I am."

"That's fucked up, Cat," I admonish, taking a look back over my shoulder to Bridger and Auralie. He's ordered her to disrobe as she's unbuttoning the lavender silk blouse she had put on with a pair of skinny jeans. My heartrate ratchets up a notch, and I can barely tear my eyes away. But I do just briefly, turning back to Cat. "Rand's a great guy. I don't want to see you fuck with his head or heart. But you're a great woman too. Don't turn your back on something good just because you don't think you deserve it."

The minute the words leave my mouth, I realize I'm talking about myself as much as I'm talking about Cat. I recognize that look on her face, and the forlorn spirit within that refuses to believe happiness is attainable merely because you think you should be punished for all your bad deeds.

If only I'd take my own advice.

I stand up from the bar as I see the bartender walking toward me with the drink, giving her a shake of my head that I've changed my mind. Putting my hand to Cat's shoulder, I say, "Go home, Cat. Go home to Rand and fix whatever the fuck you think is broken. Don't waste something beautiful on the ugly you carry around inside."

She blinks at me, tears misting in her eyes, and I'm astounded once again that I'm giving advice that I'm not willing myself to accept.

But I've said my piece and now I have something more important to do. I turn away from Cat, the bar, and my drink, and push my way through the crowd until I'm up standing before the glass wall.

Auralie's completely naked, her clothes laying in a pile on the floor. My eyes flick to the blood-red lace panties laying there, a direct thumb of her nose toward Magnus, who wants her to look virginal. My gaze slides up to her and I find her watching me, but then Bridger wraps a large hand around her wrist and leads her over to the St. Andrew's Cross.

Interesting.

If he ties her up there, she can't suck his dick and I'm liking that.

Or is that slight disappointment that I won't see her with Bridger?

I shake my head hard, confused at these contrary thoughts.

God, I'm fucked up in the head. More than usual.

I can't hear what Bridger's saying as he leans in close to Auralie and whispers something to her, but I can tell by the subtle relaxing of her shoulders that he's trying to be reassuring. They drop minutely as he leads her up to the platform the cross sits on, turning her so that her back presses into the center of the "X". She tenses up again when he lifts a wrist and shackles it in place, then her entire body stiffens when he clasps the other in place. He doesn't bother locking her ankles in. I have to think it's so she retains a measure of control, which means Bridger is as adept at reading her discomfort as I am from twenty feet away.

And Christ, she looks perfect, even without her legs spread-eagled in the clasps. Naked, pale skin with dark raven hair hanging over her shoulders and to the sides of her breasts. Said breasts heavy with nipples tightened up either from the cool air in those rooms or the scrutiny she's drawn. Her gaze moves slowly across the crowd standing outside the glassed room and then locks on me. Her facial muscles stay frozen so as not to give away her feelings to these strangers, but I can see it in her eyes. The slight warming of her blue irises so they look like tropical waters. I know it's meant to be an encouraging look to me that we'll both survive this.

I know we'll survive it, but I'm not sure my sanity will come out unscathed because I'm dreading what's getting ready to happen even as my dick twitches with anticipation.

Bridger turns into Auralie again, pushing the hank of hair that had fallen over her shoulder and breast back so her body is completely unobstructed. He says something else… too low for any sound to come close to permeating the glass barrier, and then unexpectedly drops his hand to pinch the nipple he just uncovered.

Auralie's entire body arches away from the cross and her head falls back. Her face bears a mixture of pleasure and fear, and her mouth forms a perfect "O". While the moan I know she just let loose is silent to the rest of the Silo patrons, I know exactly what it sounds like and it's vivid in my imagination.

My cock goes fully locked and loaded, straining against the zipper of my jeans, but I ignore the bastard, instead keeping my attention on Auralie as she raises her head and locks her eyes immediately on mine again. Her cheeks are flushed, but her lips are flattened in silent apology to me. I give her a smile, telling her, *It's okay. It's okay. It's okay.*

Bridger turns from Auralie, leans over, and grabs a short-handled flogger with dozens of wide strips of soft suede hanging from it. I've used that same flogger before. I know it doesn't produce any more sting than my hand on her ass last night, but it looks menacing.

Auralie swallows hard when she sees it.

Bridger says something to her.

She nods in acceptance.

His right arm flies in a backhand sweep, and he whips the lashes across her breasts. They make a resounding crack against her skin that does permeate the glass wall, but I know it hurt no more than my palm because Auralie arches her back again from the cross and cries out in pleasure. When the flogger is gone, pink marks slash diagonally across her chest and her nipples are harder than I've ever seen them before.

My cock starts leaking.

The man next to me is having a similar problem as he reaches down and rubs his dick through his pants. I want to break his fingers.

Bridger drops his left hand, brings it right in between Auralie's legs, and he pushes his fingers in between the lips of her labia. I know what he'll find there.

Sopping wet pussy.

With slick fingertips, he drags them to her clit and circles a few times. Auralie's head falls forward and her hips tilt for more friction with Bridger.

His left hand is suddenly gone and his right is sending another backhand whip to the flogger, this time right over her pussy. Auralie shrieks, her eyes glazed with pleasure and her pupils so blown, there's hardly any blue left in her irises. Bridger's left hand is back again, massaging her clit, which I'm sure is swollen enough it felt the bite of one of those straps.

Bridger does this over and over again. Lashes at Auralie's pale skin from her collarbones down to her thighs, even a few strikes to the backs of her knees. In between, his fingers go to her clit and massage it. When her hips start bucking and she's panting heavy, he pulls his hand back and lets the flogger fly again.

It's classic slap and tickle, and it's hot as fuck as I watch Bridger tapping into Auralie's love of a little bit of pain with her pleasure. So fucking hot that I am literally salivating with the need to do something… eat her pussy… fuck her brains out. The dude next to me has his pants open, actively working his dick and moaning. I don't look at the crowd past him as I'm afraid I'll get pissed at all the people ogling.

So I watch Bridger and Auralie, chanting silently to myself, *That's it. Come on, baby. Come hard.*

And then she does, with a scream and a final arching of her back so her hips press against Bridger's hand. He pinches her clit and gives it a little twist. She screams again with her head thrown back. The minute she rights herself, her eyes once again lock with mine. Pupils still large but there's more cognizance there, and I can immediately read her question to me, *Are you mad at me because that felt so good?*

I smile at her and give a little shake to my head. *No, baby. But I am going to fuck you so hard when we leave here. Hope you're ready for it.*

She smiles back at me, and then I remember something important.

I fumble with my phone. I'm able to snap a few pictures of Bridger standing there with Auralie, his hand still between her legs where he strokes lightly at her pussy… helping to gently bring her down.

That should satisfy that fucker Magnus.

At least for one more night.

BRIDGER AND AURALIE come back into the main gathering area of the Silo. Several men make moves to talk to her, but Bridger holds them off with a polite shake of his head. He gives me a pointed look and jerks his chin toward the exit door, and I nod with excitement filling me. He wants to talk. It can only be about my dilemma with Magnus and using Auralie in his con.

I turn to look back at the bar, a little bit of worry about Cat still sticking with me. However, she's not sitting there. I carefully sweep the rest of the Silo, fearful I might find her fucking someone else, but I don't see her anywhere. Not in the main area and not in any of the glass rooms. I breathe a little sigh of relief that she seems to have wizened up and left, and I hope it's to go to Rand and fix whatever seems to have broken since I saw them last together.

Bridger leads Auralie out of The Silo and I follow, across the slate path to the back door of The Wicked Horse. We all walk single file down the hallway and into his office. The music is booming inside the nightclub, but his walls and door are specially designed to block the noise and all goes silent when we're closed inside.

Bridger walks behind his desk. I come to stand beside Auralie, my hand going to the small of her back where I rest my palm there. She shifts slightly toward me but keeps her head bowed.

I lean down, put my mouth near her ear, and tell her, "That was hot, babe."

She pulls back slightly and cranes her neck to look at

me with wide eyes, wanting to believe that what she just did… what she just let Bridger do to her… did not change my desire for her. Can't say as it was entirely easy watching another man touch what I'm inappropriately starting to think of as solely mine, but I was more turned on than turned off. Of course, that's because I trust Bridger, and I'm not sure I'd feel that with another man involved.

Maybe Rand.

Possibly Cain.

But that's about it.

I nod at her and whisper, "Totally hot."

She gives me a small smile. We turn to Bridger when we hear him rustle some papers on his desk. He pushes aside a stack of documents and pulls his laptop nearer to him, opening it up and turning it on. While it boots up, he says, "I talked to a friend of mine in New York who practices law there. Name's Cal Carson and while he does mostly civil law, he knows someone at the U.S. Attorney's office."

My hand drops from Auralie and I step toward his desk, eager to hear where this is going.

Bridger continues. "While I didn't have much in the way of details to pass on to Cal, what little bit I told him about Magnus was enough for him to believe this attorney would be interested in talking to Auralie's dad. Most likely give him immunity in exchange for spilling his guts on everything he knows about Magnus."

A jolt of pure excitement runs through me as I hadn't

considered the possibility of legal means to get Auralie out of this mess. Here I was contemplating reverse cons and murder. "That's excellent—"

"You told him about Magnus and me?" I hear Auralie ask from behind me, and there's no mistaking the astonished fury in her words despite the softness of her tone.

I turn to look at her, stiffen my spine, and brace for more fury. "Well, yeah. I asked him for his advice… see if there was a way he figured we could shut this shit down with Magnus."

Auralie strides up to me, her fists clenched in anger. She gets right up in my face—has to stand up on tiptoes to do so—and snarls. "I did not ask for you to get involved in this. In fact, I told you the truth about what was going on with the assumption that you would keep that shit secret. It was a confidence I told you, and you went and fucking betrayed that."

I'm taken aback by the venom dripping from her words, but I wave it off. "Auralie… you knew there was no way in hell I was going to let you go through with this."

"Why?" she snarls. "Because it's illegal? Because it scams someone who won't miss the fucking money?"

"No," I yell back at her, leaning down closer to her face. "Because I did not want those beautiful lips of yours wrapped around someone else's cock."

"Oh," she says sarcastically. "But it's okay for your buddy there to whip and finger me to orgasm?"

"I didn't see you complaining," I bite out, feeling the need to put her on the defensive.

Gasping, she steps back from me as if I'd slapped her in the face. She glares at me for a moment, and then turns her gaze slowly to Bridger. "I appreciate your help, but I'm going to decline."

I open my mouth to argue with her because this is the perfect fucking solution as it frees her and her dad, and hopefully sends Magnus to prison. But then she spins back on me and says in a very quiet voice that still packs a sonic punch, "I would like you to take me back to my house."

Turning around, she walks stiffly to the door and exits, pulling it quietly shut behind her. This also packs a punch. I'd have much rather seen her slam it because that would indicate she's pissed and wanting to at least fight about it. Instead, it seemed like a final closing of the door on "us".

I turn back to look at Bridger. He gives me an empathetic look that says, *Sorry, man.*

Sighing, I turn toward his office door, figuring out how to do damage control on a situation that is completely outside of my control.

Chapter 20
Auralie

THE RIDE BACK to the cabin is tense and silent. Tense because this jackass is ruining everything and putting my father in danger, and silent because the minute we got in Logan's truck and he said, "Auralie... I didn't mean—"

And I snapped at him, "Shut the fuck up and leave me alone."

When he pulls into the short driveway, I snatch my purse and bolt out of the passenger door. I sort of assumed he got the hint and wouldn't follow me, but I hear him getting out and his door slamming just after mine.

"Go away, Logan," I mutter over my shoulder as I stomp up the porch steps and dig the front door key out of my purse.

"Not going to happen," he mutters back, close on my heels.

I slam the key in the lock, twist it viciously, and throw the door open, all while sneering at him, "Let me guess. That little job your buddy did on me at The Silo got you all worked up, right? Want to fuck me, don't you?"

Logan snatches me by the upper arm. I anticipate he'll spin me around to face him, but instead, he pushes me through the doorway and marches me right into the living room while growling at me, "You're goddamn right I want to fuck you."

I want to scream at him in frustration that he thinks so little of my anger and all he wants to do is use my body, but that need to scream wars with the insatiable need I have for him to fuck me. While I'll never admit it to him, what Bridger did to me in that club while Logan watched with hot, needy eyes has my panties still soaked despite how mad I am at him.

"Then do it," I hiss at him.

He makes a frustrated sound deep in his chest, but he walks me right around the back of the couch that's positioned to separate the living area from the kitchen. "Fine. I was going to talk this shit out, but if you want fucked, I'll fuck you. Never going to turn my nose up at that sweet pussy."

"You asshole," I seethe at him even as my core clenches. It clenches even harder when he pushes me right over the back of the couch so I'm bent at my pelvis with my ass is in the air.

Two seconds later, his palm is cracking down on my jean-clad ass. He mutters, "Ungrateful little snot."

"Arrogant bast—"

His hand smacks my ass again, and my traitorous body moans in response.

"That's right," Logan whispers in a voice filled with lustful excitement as his hands rip my jeans and underwear over my hips and down my legs until they're bunched tight at my ankles. His hand descends again on my bare cheeks, causing me to jerk and moan and my hands to press down hard into the couch cushions for stability and leverage.

I brace, waiting for him to spank me again, but then his face is pressed into my ass and his tongue licking at my pussy from behind as his fingers pull my cheeks apart.

"Oh, Logan," I murmur in abandon, all thoughts of anger and fight going out of me.

His mouth leaves me and two fingers press inside. "You're drenched, Auralie. Is that from what Bridger did to you?"

"No," I moan as his fingers move in and out.

"From us fighting? Want a hard hate-fuck?" he taunts.

"No," I rasp out, shaking my head vehemently. "Not hate."

"Just a hard fuck, then?" he murmurs as he pulls his fingers out of me and slides them up the seam of my ass, causing a full-body shudder. "I can certainly give that to you."

"Logan—"

"Shhh, Auralie," his voice whispers across the back of my neck as he stands to bend over me. He presses the length of his cock against my butt and grinds a little.

"Gonna fuck you and then we'll fight, okay?"

I nod frantically, because I really, really need him inside of me. I've been carrying that low burn of lust inside of me since Bridger made me come on that St. Andrew's cross.

I expect him to pull back, free his cock, and plunge into me from behind, but that's just silly, because Logan never does the expected. Instead, he grasps my legs and flips me over the couch, where I twist and land on my back. I come up on my elbows and watch as he prowls around toward me, his hands working deftly at his belt and zipper, pushing his jeans down enough to free himself.

He's thick and hard, the silky skin of his cock angry red, which is fitting… seeing as how he's angry at me still. I can tell by the way his eyes sizzle with the promise of some type of retribution for me having the temerity to be mad at him. Just the thought causes my blood to race through my veins and my breath to hitch.

Logan pulls my legs into the air to make room on the couch. He kneels before me. If I didn't have my ankles encumbered, I'd gladly spread my legs and wrap them around his waist.

But he has other plans.

Plans that don't include taking the time to strip me naked.

Instead, he pulls my legs up a bit higher and leverages my calves onto his left shoulder, causing my hips to twist toward the back of the couch. He holds my legs in place with his left arm wrapped securely around them. With a dip of his own hips, he uses his other hand to help guide his cock to me.

Not sure how he's going to do this as my legs are pressed tight to each other, but then… he's working the head of his cock into my barely accessible pussy. He pushes and grunts and twists his hips this way and that, shoving his way past the resistance of my outer lips until he reaches the wet just inside.

The thick head breaches me a few inches before he pulls back, twists his hips again, and punches in and up. He sinks halfway in and mutters, "Christ… that's tight."

And God… yes, that's so tight and I feel so full.

Ignoring the fact my legs are starting to tingle, and with no way to reach out to hold onto Logan in this position, I let my fingertips clutch onto the chenille-covered cushions as he withdraws again to the very tip. With a mighty heave, he sinks all the way into me. I know it feels good because his eyes squeeze shut and air blows so hard out of his mouth, it flutters all the way down over my face.

Logan reaches under my ass, lifts me up, and twists me more to the side so I'm laying half on my side, my body spiraled. He then leans over me, causing me to jackknife. My lungs compress and I can barely breathe, but then Logan starts pistoning in and out of me, the angle and lack of spread to my pussy causing him to grunt with every thrust.

And oh… just… oh, wow.

This feels good.

So damned good.

I suck in small pockets of air each time he pulls out, expelling the same in harsh pants when he punches back in. I'm so wet. The glide is easy and effortless, but it doesn't stop him from giving me the hard fuck he offered and I accepted.

Logan pounds me into the couch, his face etched with pleasure and his eyes darkened to a bronzed mocha. He only ups the sex appeal when he pulls his full bottom lip between his teeth and bites down on it, a clear indication that he's trying to control himself, but I hate to tell this man… it's a losing proposition.

"More," I whisper on a forced exhalation.

"Fuck me," he mutters. "My girl wants more."

So he gives me more, fucking me exquisitely and with no doubt that neither of us has ever had it this good.

From out of nowhere, my orgasm starts to build before curling inward for one brief, agonizing moment and then exploding so swiftly it leaves my scream far behind by virtue of the sheer force of the pleasure.

My mouth opens, but nothing comes out. I want to tell Logan I'm coming, but really… I don't need to. He can feel me spasming all around his cock, and I know this because he whispers, "Fuck yeah… my girl comes hard when I'm deep inside her."

I whimper from his words alone, because he said "my girl" twice in the last twenty seconds.

Am I?

His girl?

I'm not sure how I can be anything when he's thrown my entire life into disarray, but I can't think about that now. The way he continues to tunnel in and out of me is beyond distracting, and all thoughts completely abandon me when Logan slams deep, holds himself planted, and then shudders hard as he releases inside of me. I carefully study his face, the way his cheek is pressed up against the outside of my leg, still resting on his shoulder and secured to my other leg by virtue of my jeans.

Logan closes his eyes… groans… grinds against my ass and then groans again.

I want him to tell me how good that feels and how much I mean to him then I want some explanation as to why he went behind my back to Bridger and outted me. Instead, when I sense he's empty, he opens his eyes and pins me with a hard look. Any sweet words of cherishment that might have been forthcoming during that moment of bliss right after orgasm clearly not forthcoming.

Logan pulls out of me, and I feel the rush of his semen running down the crack of my ass. He lets my legs drop unceremoniously to the couch and rolls off, tucking his half hard, glistening dick back into his jeans.

"Get dressed," he says curtly. "We need to figure out the best way to get your dad to talk to this attorney Bridger's friend suggested."

He did not just say that to me.

I sit up, swing my legs off the couch, and pull my underwear and jeans up, wincing over the feel of wetness that runs down the inside of my legs before being sopped up by my pants. I give a hop, pulling my zipper up. As I'm buttoning, I tell him, "Bite me, Logan. You do not dictate my life."

He looks at me warily. "I'm not trying to dictate your life. I'm trying to help."

"By betraying me?" I ask incredulously. "Did it occur to you that you've just put my dad in very real danger… getting other people involved?"

"Bridger wouldn't have—"

"If you would have just left well enough alone, I could have finished this last job and been free from Magnus forever," I say, talking right over him. "I was so close to being done with that man and this life. I would have protected my dad in the process, and it would have all been okay. But you've screwed it all up."

"I was trying to protect you," Logan says as he takes a step toward me, arms stretched out in supplication.

"You were trying to protect yourself," I sneer at him. "You couldn't stand the thought of me being with someone else. Well, at least not with someone you deem to be unfit, but it was clearly okay to share me with your buddy."

"That's not—"

"You were protecting yourself because you're being proprietary over what you consider to be your property now, you fucking caveman—"

Logan lunges toward me, grabbing me by my upper arms and giving me a little shake before he snarls, "I don't think you're my property. I care about you, goddamn it."

I roll my eyes, completely disbelieving his words and the casual way he throws them about. "Oh, yeah," I taunt him. "You care about me?"

"Yes," he says emphatically, his hands gripping me tight.

"Then tell me what happened two years ago that caused you to run from life," I demand hotly. "Tell me what in the hell happened that caused you to have nightmares so bad you have to fuck me with lube to get rid of them."

Logan blanches and his hands fall away. He takes a step back and opens his mouth, but nothing comes out.

"Tell me," I press with desperation. "You care about me so much that you're practically taking control of my life, tell me about Logan McKay and who he was two years ago."

He gives a shake of his head and his gaze drops to the floor, lips now pressed tight together as an indication of stubborn silence.

"You want me to trust that you're doing the right thing by telling Bridger about Magnus and me. You want me to trust you in this plan to let the law get involved, in a move that could end up putting Dad and me in jail if things don't work out the way your buddy thinks they will. You want me to have all this trust in you, and yet you can't even trust me enough to give me anything of you in return."

"I've given you—" he murmurs, gaze still pinned to the floor.

"You've given me your dick and some great orgasms, Logan," I say quietly. "But let's be real… that's about all you've given me."

Okay, that's harsh and not exactly true. He's clearly given me attention and care, as well as laughter and redirection from my plight. He's trying to do right by me in the only way he knows how. But I can't admit that to him right now because I'm too hurt that he's not giving me the one thing I want.

The one thing I need if he wants me to take a very drastic turn in my life.

He doesn't respond to my taunt, so I add on, "I told you the very most secret thing about my life, and I entrusted that to you. I thought we had something… different. I thought *you* were different."

Logan's eyes drag up slowly until they're locked onto mine, and my heart starts to shrivel by what I see.

A completely blank, ambivalent, emotionless mask that looks a lot like Logan McKay but is nothing more than a two-dimensional image of the man I thought I had an amazing connection with.

There's no anger.

No hardness.

No frustration with me.

No desire.

No affinity.

No… nothing.

"I'm sorry," Logan says in a flat voice. "I'm sorry I messed things up for you, and I'm sorry I can't be what you need."

Every fiber of my being wants to scream at him in denial. That he could be exactly what I need if he would just give me a little piece of himself. I really don't need the whole thing, but I need him to show me that there's something tangible here.

I need more than just silent messages that I can read with sure clarity.

I need him to show me what we have is real.

Instead, he turns away from me, walks to the front door, opens it, and walks out, shutting it quietly behind him.

Disbelieving at what just happened, I stare at the door for a few minutes, wondering if this is a joke and he'll walk back in. Logan McKay has utterly turned my life upside down. This was from the moment I first locked eyes on him in The Silo. I knew deep in my heart my life would never be the same right in that exact moment. I just never imagined it would turn out like this… with him outing me to Bridger, ruining the con, putting my dad in danger, and then leaving me without so much as a backward glance.

With me falling for him and him walking out *without a goddamn backward glance.*

When it's clear that Logan is really gone, I turn from the door and walk over to my purse. I need to head back to The Wicked Horse, because unfortunately, I don't have a lot of play left. Magnus is coming back tomorrow, and he's going to be expecting that I've kept the con running just fine. He has no clue that it's been effectively shut down, because no way in hell is Bridger going to let this continue to go on in his club.

Which means I now need to get Bridger to work with me on this. The trick to sell my "virginity" is a bust—no pun intended—and the minute Magnus realizes that, he's going to come after my father and me. I have to make plans to get my dad and me as far away from Magnus as possible and hopefully help the police put him in prison so we'll be safe. Until that happens though, I'm going to be sleeping with one eye open and moving through the streets of New York, constantly looking over my shoulder.

Thanks a lot, Logan.

Chapter 21

Logan

SIT IN my truck and look at the entrance to The Silo. When I left Auralie last night at her cabin, I told myself that today was the day I got back on with living my life the way I should be living it.

Reserved and solitary from everyone.

It was the safest way for me to be able to live with myself.

Of course, that meant I had to give up Auralie and all prospect of something good with her. She drew the line in the sand with me, and it was clear. If I wanted something with her, I had to open up all the way. I had to trust her the way I wanted her to trust me.

And fuck that.

Wasn't about to open up my carefully constructed walls that helped keep me protected and my sanity intact.

So in order to get back on with my life and not look backward at what could have been with Auralie, I knew that meant hitting the Silo up tonight and getting my freak back on with whatever available pussy was there. I'd go in, choose someone quickly, fuck her good, and blow a nut. Then I'd be back right again.

Except I've sat in this fucking truck for going on forty minutes now and haven't made a move to get out. Maybe I'm waiting for my dick to wake up and lead me in there. Perhaps I'm waiting for some sign from above that I'm making the right choice.

I'm waiting and waiting, but nothing's happening.

With a sigh, I pull my phone out and flip through Contacts until I find Rand's number. It's only ten PM so it's not too late to call.

He answers on the third ring, sounding groggy. "What's up, man?"

"Did I wake you up?" I ask hesitantly.

"Nah," he says and coughs to clear his throat. "Just exhausted. What's going on?"

"Just checking in. Saw Cat at The Silo last night, and you weren't with her. Making sure everything's okay."

He's silent a moment and says, "No clue if anything's okay, but yeah… I knew she was there."

"She didn't stay," I say quickly, so he knows she didn't fuck around on him.

"I know," he says with a heavy sigh. "Bridger was keeping an eye on her for me and told me she left."

"Dude… what's going on?"

"I'm giving her a bit of space to try to figure out what she wants," he says in a tired voice. "I'm actually in Vegas right now. Tracked her mom down to see if I could get some info on her dad."

I whistle low through my teeth. "And did you?"

"Yeah. Flying out to North Carolina tomorrow."

I digest this, thinking of the lengths Rand is going to for a woman who was sitting alone without him at a sex club last night. Granted, she didn't do anything, but she was there.

Had to be considering it.

My gaze goes to The Silo, because seems like I'm getting ready to do the same thing Cat was contemplating just last night. Perhaps making a decisive move to kill the final connection to someone?

"Why was she in The Silo?" I ask, thinking maybe Rand has some sage advice on the subject of people who might want a relationship but think they can't handle it.

"She needs to figure herself out," he says simply. "Figure out what she wants and what's most important to her. Most of all, she has to decide whether or not she thinks she's good enough for me, because she's got some fucked-up idea in her head that she's not."

Yeah… I can totally understand that shit. Seems like Cat and I have something in common.

Movement in the parking lot catches my attention. I narrow my eyes as Magnus pulls his Porsche into a spot nearer to The Silo than where I sit. He gets out, aims the key fob at the car door to lock it, and walks inside.

"Listen," I say as I get out of my truck. "I've got to go, but dude… I hope that shit works out with you and Cat."

"Thanks, Logan. Me too."

I don't bother locking my truck as I say, "Later," and

disconnect the call. Shoving my phone in my back pocket, I walk into The Silo, my nerves a jangled mess. I have absolutely no idea what I might find when I go inside. I haven't talked to Bridger all day, mainly because I'm afraid of what he might say to me. I'm pretty sure it would be something like, "Man, the fuck up".

I also have no clue where Auralie is. Magnus just walked in alone, so I know she's not with him.

Unless she's already in there, but no… no way is Bridger going to let that shit go down when he knows the virginity sale is a scam.

Unease slithers through me as I consider the consequences to Auralie of what I've done. It's not the first time I've thought about the dangerous repercussions I laid on her doorstep without even bothering to clue her in on what I was planning to do. I'm not sure how she's going to wrangle out of this mess, and for the most part today, I stuck my head in the sand and just sort of hoped that Bridger would work something out for her.

I'm a fucking coward in that respect, and I know it. But it was easier than dealing with my muddled feelings about what I had and what I subsequently lost because I refuse to open myself up fully to a woman.

I walk into The Silo. As I come out of the short hall that leads to the interior, I see Magnus stalking toward Bridger, who's talking to a group of people outside the Black Room. Inside, a woman is on her hands and knees, taking it up the ass. She seems to be enjoying it by the sounds of her moans, which are having no problem permeating the glass wall because they're so loud.

I follow Magnus as he approaches Bridger, so I'm close enough to hear him demand, "I need to speak to you, Mr. Payne."

Bridger cuts a hard look at Magnus for his interruption, but he murmurs an apology to the group and steps toward Magnus. "What's up?"

"Where's Auralie?" Magnus challenges with as much menace as his prissy ass can manage.

"No clue," Bridger says with a shrug of his shoulders.

"I flew in this evening and she's not at the cabin," Magnus says, and his voice is near panicked. "All of her clothes and personal items are still there though."

"Did she tell you she was going somewhere?" Bridger asks nonchalantly.

"I talked to her right before I got on my plane connection in Dallas," Magnus says. "She said she'd see me when I got here. She's not at the cabin so I came here, but I don't see her."

Immediate dread fills me that, based on what Magnus is saying, Auralie seems to be missing. I'm not sure where I thought she would be, but again… that was part of me being an ostrich and sticking my head in the sand. But the fact that Magnus seems to be worried about her has me worried about her.

Bridger shrugs. "Not sure what to tell you, Mr. Albright, but I haven't seen her since last night. But you did miss quite the show she put on. I'm interested to see the price of the bids that come in for her virginity once you open it up. I'm more than interested to see what you do tonight... provided she shows up, that is."

I jerk, startled by Bridger's proclamation.

He's going to let this farce go on?

I had underestimated the lengths he'd go to so that Auralie remains protected. Really didn't think he'd give a damn to be honest.

Magnus sighs, looking around the club as if Auralie will mysteriously appear. I do the same, scanning the interior... hoping for a glimpse of her so I know she's okay, and then I can tell her...

What?

What exactly would I fucking tell her?

Bridger claps Magnus on the back. "Have a drink. Relax. I'm sure she'll show up. She's probably just making a grand entrance or something."

Magnus looks disgruntled but nods in agreement before turning toward the bar.

Bridger's gaze comes to me but then slides right past without any real acknowledgment before he starts to walk by me toward the exit of The Silo.

"Where's Auralie?" I mutter as he strides past.

"What's it to you?" he challenges with a quick glance over his shoulder at me, and then he continues on his path without falter.

"Cut the shit," I growl as I turn to catch up to him. "You clearly know where she is. Magnus may have bought that crock you just handed him, but I don't."

Bridger doesn't even look at me but walks right out

of The Silo, with me following behind him. When the door closes behind us both, he says, "I repeat. What's it to you? Auralie said you left her last night—that things were over between you two."

"They are," I mutter defensively, and fuck… why does that make me physically sick to my stomach to even say that? "But don't begrudge my worry about her."

Bridger opens the back door to the Wicked Horse and steps through as he says in a bland voice. "I don't begrudge you anything, but why you waste effort on this woman is beyond me. She's a scammer. A con artist. Apparently a great fuck, but still… plenty of those around here."

Rage strikes me in a hot, blistering wave and I lunge at Bridger from behind, both my hands slamming into his shoulder blades and knocking him forward. He's not expecting the attack, and he goes flying forward several feet before he catches himself.

He spins on me, bracing for another attack, and I don't hesitate, snagging fistfuls of his t-shirt and spinning him toward the wall before slamming him back into it. His hands come up to grip onto my wrists, but he makes no effort to fight back at me or push me away.

"You fucking asshole," I snarl as I put my face right into his. "You don't know shit about Auralie or the reasons she had to do what she had to do."

"Then why don't you enlighten me?" Bridger taunts with a quirk of his lips, and I can tell my shoving him around amuses rather than intimidates. "Because I truly don't understand why it matters to you. You left her last night. Left her to fend for herself now that you ruined her game. So why the fuck does it even matter to you?"

"Fuck you," I yell as I release him to turn away, my frustration boiling over because I don't know why it matters to me. I let her go last night.

Or rather, I refused to stay and give her something she wanted.

Was probably entitled to, actually.

I look down the hallway toward the interior of The Wicked Horse just beyond. It's not overly packed, but then again, it's a Wednesday night. An ordinary night where I might be in there myself, drinking a beer and perusing potential fuckmates. Most likely, I wouldn't indulge because most women in there required work. Conversation, flirting, etc. If it wasn't an easy lay, I wasn't interested. So I'd usually head over to The Silo.

That would be my ordinary Wednesday night in my ordinary life here in Wyoming. I was satisfied with that.

Until a raven-haired beauty with innocent eyes but a fun and kinky side won me over, and I have no clue how it happened.

Why we connected.

Why I felt something with her I never felt for another woman.

Fuck that… for another human being, except for…

Nope. Not going to think about that.

Except, fuck if I can stop thinking about Auralie and the way she's made me feel since I locked eyes on her.

And I'm not talking about the way she makes my cock feel. I'm talking about the way we connect. The way we can speak silently but still deeply with each other. The natural feeling of ease in her presence. As if I don't have to prove myself, but she accepts me for who I am. Or the way she laughs, whether it's because she finds me funny or she's being mischievous. Or the way she lays in my arms. Or shrieks in excitement when she catches a fish. Or sucks my dick on a riverbank. Or just about fucking anything she does turns me on physically, mentally, spiritually, emotionally…

Christ, I'm fucked in the head.

Mostly though… I can't stop thinking about what a survivor she is. To be raised the way she was, and, yet, she found her own moral compass to break away from that life. Granted, she was in the middle of a con when I met her, but she wasn't doing it for herself and she wasn't doing it for the almighty sin of greed. She was doing it to protect someone she loved, which made me respect her even more.

Auralie's a woman who has given me every reason to hope for something better in this life. Yet, I'm still too afraid to reach out and grasp onto that with ambitious determination. I'm still hiding from the world because it's become easy for me to do so.

But still… I have to make sure she's okay.

I spin around to ask Bridger again where Auralie is because no matter the bullshit he just tried to hand me about having disdain for her, I could tell that was nothing more than him baiting me. Bridger works with ulterior motive most of the time, and I get what he's trying to do. He's telling me to shit or get off the pot.

Not really ready to do either, but I need to know Auralie's safe.

Except when I turn around, Bridger's gone, but his office door is standing wide open. I take this as a clear indication I'm invited in to continue this "discussion".

I walk in, shutting the door behind me to close out the country music blaring in the club. Bridger's sitting at his desk, flipping through something on his iPhone. He doesn't even look up at me when I take a seat opposite him, but merely says, "She flew out around mid-morning to New York. Met with my buddy Cal and the federal prosecutor, woman named Dee Switzer, late this afternoon—east coast time, of course. Don't know anything more than that."

My stomach clenches to know she's not here in Wyoming because I think I was hoping, deep down, that maybe there was a chance I'd get to see her again. Maybe to fight again—maybe to fuck. Maybe even to find a way to give her what she wanted without destroying myself in the process.

It also clenches because now she's made her break from Magnus. The thing that's been bothering me the most about what I did is that I put the wheels in motion to force her to do something dangerous. To turn her and her father against a man who had the clear means to make people go *poof*. And I know one thing I would never survive is if I caused someone to be hurt or worse yet… killed.

I cannot survive that again.

There's no way.

"How do you know this?" I ask neutrally, trying to act not all that interested, but I'm not fooling Bridger.

I know I'm not fooling him because he cocks an eyebrow at me as he smirks, but then enlightens me without making me feel like too much of an idiot. "Because she came to me last night after you left her. She told me everything. All about her life as a grifter with her dad. How she wanted to break away and almost did, and how she was working this one last con to protect her dad."

"She had no choice," I say in defense of her actions.

Bridger raises his hand to wave me off. "I get it. Not mad at what she was trying to accomplish. I'd do the same thing if I were in her shoes. Which is why I pushed hard at her to take the offer by Cal to go to the authorities on this and put Magnus in prison. It's her best option."

"Her only option after I ratted her out," I mutter, wondering why I feel such guilt over betraying her that way. I honestly was hoping to help, but I realize… I should have talked to her about it. For all my prattling on to her about wanting to help her out of her situation, after finally forcing her to let me in on her secret, I should have given her the respect of mutual discussion on how to best attack the problem. I acted like a fucking caveman, brought Bridger into this when really… maybe

I should have let her finish the scam so she could be free.

But it's too late to cry over that now. It's done.

"Will the federal prosecutor help her? Protect her and her dad?" I ask hesitantly.

"No clue," he says with a shrug. "Not my problem either. I helped her out best I could. I'm also going to do one more solid to her by putting Magnus off her trail a bit."

"You had her leave all her possessions behind," I surmise. "So Magnus wouldn't know she ran."

"It will hold him off maybe a day," Bridger says with a casual shrug. "But I'm guessing he's going to go after her come tomorrow."

"What the fuck?" I snarl as I shoot up out of my chair. "You say that as if you don't give a fuck she could be in real danger."

"I don't," he says, pinning me with a hard look. I feel my blood pressure skyrocketing at his further bait tactics. "She's not my problem."

She's not mine either.

Except… goddamn it all to hell. She is my problem.

But not really a problem.

More of a miracle actually.

And one I didn't anticipate I'd ever be worthy of, but the thought of that being snuffed out and taken away from me forever spurs me into action, even if I'm not quite accepting of the fact I deserve this.

"You're an asshole, Bridger," I mutter as I turn away from the desk. I hear him snort behind me before he gives a bark of a laugh. I refuse to smile, but I grudgingly say, "Thanks for helping her out," as I walk out of his office.

"Have a nice flight," he says, again taunting me, but I deserve it.

I deserve every bit of shit he might choose to give me for my pigheadedness. I know I've had my head stuck up my ass, and I have to do something to remove it. But that's a secondary worry.

For now, I have to get to New York and make sure Auralie is safe because I'm sure Magnus won't be far behind.

Chapter 22
Auralie

"**D**ID WE DO the right thing?" my father asks as he sits back in his recliner and sips on a beer.

"No crawling out of the rabbit hole now," I murmur as I sit in the window seat, looking down at my Vinegar Hill neighborhood below. And I use the term window seat loosely. It's really just a window with a sill that's larger than average, about a foot wide, and I'm barely able to sit my ass on the splintered wood that's about fifteen years overdue for a re-paint.

But the sun is shining and warm upon me as I rest my chin on my knees and try to shake myself out of my doldrums.

"Magnus will be gunning for us hard," he says pensively, and my stomach knots up. That is an absolute fucking understatement.

"We had no choice," I tell him, trying to sound confident, but I'm far from it. I have no clue if we're doing the right thing, but as I just said.

No choice.

Logan saw to that.

And yet, I can't find it in myself to be really mad at

him. When it boils down to its simplest form, there were actually three choices we had available to us when my father landed himself in hot water with Magnus.

First, and not ideal at all, we could have run. Dad and I could have packed up and moved somewhere across the country. Hoped Magnus wouldn't want to waste his precious resources trying to find us. It wouldn't have been hard to set up elsewhere. We could have had a meager but decent life back on the grift.

Second, we've always had the option of flipping on Magnus. Can't say as I ever really gave it much serious thought, but as I watched Magnus pull my father deeper and deeper into his web, not going to say it didn't cross my mind on occasion to rat him out. Of course, I never considered having my father do this as I knew the risk of pissing someone like Magnus off, but still… it was an option.

Third, and the option I chose, was to assist Magnus in one last con to get my dad back in his good graces. It was the easiest choice, and I was deluded enough to allow myself to think Magnus would accept this as my final payment to him and that he'd release me forever. Deep down, I probably knew it wasn't ever going to turn out like I'd imagined it, because people like Magnus never let go of what they considered their rightful property. And no doubt… he felt he owned my dad and me.

Ironically, pursuing choice number three ended up ultimately leading us to use choice number two to get out of this pickle, and in hindsight, it's easy to wish we'd just done that to begin with.

But had we gone to the police from the start, then I would have never gone to Wyoming and met Logan. I would have never known a man existed who was probably my soulmate. And while it ultimately didn't work out between us—a thought that still has me on the verge of tears when I think about how stubborn he is in his refusal to let me all the way in—I can't regret the time I spent with him and the hard way in which I fell for him.

"Where do you think Magnus is right now?" my dad muses, but not in a lighthearted way. I can hear the fear coating his voice, and I know he's not fearful for himself. He's fearful for me since I'm the one who royally fucked Magnus over this time. I didn't tell my dad all the details, because he has no idea what the real con was, but I told him enough to make it clear the police was our only option.

I pick up my phone, flip through my text messages, and see the one Bridger sent me just a few hours ago.

Magnus flew out at noon. He'll be back in NYC this evening.

Bridger has kept in contact with me since I left Wyoming yesterday morning. He'd been instrumental in giving me guidance the night I went to see him after Logan left me. He got me on a plane the next morning, had Cal Carson pick me up at the airport, who in turn swung by my dad's apartment and picked him up, and then stayed with us all afternoon as we answered Dee

Switzer's questions about all of Magnus' illegal operations.

Cal is great. It turns out, he and his wife, Macy, know Bridger well, but I'm not sure how. Dee is also great; a tough old broad who smokes like a fiend inside her "non-smoking" government-issue office and doesn't give a shit who it offends. She's tough on criminals, but she wasn't judgmental about me and my dad's involvement in said crime. She's more interested in pulling a big fish out of the sea of crime in her city, and once my dad told her about the mini-Ponzi scheme Magnus started nine months ago, her eyes glittered like a child on Christmas morning.

My father gave Dee enough information, including turning over documents proving Magnus was defrauding investors by giving fake returns from new investor money—classic Ponzi maneuver—and she was preparing an arrest warrant but wasn't sure when it would be executed. Sadly, while Magnus was in serious trouble over the various fraudulent cons he had going on, he wasn't so big a fish that we warranted any type of police protection. The most Dee could say was that we needed to be careful and that once Magnus was brought into custody, it would be made clear he would be under very intense scrutiny from the police. We all hoped that would be enough to make him want to keep his nose clean and not add a murder charge to his rap sheet. I did not want my father or me going *poof*.

Of course, there was still the option of us packing up

and moving away.

Possibly starting over somewhere new.

Never thought I'd say that because I love New York and it's my home.

But the time I spent in Wyoming has given me new perspective. Maybe because I was with a man who showed me I could have a really amazing life somewhere else? Well, at least until things went to shit really fast.

And my heart got broken in the process.

I mean, really broken.

"You okay, darlin'?" my dad asks.

I tilt my face away from the street to look at him. He has no idea the things I went through to save him. I could never tell him the level to which I stooped, not only because he'd be devastated to know what I'd done for him, but also because while Mickey Foster is a non-violent man, he'd never give up a quest to kill Magnus for the type of con he involved me in. My father may not have had qualms with me cheating, lying, and stealing to make a living, but he'd never forgive the injustice of Magnus forcing me to essentially prostitute myself if he knew the real truth. As it were, I'm just thankful my dad accepted me at face value when I told him that the con was a bust and that our only option was to help the police bring him down.

"I'm fine, Daddy," I say softly. "Just… worried."

"Looks like more than worry on that sad face of yours," he observes.

I take in my dad's kind face with his laugh lines, and

even smile to myself over the inherent sparkle of deviousness in his eyes that is the telltale sign of a lifelong con artist. I love him for his faults and despite them, and when all is said and done, I can never regret my actions to save the one man in my life who loves me unconditionally and holds nothing of himself back.

"Ever think about leaving New York?" I ask him in an effort to not only change the subject away from my sad thoughts about Logan, but also to actually put some thought into the best way to keep us safe until Magnus is put in prison. That was not going to happen overnight, and I was not looking forward to sleeping the next several months with one eye open. "We could start over somewhere. Maybe southern California where it's always sunny and warm?"

"Hate to leave our home, baby girl," he says morosely. "But like you… I'm worried about what Magnus is going to do. At the very least, you should leave."

"I'm not going anywhere without you," I rebuke. "We're a team."

"Always a team," he says and holds his beer up in salute to me. "So maybe California isn't a bad idea."

I give him a lukewarm smile and wonder what it would take to start over. Dad has no job skills, but he can grift anywhere. I could help out… maybe still go to school. I give a mirthless internal giggle over that. The College Grifter. I bet I'd be one of a kind.

A knock on the door has me freezing in place, my eyes the only things moving toward my father. He lowers the recliner slowly, wincing as it creaks a little, and sets his beer on the table. Reaching down to the side of his chair, he picks up the baseball bat he keeps there. Like I said, he's generally a non-violent type and doesn't believe in guns, but living the type of life we do… you have got to have some protection.

I swing my legs off the windowsill, placing them on the floor to stand up, but my dad shakes his head at me in silent admonishment. With a jerk of his chin, he motions me to go to my bedroom.

I shake my head in denial, considering the large butcher knife in the kitchen.

"Get in your room now," he whispers at me with that stern father look that's not to be disobeyed.

My pulse spikes in fear, but I refuse his order, instead darting into the kitchen and grabbing the knife out of the wooden block. I creep back into the living room, my father giving me a harsh glare before moving to the door.

I pad silently behind him on bare feet and watch as Dad puts his eye to the peephole. He stares a minute and turns to face me, giving me a silent shrug to indicate he doesn't recognize who's at the door.

This relieves me slightly because it's clearly not Magnus, but it doesn't mean he wouldn't send a messenger over to find out if I was here. There's no way he knows about our involvement with the police yet, but I'm sure he's more than pissed he couldn't find me in Wyoming.

I push past my father and put my eye up to the peephole, perhaps able to recognize one of Magnus' henchman or even better yet, the apartment manager who might be here to collect our rent, which always seems to be overdue.

Instead, I see Logan's beautiful face staring at the door and I jerk backward, knocking into my dad.

"Who is it?" he whispers to me.

"Logan," I whisper back involuntarily. I look back through the peephole and take note of the swell of joy and anger that sweeps through me.

Without another thought, I pull the chain free of the lock and swing the door open, fashioning my most malevolent stare at the man who managed to drive me higher than I've ever been in my life, only to drop me from the stratosphere to crash back down to earth.

"What do you want?" I ask, my tone appropriately icy.

Logan's eyes roam briefly over my face before looking down to the butcher knife in my hand, and he winces. And because I apparently have some sort of mystical connection to his emotions, I read his guilt loud and clear.

I put you in danger, and now you have to carry a butcher knife around your apartment.

But he quickly schools his features and says, "I came to check on you. Make sure you're okay."

I can't help the sarcasm. It comes pouring out. I hold the knife up and say, "I'm just peachy, Logan. Just waiting for Magnus to come bust into my apartment and whack my father and me."

I open the door up a little so he can see my dad standing there with the baseball bat and jerk my chin toward him. "See. Dad's got a bat. I got a knife. We're fine. So you can just mosey on out of here and head back to Wyoming."

"You're clearly not fine," he grits out as he pushes his way past me into the apartment.

"Well, make yourself at home," I mutter as I step back and then close the door behind him.

"Don't mind if I do," he snipes back.

I roll my eyes at his back before asking with resignation, "Seriously, Logan... what are you doing here?"

I pretend not to notice how damned good he looks in faded jeans, his hiking boots, and a long-sleeved dark blue Henley, even as I feel my skin tightening all over just from his presence.

Logan spins on me, scrubs a frustrated hand through his hair, and admits, "I was worried about you."

I throw my hands out, one still clutching the knife, and say with exasperation, "Well, as you can see... I'm fine. So you can just go."

"I'm sorry I got you into this mess," he blurts out, his face lined with guilt and worry.

"He got you into this mess?" my dad asks from behind me.

I wince, because I'd forgotten my dad was witnessing this painful exchange. I also cringe because my dad has no clue who Logan is or that he played a part in our current predicament. All I told my father when I came home was that I couldn't continue on with the con because I felt it was too dangerous, and that I met someone in Wyoming—that would be Bridger—who had a way to help us out of this mess.

To my dad's credit, he tried to question me on what type of danger Magnus had put me in, but I'd stubbornly refused the details and said he'd just have to trust me. There was no way I could ever tell my father the sordid details of the con, much less how I fell for a man who was trying to help me out but put me in a worse pickle than I already was. I certainly couldn't tell him that now, or else he'd take that bat to Logan, and I liked his face all pretty the way it was.

With a sigh, I say, "Dad... this is Logan. A friend. He had my back in Wyoming... like my friend Bridger."

This was not a blatant lie, because if I were to look at it solely from Logan's perspective, he did have my back. He just went about it the wrong way.

Logan cocks at eyebrow at me, clearly surprised I'd reference him as a friend or that I'd even dare to say he had my back. And then he goes on to make matters worse, when he asks me dryly, "A friend? I think I was more than that."

"Seriously?" I ask in exasperation. "You want to lay that innuendo out like that right in front of my father? Who you just met and who is also holding a baseball bat that he is not afraid to use?"

And he did not just quirk his lips up in amusement at me...?

Before I can slap the smirk off his face, he steps past me and holds his hand out to my father. "Mr. Foster… I'm Logan McKay. As Auralie said, I'm a friend of hers. And I hope I'm more than that."

I growl low in my chest as my dad's eyes cut to me with surprise before he looks back to Logan and offers his non-bat-bearing hand to shake. "Pleased to meet you."

Logan nods at my dad before turning back to me. "Bridger told me you met with the federal prosecutor."

"Yes. My dad gave enough information and proof that they're going to issue an arrest warrant for Magnus," I tell him grudgingly. "No clue when they'll serve it though."

"He's going to come after you," Logan states a simple fact I already know. "First and foremost because you ditched him in Wyoming."

"This I know," I say, sarcastically waving the knife in front of my face again, which is really a childish maneuver but whatever. "Hence the reason we're armed."

Logan snorts at our pitiful defense system and walks back to my door. I'm stunned for a moment, thinking my sarcasm has driven him off before I can really look at him and get my fill of all his magnificence before he leaves me again. I almost call him back once he opens the door, but he halts there and sticks his head out into the hallway, looking down to the left.

"You guys can come in," he says to someone in the hall.

Logan steps back and admits two burly men in their

early thirties. Both dressed in street clothes… jeans, t-shirts, and jackets. Fairly non-descript except for the air of menace they both carry about their personas.

Logan turns to me. "This is Wade and Wilson. They're going to be your shadows until Magnus is behind bars."

My eyebrows shoot sky high as I look at the men standing there before me, both with their hands clasped behind their backs as they stand at almost military attention.

"Come again?" I ask Logan in shock.

"They're protection for you and your dad," Logan says briskly. "They'll switch out with another team for the night shift, but they're on you until Magnus is taken care of."

"Protection?" I mutter, still not able to comprehend what Logan is doing.

Logan's eyes slide to the knife I'm still clutching. "Yeah… they're much better than knives and bats."

"I don't understand. You what… hired bodyguards?"

"No," Logan says sarcastically, but it's a sarcasm laced with amusement. "I went to St. Margaret's School for Wayward Children and hired mercenaries."

"Huh?" I ask, completely lost in the conversation, not because it's confusing as hell, but mostly because my brain has been pure mush since Logan walked into my apartment.

"Didn't you see *Deadpool*?" he asks me.

"No, I didn't," I murmur.

"Well, never mind… you're going to have twenty-four-hour protection," he says confidently. "They'll stay out in the hallway, but if you need to leave, they'll go with you. I've also hired someone from their agency to track Magnus down to deliver a very strong message that you are under protection and that orders are shoot to kill if someone comes after you."

I blink in astonishment, and my dad mutters, "Holy shit."

Logan turns to Wade and Wilson, nodding toward the door, "You guys can go ahead outside. You're officially on the clock."

"Yes, sir," one of them says in response, and I'm not sure if it's Wade or Wilson, but then they both turn and walk out the door. In a daze, I bend over and place the knife on the coffee table, clearly not needing it right now.

When I look back to Logan, I ask with narrowed eyes, "We can't afford this. And I know you can't afford it, so who's paying for this protection?"

"I actually can afford it," Logan says. With apologetic eyes, he adds on, "It's the least I can do for you."

I do not like that at all, because now I know he's here only because he's driven by guilt for putting me in this situation to begin with. It was stupid to think he'd come all this way because he wanted a relationship with me.

"Well, thank you," I snap at him. "I appreciate the offer, and we'll accept it. So now that you have that burden off your shoulders, you can go ahead and go now."

Logan stares at me for a moment, and it's the only time I've not really been able to read what his silence says. Finally, he nods at me and then turns to my father. "It was nice to meet you, Mr. Foster."

"You too," my dad says, sounding every bit as shell shocked as I feel.

Logan turns to the door. My heart cracks as he turns the knob and pulls it open. Before he steps through though, he turns to me and says, "I also came to tell you my story. Who I was two years ago and why it's led me to do the things I've done."

My jaw drops open wide and my heart squeezes even more painfully.

He gives me a wink. "When you want to hear it, I'm staying at the Marriott on Adams Street. Room 4319."

Then he walks out the door and shuts it softly behind him.

Chapter 23
Logan

AURALIE ARRIVES AT my hotel room a mere forty minutes after I do. I estimate she took a shower because her hair is still damp and she's wearing different clothes. The subtle smell of jasmine hits me as I open the door, and I have to suppress the urge to jerk her inside, strip her naked, and feast on her for hours.

Hopefully, that will come later.

I step aside and Auralie walks in without comment, taking in the small, cramped room that's typical of New York hotels as the need to cram as many people in as possible eats up the usable square footage. I shut the door and follow her in, shoving my hands in my pockets.

It's a nervous gesture, and I'm not going to lie… my pulse is out of control with fear and dread over what I'm getting ready to lay at her feet. I'm going to tell her the basis for my nightmares. I'm divulging to this woman the part of me that's a monster and not nearly good enough for the likes of her.

But it's what Auralie wants.

It's what she needs.

And I want to give her the world, even if I have to

crush myself and possibly her in the process.

She's nervous too, I can tell as she turns around to sit on the edge of the king-sized mattress covered in a blanket done in browns, tans, and lime-green geometric designs. It's all too contemporary and modern for my taste, but then again… I've been happy living in a tin trailer for the last two years with a ratty old blanket I'd picked up at Target when I started my travels.

"Want something to drink?" I ask, only to buy time. I haven't quite figured out how I'm going to start my tale.

Auralie shakes her head. "No. I want to hear your story."

"I won't stop you from running once you hear it," I tell her, already preparing myself for the end of something that really never got off the ground in a good way.

"I'm not going anywhere," she says quietly.

Confidently.

It should bolster me, but it doesn't because she's naive to think I can be good for her.

But still, I give a resolute sigh and walk past her to look out the window at the Brooklyn Bridge. I can't bear to look at her as I start to deliver the speech I must have practiced a hundred times on the plane once I made the decision to fly to New York for her.

The minute I walked out of Bridger's office last night, I knew I was going to open myself up to her, because I had nothing to lose at this point. Auralie was something I didn't expect in my life, but once I got a

taste of her and then subsequently lost it, I figured…
what the fuck do I really have to lose at this point?

"I was married once," I start off saying, and she gives
a small gasp of surprise. "I was also a doctor."

Another gasp, this one deeper, and she blurts out, "A
doctor?"

I look over my shoulder at her and give a wry smile.
"Hard to believe, right?"

"Actually, not really," she says quietly. "I mean… I
think you're brilliant so why wouldn't you be a doctor?
But I do have to wonder how you went from doctor to
fly-fishing guide."

I turn away from her, looking blankly out the window. "I was a general surgeon in Chicago, where I was
born and raised. Returned there after med school and my
residency. Joined a prominent practice. Got married
while I was early in my residency—her name was Donna—and we lived a pretty fucking charmed life."

"A doctor," Auralic says in awe.

"I was a jackass," I say with no small amount of bitterness in my voice. "I was young but had a God
complex. Thought I was hot shit because I graduated top
of my med school and was head and shoulders above
everyone else in residency. Didn't think there was a
problem I couldn't cure or fix. I had an ego the size of
the universe and the track record to back it up. I was just
fool enough to think nothing could bring me down."

"What happened?" she whispers fearfully.

I swallow hard, fight back the nausea, and tell her, "A

little girl was brought into the emergency room when I was on call. Just five years old. She took a bad fall off some schoolyard equipment and landed on a railroad tie, causing a crush injury to her ribs."

"Oh, no," Auralie breathes out from behind me.

"A CT scan showed her spleen was ruptured, but no other major injuries. It was a simple enough surgical fix—quick in and out with a laparoscope to remove it. A procedure I'd done many, many times."

She waits silently as I barrel forward with my story, the words getting harder and harder to get out. My heart thunders, echoing through my brain so I almost can't hear myself when I admit with crushing defeat, "The other surgeon on call... he told me not to take the case. That he'd handle it, but I wouldn't listen. God complex and all. I thought I was the best man for the job, despite knowing deep down I should stay away."

"I don't understand," she murmurs in confusion.

I finally turn toward Auralie, because I need to look her in the eye when I tell her the very worst thing about myself. "It was my daughter... Carrie."

"What?" she asks, and she actually rears backward from my revelation.

I can't maintain eye contact, so I drop my gaze in a cowardly fashion to the mocha-brown carpeting. "Lots of unwritten rules in the profession of medicine, but you never treat a family member. I was told to back away, but I was too much of a conceited asshole to listen. I didn't trust anyone to do the job right but myself."

"What happened?"

Fuck… what didn't happen is the question?

"I screwed up," I say, managing to drag my gaze back up to hers even though it about kills me to see the pain reflected in her beautiful blue eyes. "Got her spleen out, but I missed a bleeder. Closed her up, watched her in recovery for a little bit, and then left to handle another surgical case."

Auralie's eyes fill with tears. "Missed a bleeder?"

I nod, my own eyes filling up with tears I've refused to let fall since the day I buried my sweet girl. "The recovery nurse realized pretty quickly that she was in trouble when her blood pressure dropped. The other surgeon on call opened her back up, gave her blood… but it was too late. Her organs shut down, and she—"

Auralie flies off the bed suddenly and slams her body into mine with a cry of dismay. Her arms go around my back and she plasters herself against me—tries to crawl inside of me—as she sobs, "No. Oh, Logan. No."

As I blink, the tears spill down my face. I want to wrap my arms around her. I want to accept her comfort, but I can't. I have to get it all out. "It was my fault. I killed my daughter. Donna told me so. She reminded me every day after Carrie died, even as we lowered her into the ground. She reminded me when she served divorce papers to me."

Auralie makes a distressed sound in her throat.

"I gave up after that," I murmur in quiet reflection. "Gave up the practice of medicine. Gave up my life. I just left. Left it all behind and never looked back. It's why I don't talk to my parents anymore… because I killed their only grandchild."

"No, no, no," Auralie chants as I feel her tears soaking through my shirt. "No, it wasn't your fault. Mistakes happen all the time."

I don't disagree with her because that's a basic risk of all medicine. Missing a bleeder can also be a normal consequence of just such a surgery, but fuck if I'll ever accept anything but full responsibility for my dark-haired angel dying on an operating table. For the pain I caused Donna and her parents and my parents.

Now the pain I've caused myself?

I'll accept that because it's my punishment. I'll bear it until the day I die.

Auralie releases her hold on me, reaches back, and grabs my wrists. She pulls my arms up and wraps them around her back. When they go lax in a subconscious move on my part to refuse her comfort, she pulls at them again, squeezing me to insist I hold onto her.

I suck in a breath, rapidly blink my eyes again, and when Auralie squeezes harder at me, I finally engage my arm muscles and hold them loosely in place around her. She doesn't accept that though, burrowing in tighter to me, pressing at my arms to lock tighter around her body. It's a silent plea, one that I read clear as day because I never miss a message this woman sends to me, that she is offering herself as a rock-solid means of support to me right now.

I don't fucking deserve it, but I'm such a selfish bastard, I go ahead and take it. Pulling her in close to me, I press my nose into the top of her head and breathe in her scent. I listen to her as she starts to cry in earnest, and now I'm the one who wants to console her.

"Don't cry, baby," I whisper. "I'm not worth it."

"You're so fucking worth it," she mumbles into my chest, squeezing me so hard I can barely breathe. "You're mine and you are worth every goddamn tear I choose to shed on your behalf."

"I don't deserve—"

"Shut up," she cries as she pulls back and looks up at me with tear-streaked eyes. "You deserve happiness, Logan. I don't care if you made a mistake or if it was God who decided to take your baby from you. You're a good man. A righteous man. You are my man, and you are not going to bear this alone. I swear to fucking God, so don't even think about trying to use this as an excuse to push me away."

"Auralie," I say, because I'm stunned by the vehemence in her voice.

"You forgive yourself, Logan," she presses on me urgently. "Your forgive yourself right this moment, and if you can't do it right this moment, then I'm going to remind you every single day for the rest of your life that you deserve some peace. And I'm going to remind you because I deserve some peace and happiness too, and you're the only one who can give it to me, so I'm not going to let you leave me again because you've got some misguided notions about suffering for something that you've already suffered enough over."

Fuck… this woman.

Goddamn this woman for giving me hope.

"When I fucked you that last time," I tell her slowly. "I saw it in your eyes. You demanded to know about my life, and I knew if I told you, this is what you'd do. That you'd accept the broken and fucked-up Logan McKay into your life, and that you'd forgive me my trespasses because I didn't have the strength to do it myself."

"I'd forgive you anything," she whispers before pressing a kiss into the center of my chest.

"I'm not sure I deserve that type of unconditional acceptance," I tell her truthfully. "But I am giving you what you wanted… to know about the real me."

"I don't care what you think," she says, leaning back to look at me. "And I'm falling hard for the real you. I want you to fall with me, okay?"

"Already did that," I murmur, nuzzling into her head… feeling the softness of her hair against my cheek.

"Then it's agreed," she says. Although I can't see her face, I can hear her smile. I can feel that fucking smile… soft, sweet, and utterly devoted. "We've fallen for each other."

"I'm fucked up, baby," I say, in a last-ditch effort to put her off. To make her see reason. To save her from a life with a fucked-up man.

"Maybe you are," she says. "But I'm not going to let you stay that way. Like I said, I'm going to remind you constantly that you deserve more. That you deserve me. That right there is saying something because I'm no picnic half the time."

A small chuckle escapes me, testament to the fact that despite the heaviness of this moment and the unburdening that just occurred, I apparently still have room for some measure of happiness.

Maybe… just maybe… I have room for even more.

"Logan," Auralie murmurs as she nuzzles against my chest again for a brief moment before pulling back enough to look up to me.

Her face is still wet with tears. I loosen my arms from around her waist to bring my fingers to her cheeks so I can wipe them dry. "Yeah?"

"I want you inside me," she says softly, her eyes warm and inviting. "Is that inappropriate?"

I smile back at her… my expression tender and full of emotion that I can't contain. "Not inappropriate."

"Then what are you waiting for?"

"For this," I answer huskily and bend to kiss her.

Slow and deep, with nothing but a soft moan against her mouth that hopefully conveys my need for her.

Clothes hit the floor.

Her body hits the bed.

Then I'm inside of her and fuck almighty… how could I have ever have thought to walk away from this?

You didn't walk away, moron, I tell myself. *You went after her and bared your soul, and she invited you into her body. She invited you into her soul.*

Auralie's hands roam all over me, almost as if she can't believe I'm real and she's testing to ensure I'm not a mirage. Every glide of her fingers over my skin fills me with a fullness I never experienced before.

Fullness of heart, for sure.

But something else.

Life.

For the first time in years, my life feels… overflowing.

Complete.

I fuck Auralie slowly and sweetly, a first for both of us. Seems like it's straight from a fucking fairy tale, but we both come together, groaning into each other's mouths, which haven't lifted from the other since I pushed my way inside her body.

When I empty myself in her, I wait for that blissfully blank space I normally go to. That place where sex usually leads me. A safe, insulated place where only I exist.

Except now, it feels completely different because I'm not there alone. Auralie is right there with me. It feels so fucking good that I'm not ever going to let it go.

Chapter 24
Auralie

Three weeks later…

"WELL, I THINK it's okay for Logan to call off his guard dogs," my dad says in exasperation.

"Dad," I say in warning. "Until Magnus goes to trial—"

"He's in jail, Auralie," my dad points out. This I already know as he was arrested almost two weeks ago after the prosecutor tallied all the evidence from my dad as well as some other witnesses, including the Ponzi investors. Because of the nature of the white-collar crimes, all of Magnus' assets were seized by the government at the time of his arrest, so he was without funds to make bail.

"Yes, he's in jail," I agree. "But he still has contacts out in the world, and you're the primary witness against him. So keep the guard dogs."

"It's hard to run a scam with them looking over my shoulder," he grumbles, and I have to laugh. I mean, it's not funny that my dad makes his living on the streets, but it's what he knows. I'm trying to change that though, and Logan and I are hoping to talk him into a move here when he comes out to visit later this week.

"Dad, those guys don't care what you do," I remind him. "They're not police. They're—"

"Guard dogs," he inserts.

"Woof-woof," I bark at him, and he laughs at me.

I laugh back, and it's easy, natural and fun. I can do it because my life is set right again, and I have so much to laugh about.

"Okay, Dad," I say into the phone as I hold it between my ear and shoulder at the same time I'm trying to put new sheets on the mattress. It's a difficult enough task to do on its own, but it's nearly impossible when I'm on the phone, because Logan's little bed extends from wall to wall with no room to walk on either side. Add in the fact I'm trying to carry on a conversation with my dad has me grimacing in frustration as one corner pops off as I try to pull another tight. "I'll see you in a few days, and we'll have so much fun when you get here."

"Can't wait, darlin'," my dad says. "Love you."

"Love you too," I mutter, dropping the phone from my shoulder where it clatters to the floor. I then pull the one corner tight, crawl across the bed and pull the other tight, before rolling off and holding my breath, hoping the sheet stays in place.

The door to the trailer opens, and Logan stomps inside. I look over my shoulder at him, and he laughs.

"What's up with the look of consternation?" he asks as he comes up to stand behind me.

I turn to look back at the bed and warn him, "Don't move too suddenly… that damn sheet might pop off at the slightest provocation."

Logan laughs again, and oh… I love that sound.

"I don't know," he says between chuckles. "It looks pretty solid to me."

"You didn't just spend the last fifteen minutes wrestling with it," I mutter.

"Well, let's test it out," he says.

Before I know it, I'm hauled into the air, twisted around and then sailing toward the mattress where I land with a bounce, then another, before Logan is jumping on top of me.

He straddles me at my waist and looks down at me with a grin. "See… sheets held tight."

"So I see," I say dryly.

"Let's give them a real work out, okay?" he says as his hands go to my shirt to whisk it off me.

I giggle and make a half-assed attempt to push him away, but then his hands are on my breasts and his fingers are plucking at my nipples through the thin material of my bra.

Sighing in contentment, I then start to squirm under his ministrations, which are sadly brief because his hands are at my jeans and they're being pulled unceremoniously from my legs.

I stretch like a cat as he crawls back up my body and lays part of his weight on me, the rest being held up by his strong arms locked at my sides.

"Your dad good?" he asks as he peers down at me.

I nod as I pull my bottom lip between my teeth

briefly, let it pop free, and say, "He's excited about coming to visit. Thank you for buying a ticket for him and putting him up in a hotel."

"You smile at me like that more often, and I'll buy you the world," he quips.

Turns out, Logan might not actually be able to buy me the world, but he's far from a poor Wyoming fisherman. That night almost three weeks ago when Logan came to me in New York, and after he confessed what he deemed to be unforgivable sins, he told me all about his prior life.

He was able to talk more freely once we got past the tragic circumstances of Carrie's death, and he clued me in on a few things. Although Logan had just finished his residency, he had made good money. Add on his wife was also a surgeon and that they were both fairly frugal, and that meant they had a nice savings when they split up. He got half of all assets in his divorce, including the equity when they sold their home and those monies have sat in investment accounts getting bigger and bigger while he led a meager life the last two years. It didn't make Logan super wealthy but it gave him enough money to hire protection for me and my dad.

My heart contracts painfully now as I think about Carrie. After that painful unloading that day, we've talked here and there about his daughter. I think if Logan has his way, he wouldn't talk about it ever again, but I'm not about to let that happen. He needs to remember the good times with her, and he can't do that when he shuts everything about his past out. I've also encouraged him to reach out to his parents and they've had some tentative talks via phone. They're pushing to come here for a visit but I don't think he's quite ready for that yet. Doesn't mean I'm not going to bring it up whenever I can, because he needs to reconnect with them. He needs to have them back in his life.

Sometimes he gets frustrated with me for continually pushing him to confront his past, but I've also noticed positive changes since I've been hounding him.

The nightmares for one thing.

They've dwindled to coming very infrequently, and when they do come, I'm there waiting for him to use me in the way that he best needs. It's never like it was that one night when he needed me so badly that he couldn't even take the time to get me wet, but rather, if he has a nightmare, he'll wake me up first from slumber, then he wakes my body up with his mouth and hands. After that, he fucks me, usually quite urgently but with no less care than he's given me since that day we reconnected in New York City.

That day… it was the start of my new life.

Logan's too.

I packed my bags and returned to Wyoming with him three days after he arrived, content to live in Logan's little tin trailer for the rest of my life, although he's mentioned a few times perhaps we'll move to a condo with a bigger bed and better kitchen. While I still could never tell my dad everything that happened between

Logan and me, because that would include having to clue him in on the terrible things Magnus had me do, I told him enough that he was content with the knowledge his daughter was falling in love for the first time.

And since I returned with Logan, I've continued to fall for my doctor-turned-fisherman.

Helplessly, deeply, irrevocably, and forever in love with this man.

"Baby… that look on your face makes me want to eat your pussy until you come about fifty different times," Logan growls, and I focus in on his face.

So intent.

So serious.

Filled with lust and something I think is love, but I'm not quite sure.

But one thing I've come to realize over these past three weeks living my new life with Logan is that he's still hesitant to accept the good. He's still fearful it will be ripped away. He's afraid to believe that I'm here to stay.

So I attempt to make it easy on him.

My hands go to his face. I rub my fingers against the bristles of the beard he claims he's going to grow for the winter months. "I love you, Logan."

He sucks in an astonished breath and his eyes go slightly blank… as if he's afraid to believe my words and he's distancing himself from the pain of rejection.

"It's true," I say, making my tone matter of fact while pressing my fingers into his cheeks to make sure I have his attention. "I've gone and fallen right down the rabbit hole of love with you, Logan McKay."

He blinks down at me, and I see a slight flicker of hope in his eyes.

"Yup," I continue on lightly. "No clue how it happened, but now that I've given into it, I'm rolling with it. And it feels right, you know?"

He gives a slight nod, and I beam back at him.

"Be honest with me," I say to him seriously. "I'm not too crazy to be feeling that, right?"

He doesn't hesitate in the slightest, just shakes his head at me. More hope fills his gaze and it's almost painful to watch, but I press forward.

"And it's okay if you don't feel the same," I say neutrally. "I can wait for you to—"

"I love you," he blurts out. Giving me a look of fear, he waits to see my reaction.

That breaks my heart that he's so out of tune with his own capacity for love, but I put on a brilliant smile. "Well, of course you do," I say brightly. "What's not to love about me?"

"There's everything to love about you," he murmurs.

I watch, spellbound, as all the apprehension finally melts away and he's staring back at me with nothing but abject devotion and tenderness.

My eyes mist up briefly, but I know I can't make this moment too heavy for Logan. He's still sensitive to the newness of expressing emotion, and I don't want him to retreat or think on it too much. So I slide my hands around the back of his neck and press my fingers into his muscles.

"Soooo," I drawl out as I wiggle underneath him. "I think you said something about fifty orgasms."

That's usually enough to get him focused, but the usual flare of heat my seductive words would cause doesn't come. Instead, he looks down at me with that same mix of sweet tenderness with a slight bit of unease because we just got done exchanging very important words that cement our bond even stronger.

I tilt my head and silently ask him, *What's wrong?*

"I love you," he says firmly, enunciating the words so they ring clear and true. "I. Love. You."

I let out a quavering breath. My insides turn to absolute mush as I realize that Logan is not only telling me how he feels, he's also communicating to me that he is fucking owning these emotions, and he's doing it so bravely and without fear that it will all get jerked away from him at some point.

"Oh, baby," I whisper, pulling him down to me. His head goes to my shoulder and his arms lock around me. I hold him tight to my body, and I revel in this man surrounding me.

This man who has invaded me and now controls my heart.

My life.

"Auralie," he says as he turns his head into my neck. "I'm accepting it."

"What's that?" I ask, but I already know the answer.

"That maybe it's okay if I have something great in my life."

"Yeah, honey," I say with a smile on my lips and lightness in my heart. "It's totally okay to accept that."

We're silent for a moment, just holding on to each other.

Then he shifts, lifts his head, and peers down at me. "Now I think I'll hand out some of those orgasms we were just discussing."

I smile at him, unable to stop my body squirming at the thought. "That's something I can totally accept too."

Epilogue
Bridger

I WALK INTO my cabin that sits on Double J property, completely exhausted. I stayed at The Silo until the last customer left because we had a packed house, and when you get a whole lot of people doing freaky fucking, the hormones and pheromones that circulate can make people crazy.

As it turns out, I had to break up a fight between two girls over some dude's huge pierced dick, as well as stop a whipping session that got out of hand because the fucker wielding the whip had no clue what he was doing. He drew unnecessary blood on a woman that she didn't want and wasn't prepared for. And although she was fully consenting and it was in fact her idea to let her "date" try some new kink on her, I knew she was going to be in a world of hurt if I let it go on. The dude was pissed and threatened to pull his membership. I grabbed him by the back of the neck, dragged his sorry ass out of The Silo, and before I slammed the door in his face, I told him his membership was revoked. The fucker then had the balls to beat on the door. When he wouldn't stop, I opened it up, stepped out, and beat his ass. It wasn't much of a fight as two punches—one to his jaw and then one to his right kidney—had him down moaning like a bitch. I'm sure he'll be pissing blood tomorrow. I had one of the male bartenders take him home with strict instructions to impart to him he'd get more if he came back on the property again.

After, I went back in and fucked the girl he was whipping, because she was all worked up despite his lousy job. Fucked her right in the same room her blood was first drawn with The Silo crowd watching. I did it dispassionately, although I did get her off too. I put her on her hands and knees, ignored the people pressing their faces in on the glass because I really don't care for public sex but it won't stop me if the mood strikes, and I banged out an effective orgasm.

As per usual, the minute I felt my balls pull up with the need for release, I pulled out of her, whipped the condom off, and shot all over her back. I gave her a sharp slap on the ass at the same time, dragged my thumb through the wetness on her back, and shoved it up her ass. She went off like a firecracker again, and my job was done. Left her on the floor panting as I tucked my dick back in and walked out.

So yeah… exhausted and more so than normal. It's been getting harder and harder to maintain my role as the head of The Silo, and I'm not sure if it's because I've been doing it on my own for almost six months now since Woolf left or if I'm just losing the taste for all the kink. There was a time in my life that this shit was the only thing that kept me sane and grounded, but I'm finding I'm actually developing a bit of an intolerance for it. It's why I spend so much time holed up in my office at The Wicked Horse, depending on some of my most trusted Fantasy Makers to make sure things run smoothly.

Sadly, those people I can depend on are dropping like flies. First Woolf exited the business when he got involved with Callie Hayes. I don't begrudge my best friend happiness at all, and I'm still happy for him to this day, although I do miss him as we see each other very infrequently now. Then Cain fell for Sloane, Rand for Cat, and just recently, Logan gave it all up for Auralie. While these guys will always love to mix in kink in their fucking, they're also the type that once they commit to a woman, they're giving up the days of debauchery. It's not unheard of for monogamous couples to frequent The Silo, but while those couples do indeed have an amazing amount of trust to lead this lifestyle, I've always known there's something missing from their relationship that leads them here.

Woolf, Cain, Rand, and Logan?

They have everything they could possibly want waiting in bed for them at home, so yeah… their days in The Silo are over, and it's really just me left.

Sighing, I head into the kitchen and pull a beer from the fridge. I twist the cap off, lobbing it into the garbage can before taking my first pull. It goes down nicely, and before I can even take a second sip, I'm craving another beer already. It appears I'm well on my way to getting shit faced tonight.

Again.

It's become a habit because I'm finding it harder and harder to fall asleep.

Heading into the living room, I sit down on my leather recliner and put my beer down on the table beside it. I take off my boots—cowboy tonight although on any other day, it could be biker boots—and then I kick the recliner back. I pick up my beer from the table, along with the necklace that lays there.

It's silver and tarnished with age with a simple lobster clasp that was broken years ago and never repaired. On the blackened chain rests a silver men's wedding ring, which doesn't come off as I ended up tying the ends of the thin chain into a knot. I hold the ring up, which is also changing color with the passage of time, and I let memories take me over.

I don't want them to take me over, but they do anyway.

They do every fucking time I look at this necklace and ring, and I look at it frequently.

Flat on my back, tied up. Wrists to headboard, but my legs are loose and lying flat on the dirty, stained mattress. I let myself be tied willingly, but I'm not here willingly. I'm there through no choice of my own.

She rides my cock slowly, hands to my chest, using it for leverage to slide up and down my shaft. The needle marks on her arm are like bright beacons, and I focus on them so I don't have to look at that fucking necklace and ring swaying back and forth as she fucks me.

"Feels good, doesn't it, baby?" she murmurs in a raspy voice thick with lust, but not drugs. She's always sober when she wants to fuck because she doesn't want the sensation of what she does to me dulled. She'll shoot up as soon as we're done.

I grunt in unwanted acknowledgment because as much as I hate this fucking bitch, my cock will give her what she wants.

I concentrate on the feelings… wet slide of flesh, my balls tingling with the need for release—not because I want it or crave it, but only because I want this done and this skank to get off me.

"Give it to me," she moans, moving on me faster. "Come inside me, Bridger, love. Give me that spunk."

I grit my teeth. Her words are foul, grating on my ears, even as they do their job and force my orgasm closer. I want it, and I hate it. I'll hate myself even worse once I give it up.

"Mmmmm," she taunts me. "Maybe one day, I'll even let you knock me up. We'd make a beautiful baby together, wouldn't we?"

She recognizes her mistake right away as my eyes go blank and every bit of hated lust that I'm feeling starts to slide away. My dick even starts to deflate, so she backpedals quickly. By that, I mean she reaches out and viciously twists my nipples. They're already reddened from the belt she used on me before she climbed aboard. The pain fires through me and gives her the intended results, my cock going rock solid again inside her well-used pussy.

She bounces harder and faster, and then she taunts me further by grabbing the ring swaying from the necklace in one hand and bringing it to her lips. Pushing it into her mouth, she sucks on it as she looks down at me in triumph before she spits it back out and pants, "You're so fucking good, baby. I'll never get tired of this cock, you know."

I'm on the edge and she knows it, so she propels me along by reaching a hand back and giving a vicious squeeze to my balls. They shrink and harden as the pain drives through me. With utter silence, I unload inside of her. I do it silently because it's the one way I can show this bitch that my body might react to her—and only because it's been brainwashed to do so—but that's the only acknowledgment she gets.

She watches me with interest as the orgasm ripples through me, and she comes to a complete rest with my spent cock inside of her. She climbs off, not having achieved her own orgasm, but I'm not sure she's even capable of it. I've never seen it, and she doesn't fuck me to get off. She fucks me because she's a sick bitch who likes the power and control.

With a calm that shows just how whacked she is in the head, she undoes the ropes around my wrists and releases my bondage. She looks down at me with that smug look of superiority tinged with madness before bending over and placing a light kiss on the tip of my nose. It's an endearing kiss. I suspect in her own fucked-up world, she's doing this to show she loves me.

The thought causes my flesh to crawl and fury to wash through me.

She gives me a condescending pat on my chest and starts

to scoot off the bed. Before I can even reason with myself what I'm doing, my hand flies out and catches her around the back of her neck. Her eyes flare wide for a brief moment, sizzling with both anger and lust that I'd dare make such a move.

My other hand strikes, grabbing the necklace and jerking it from her body, the weak clasp easily shredding.

"Bridger," she shrieks, making a grab for the necklace.

I roll swiftly, using my grasp on her neck to flip her over me and down onto the mattress, where I throw a leg over her wasted body and straddle her.

"Get off me," she yells, and the fear in her eyes motivates me.

Motivates me to take my life back.

My hands wrap around her neck, the silver necklace wound through my fingers and the ring coming to rest at the hollow in her throat. I squeeze, and, for a brief moment, her eyes flash with lust.

This motivates me greatly.

I squeeze harder, moving my thumbs to rest over her windpipe, and I press them down.

The lust turns to fear instantaneously, and fuck my soul to hell… that motivates me further.

Tightening my hands, I start to choke the ever-loving shit out of her. I watch in fascination as she gasps, her hands now scratching and clawing at my hands, her legs frantically kicking underneath me. She tries to buck me off, but the lack of oxygen and the fact she's weak of body makes her attempts futile. Her face turns a beautiful shade of red… not nearly as red as the belt marks on my chest, but enough to satisfy me.

It then turns purple, and her eyes start to bulge as they leak copious amounts of tears. I watch as blood vessels bloom and burst in her right eye, and that fascinates me too.

Leaning down, I hover my mouth right over hers, which is opening and closing like a gasping fish, and I whisper to her, "I'm. Done. With. You."

Her eyes are blank, mostly because she's oxygen deprived. I'm not sure she even understands me. I make my point by releasing my hands from around her neck, taking only a moment to enjoy the red marks there that I know will turn purple as well, and roll off the bed. Bending down to the floor, I pick my clothes up and walk out of the bedroom.

Getting dressed in the hallway, I shove the necklace and ring in my jeans pocket. I grab my wallet off the kitchen counter that is stained with dried food and make my way through the living room, where drunk and drugged-out people lay scattered all around, a few of them fucking on the filthy carpet.

I open the door and walk right out of my stepmom's house.

I'm just fifteen years old, and I'm never coming back.

A loud banging on my front door jolts me out of the memory, and for a moment, I'm confused as to what the sound is. But it comes again, louder this time.

BOOM, BOOM, BOOM.

Kicking my legs down, I put the recliner back in an upright position and place my beer and the necklace on the table. I stalk across my living room as pounding that is more insistent reverberates through the house.

Without bothering to look to see who is outside, I throw the door open and glare at the intruder, only to have my jaw drop wide open.

Kyle Sommerville stands there, holding something cradled in his arms.

A woman.

An unconscious woman by the looks of it.

"What the fuck?" I say in astonishment, but then Kyle is barreling past me and causing me to step backward so he can make an entrance. I shut the door, turning to watch him walk over to my couch and lay the woman down with incredible care.

"Jesus fucking Christ, Kyle," I growl at him, my eyes cutting down to the package he just deposited.

He spins on me, his face grim. "I need your help."

I stomp over to the couch and look down at the woman. Her eyes closed, face pale with dark lashes fanning bruised skin underneath. Her brown hair is dirty and matted with what looks like blood, and there's dirt streaked all over her face. Her clothes are filthy as well.

"Who the fuck is that?" I ask as I point down to the woman.

"Listen to me," Kyle says urgently as he steps into me. "I am sorry for fucking involving you, but I had no choice. She is in serious fucking danger, and I need you to hide her for a bit."

"Are you out of your goddamn mind—?"

"Bridger," he shouts. "I'm not fucking around on

this. She has one foot in the grave if you don't take her in."

"You cannot leave her here," I shout back at him, because I have no clue what this crazy son of a bitch biker has gotten himself into and I want no part of it. "Take her to the police or something."

"I am the goddamn police," Kyle snarls at me in frustration, and I take two unsteady steps backward.

"What?" I ask in bewilderment.

Kyle takes a deep breath, scrubs his hands through his long, blond hair, and says, "I'm ATF, and I've been deep undercover with Mayhem's Mission for over three years now. Investigating illegal firearms, drugs, and a sex-slave ring they're running through all the clubs throughout the Midwest over to the West Coast."

I can't even comprehend what he's telling me. This is Kyle Sommerville, badass biker who is yeah… a friend… but not a good one. I know him marginally, and never once did I ever get a whiff that he's law enforcement. I can't even begin to process because I've seen this fucker do shit that's highly illegal. I've watched him clean what I'm sure are stolen guns and snort coke. Watched him fuck club pussy in the nastiest of ways, and I watched him cut a guy up at a party once because he just seemed to feel like it.

"I don't believe you," I say uncertainly.

"Why?" he mutters. "Because I'm really, really good at my undercover job? When you immerse yourself in this shit, Bridger, you go all in. You have to do the nasty with the people you get in bed with or else they won't fucking buy the cover."

That makes sense.

Sort of.

But shit… I thought that stuff only happened in the movies.

My eyes cut back down to the woman, and I must believe some of what he says because I ask, "Is she part of the sex-slave trade?"

He shakes his head. "No, she's part of something bigger, and I need you to keep her hidden."

"Why me?" I ask with narrowed eyes.

"Because if I didn't get her out of there tonight, she was going to be dead by morning," he says ominously. "And I am not ready for this bust to go down. I've got three fucking years invested in this operation, and I've done stuff that has ruined my soul. I've given up my life to bring these fuckers down, and I cannot let it be ruined. I have to see it through. But I couldn't let her die, either, so I'm begging you. Just keep her safe until this is over."

"How long?" I ask, completely disbelieving I'm even considering this lunacy.

"I don't know. Weeks?"

"What's wrong with her?" My eyes cut down to the frail woman lying unconscious on my couch.

Kyle's body shifts and his head inclines, and I know he's looking down at her too.

"Everything, man," he whispers almost fearfully. "Everything's fucking wrong with her."

If you enjoyed *Wicked Ride* as much as I enjoyed writing it, it would mean a lot for you to give me a review on your favorite retailer's website.

Connect with Sawyer online:

Website: www.sawyerbennett.com

Twitter: www.twitter.com/bennettbooks

Facebook: www.facebook.com/bennettbooks

Other Books by Sawyer Bennett

The Off Series
Off Sides

Off Limits

Off The Record

Off Course

Off Chance

Off Season

Off Duty

The Last Call Series
On The Rocks

Make It A Double

Sugar On The Edge

With A Twist

Shaken Not Stirred

The Legal Affairs Series
Legal Affairs Sneak Peek (FREE)

Legal Affairs

Confessions of a Litigation God

Clash: A Legal Affairs Story (Book #1 of Cal and Macy's Story)

Grind: A Legal Affairs Story (Book #2 of Cal and Macy's Story)

Yield: A Legal Affairs Story (Book #3 of Cal and Macy's Story)

Friction: A Legal Affairs Novel

Stand Alone Titles

If I Return

Uncivilized

Love: Uncivilized

The Sugar Bowl Series

Sugar Daddy

The Cold Fury Hockey Series (Random House / Loveswept)

Alex

Garrett

Zack

Ryker

Hawke

4 Book Bundle – Alex, Garrett, Zack, Ryker

The Wicked Horse Series

Wicked Fall

Wicked Lust

Wicked Need

Wicked Ride

The Forever Land Chronicles

Forever Young

About the Author

Since the release of her debut contemporary romance novel, Off Sides, in January 2013, Sawyer Bennett has released more than 30 books and has been featured on both the USA Today and New York Times bestseller lists on multiple occasions.

A reformed trial lawyer from North Carolina, Sawyer uses real life experience to create relatable, sexy stories that appeal to a wide array of readers. From new adult to erotic contemporary romance, Sawyer writes something for just about everyone.

Sawyer likes her Bloody Mary's strong, her martinis dirty, and her heroes a combination of the two. When not bringing fictional romance to life, Sawyer is a chauffeur, stylist, chef, maid, and personal assistant to a very active toddler, as well as full-time servant to two adorably naughty dogs. She believes in the good of others, and that a bad day can be cured with a great work-out, cake, or a combination of the two.

Made in the USA
Columbia, SC
16 November 2020